THE ILLINOIS
DETECTIVE AGENCY:
THE CASE OF THE
MISSING CATTLE

THE ILLINOIS
DETECTIVE AGENCY:
THE CASE OF THE
MISSING CATTLE

ETHAN J. WOLFE

FIVE STAR
A part of Gale, a Cengage Company

GALE
A Cengage Company

LIBRARY OF CONGRESS CATALOGING-IN-PUBLICATION DATA

Names: Wolfe, Ethan J., author.
Title: The Illinois Detective Agency : the case of the missing cattle / Ethan J. Wolfe.
Description: First edition. | Waterville, Maine : Five Star, [2021]
Identifiers: LCCN 2019041847 | ISBN 9781432871192 (hardcover)
Subjects: GSAFD: Mystery fiction. | Western stories.
Classification: LCC PS3612.A5433 I45 2020 | DDC 813/.6–dc23
LC record available at https://lccn.loc.gov/2019041847

First Edition. First Printing: February 2021
Find us on Facebook—https://www.facebook.com/FiveStarCengage
Visit our website—http://www.gale.cengage.com/fivestar
Contact Five Star Publishing at FiveStar@cengage.com

Printed in Mexico
Print Number: 01   Print Year: 2021

THE ILLINOIS DETECTIVE AGENCY: THE CASE OF THE MISSING CATTLE

CHAPTER ONE

Charles Porter the Third sat in his plush chair behind his large oak desk and sipped tea from an expensive china cup. At sixty-four years of age, he retained the hulking stature of his youth, if a bit more portly.

His hair was snowy white, his beard gray and speckled with strands of black, a holdover from his youth.

Forty years ago, when he was a young cowboy out of Nebraska, he put the skills he learned serving as a cavalry sharpshooter to good use when he took the job of stock detective for the local ranchers in New Mexico. At one time or another, Porter worked for every large rancher in the country, including John Chisum and Henry Hooker.

They called it the Stock Growers Association when they banded together across the west to achieve political clout in Washington.

Twenty years ago, when riding the range became too much of a chore for Porter to endure on a regular basis, he formed the Illinois Stock Detective Agency and chose Springfield as his headquarters. Years later, he shortened the name to just the Illinois Detective Agency.

Springfield seemed an ideal location as it was in close proximity to the stockyards in Chicago, Kansas City, and Dodge City and a short train ride from the open ranges of the west.

He employed experienced cowboys who had served in the military to investigate stolen cattle across the west, and after ten years, Porter expanded the business to include private detectives and modern-day forensics.

Porter employed not just tough, experienced men, but men well versed in the law and modern police techniques. Many had military backgrounds. Some were dissatisfied police detectives. All were unmarried, something he insisted upon. All were handpicked by Porter after undergoing rigorous testing.

As he sipped his tea, Porter listened to his potential client, J. Douglas Trent.

Trent, president of the Montana Cattlemen's Association, was most concerned with the rash of cattle thefts his state was experiencing. At first, it was just a few dozen strays that disappeared, but when the losses added up to the hundreds, ranchers became concerned.

When losses totaled thousands, panic set in, and Trent was asked to take action.

At eighteen- to twenty-dollars a head, financial losses were piling up. If left unchecked, ranchers could be forced out of business, which would cause the stock markets to plummet.

"I can appreciate the seriousness of your situation," Porter said. "It seems that no matter how many cattle thieves are hanged, someone always thinks cattle theft is an easy way to get rich."

"Mr. Porter, Montana needs its cattle ranches," Trent said. "We are just a few years away from achieving statehood. We only have a hundred thousand people in the territory, but how are we to grow a population and be admitted to the union if we are seen as a lawless territory where man and cattle aren't safe?"

"I understand perfectly," Porter said. "Wyoming, the Dakotas, and Washington are dealing with similar challenges facing statehood."

"My concern is with Montana first," Trent said.

Porter nodded. "My retainer is ten thousand dollars," he

said. "If you have that, you have hired the best agency in the country to solve your problem. If we don't solve it, there is no additional fee. Upon a successful conclusion, the balance is an additional fifteen thousand, plus all expenses."

"Every rancher in the territory chipped in," Trent said as he withdrew his checkbook. He wrote a check for ten thousand dollars and set it on the desk.

"My men will meet you in Montana in a week," Porter said. "Where is your home exactly?"

"Just north of Miles City," Trent said. "Anybody there can point you in the right direction."

"I'll wire the day of their arrival," Porter said.

"Montana can't fail, Mr. Porter," Trent said. "We're too close to statehood now to fail."

"Rest assured, Mr. Trent, you have the full backing of my agency and my men," Porter said.

Both men stood and shook hands.

After Trent left the office, Porter picked up the wood cone on his desk. The cone was attached to a copper tube that ran down the desk into the floor and emerged at his secretary's desk in another room.

"Miss Potts, can you come in here, please," Porter said into the cone.

A few moments later, the door opened and Miss Potts entered.

"Yes, Mr. Porter?" she said.

"Duffy and Cavill, where are they?"

"Mr. Duffy is in Chicago, attending a lecture on the law, Mr. Porter," Miss Potts said.

"And Mr. Cavill?"

Miss Potts lowered her eyes briefly.

"Come, come, Miss Potts, don't cover for Mr. Cavill," Porter said. "Your schoolgirl crush on Mr. Cavill is already well known."

"He's . . . at a boxing match in Peoria, Mr. Porter."

"Attending?"

"No . . . fighting."

Porter sighed. "Send each man a wire immediately and tell them to come home," Porter said.

"Yes, sir."

"And then take this check to the bank, and then you may take the rest of the afternoon off," Porter said.

"Yes, sir."

Miss Potts picked up the check and was about to leave the office when Porter said, "Miss Potts, did you know beforehand that Mr. Cavill would be fighting in a bare knuckles fight in Peoria?"

"Yes, sir."

"Next time would you please tell me," Porter said.

Miss Potts nodded. "Yes, sir."

CHAPTER TWO

James Duffy sat in the rear of the lecture hall at the University of Chicago Law Department. He found the speaker's voice amplified in the horseshoe-shaped hall, and he could actually hear better in the rear seating.

Two years away from receiving his law degree, at thirty-four years old, Duffy got a late start on his studies, having served six years in the army before deciding on attending law school.

Working for Mr. Porter also slowed his studies, but the job paid the bills and allowed him to live comfortably enough while he progressed toward his degree.

He stood six feet tall, about four inches above the average height of a man, and while he didn't possess the stature of Cavill, Duffy weighed in at a solid two hundred pounds.

He harbored no thoughts of marriage. He didn't even have a steady woman in his life because work and studies took up most of his time, but when he earned his law degree he figured there would be plenty of time to think of marrying and having children.

Duffy learned shorthand from Miss Potts and had little trouble keeping up with the lecturer, even though he spoke quickly.

The allotted time for the lecture was two hours. It had just concluded and as Duffy left the crowded hall, a Western Union delivery man stood in the hall, holding up a sign with his name on it.

"I'm James Duffy," Duffy said as he approached the delivery man.

The telegram was from Porter, requesting that he return to the office at once for assignment.

Jack Cavill sat on his stool and waited for the ninth round to begin. Because bare knuckle boxing was banned inside the city limits, the fight was being held on a barge in the Illinois River.

Cavill had been bitten by the boxing bug while serving in the army and boxed on his regiment's team, beating the navy champion four consecutive years.

His one goal in life was to fight and beat the great John L. Sullivan in the ring. At six foot, four inches tall and a solid two-hundred and forty pounds, he was taller and heavier than Sullivan.

Hundreds of people were on the barge; a thousand more lined the banks of the river and watched with binoculars.

The betting was heavily in favor of Cavill's opponent, a local man named Gould. Gould was taller and heavier than Cavill, but he carried a thick layer of blubber around his middle.

The betting money was on Gould to win by knockout in the ninth round.

So for eight rounds, Cavill carried Gould and allowed the betting crowd to think their man was in charge.

At the start of the ninth round, Cavill rushed off his stool, met Gould in the center of the ring, dodged a right haymaker, and drove his right fist squarely into Gould's liver.

Gould dropped like a brick thrown from a roof. The crowd fell silent, stunned by how quickly the fight ended.

As the barge docked and Cavill stepped off among loud boos, a Western Union delivery man handed him a telegram.

Duffy, wearing a charcoal gray suit, sat on the edge of Miss

Potts's desk and chatted with her while they waited for Cavill to arrive.

When the door opened and Cavill entered, Miss Potts immediately grew nervous, as she always did when Cavill was around.

"Miss Potts, you look lovely as always," Cavill said.

Duffy shook his head as he watched Miss Potts blush a light shade of pink.

"You're late," Duffy said to Cavill.

"No, I was on time. The train was late," Cavill said.

Duffy stood up and looked at Miss Potts. "Could you announce us, please?"

Miss Potts picked up her cone amplifier and spoke into it. "Mr. Porter, Mr. Duffy and Mr. Cavill are here," she said.

The amplifier worked so well that Duffy and Cavill could hear the reply. "Send them in, Miss Potts," Porter said.

Cavill looked at Miss Potts and winked. "Don't go anywhere," he said.

"Are you boys clear on your assignment?" Porter said.

"Very much so," Duffy said.

"Mr. Cavill?"

"Absolutely," Cavill said.

"Pick up your expense money and train tickets from Miss Potts," Porter said. "Then go to our stables and draw horses. Wire when you reach Billings and then when you can with updates. Good luck, men."

Duffy and Cavill left Porter's office and returned to Miss Potts to claim the tickets and expense money.

"One of these days, I am going to request that you accompany me on assignment, Miss Potts," Cavill said.

Duffy glared at Cavill as Miss Potts blushed a deep rose color on her cheeks and neck.

As they walked to the stables, Duffy said, "Why do you torture that woman, Jack? You know you're never going to take her to dinner or a dance. You should leave her alone."

"She looks forward to my teasing her," Cavill said.

"She does not, and I see by your knuckles you've been brawling again," Duffy said.

"I wasn't brawling," Cavill said. "I was engaged in a match of pugilism."

"Otherwise known as fighting," Duffy said.

"Exhibition match," Cavill said. "Fighting is banned inside city limits, you know that."

"How much did you make for your end of the exhibition?" Duffy said.

"One hundred dollars for the fight, about three hundred on the side bets," Cavill said.

They reached the company stables and entered. Old man McCoy was tending the twenty horses as usual. In the old days, McCoy had partnered with Porter on many occasions as a stock detective.

McCoy was grooming a large mare when they entered the stables.

"Charles told me you'd be by today for horses," McCoy said.

"Let me ask you something," Cavill said. "You've known Mr. Porter for forty years. Why do you always call him Charles?"

"That's his name," McCoy said.

"I'll take Blue," Cavill said.

McCoy looked at Duffy. "I suppose you want Bull?" he said.

"We'll be back in two hours to pick them up," Duffy said.

As they left the stables, Cavill said, "Why do you always ride that nag of a horse?"

14

"Bull just takes some getting used to," Duffy said. "He's a fine horse."

"Blue suits me better," Cavill said.

"Meet you back here in two hours," Duffy said.

At his small townhouse, Duffy cleaned his Smith & Wesson revolver, loaded it with .44 caliber cartridges, and placed it into his tan holster. He clipped on a field knife and then loaded his Winchester rifle.

He changed into denim trail clothes, loaded his saddlebags with extra clothing, a first aid kit, ammunition, and a bottle of whiskey, and then left to meet Cavill.

At his townhouse, Cavill selected his prized Colt Peacemaker he'd had fitted with custom-made black grips, his Winchester rifle, Henry rifle, and Bowie field knife. He dressed in black trail clothes, including his Stetson hat. He loaded his saddlebags with clothing, ammunition, and a bottle of whiskey and then returned to the stables to meet Duffy.

Duffy was already waiting beside Bull when Cavill arrived.

"Our train leaves in one hour," Duffy said.

McCoy handed Cavill the reins to Blue, and Cavill mounted the saddle in one quick, smooth motion.

"Let's go," Cavill said.

CHAPTER THREE

"I don't fancy two days on this stinking train," Cavill said.

Duffy and Cavill were in a riding car on a ten-car passenger train. Duffy was reading a law book, while Cavill had a Chicago newspaper.

"Every case can't be undercover work in Chicago exposing corruption," Duffy said. "Besides, I thought you liked playing cowboy."

Cavill slapped the newspaper. "Look at this. It says Sullivan is fighting in Montana come this December," he said.

"Jack, it's only the first of May," Duffy said. "We won't be in Montana come seven months from now."

"I don't fancy two days on this damned train," Cavill said. "I'm going to get a cup of coffee."

Duffy grinned as Cavill stood up and left the riding car. Duffy continued reading his law book and made notes in the margins in pencil. After a while he closed the book and decided to join Cavill in the dining car.

Cavill sat at a table with a pretty young woman when Duffy entered.

"Why would I want to go to your berth to see your custom-made Colt?" the woman said with a sly grin.

"It's one of a kind," Cavill said.

"As tempting as that offer might be, I see my husband entering the car," the woman said. She stood and greeted a man of about sixty as he entered the car and they took a table.

16

Duffy sat with Cavill.

"You never learn, do you, Jack?" Duffy said.

"What?" Cavill said.

"Never mind," Duffy said. "When we reach Billings, we have a five-day ride to Miles City. We need to think about a plan to stop the rustling going on out there."

"What plan? We find them, take them in, shoot them or hang them," Cavill said.

"Everything is simple to you, isn't it?" Duffy said.

"I'm a simple man," Cavill said.

"That's something we can agree on," Duffy said.

"What's that mean?" Cavill said.

"Nothing. Try to stay out of trouble. I'll meet you back here at six o'clock for supper."

Duffy brought a mug of coffee back to his seat and continued reading his law book. After about an hour, he noticed several men excitedly enter his car from cars ahead and rush to the rear doors and exit.

Several more followed, and then several more after that.

When another group came rushing is, Duffy stopped one man and said, "What is going on, sir?"

"Fight in the last car," the man said and dashed away.

"Fight? Aw, Jack," Duffy said.

Duffy left his seat and walked to the final two cars. Both were boxcars, reserved for horses. The first boxcar held Blue, Bull, and two other horses.

The second boxcar was crammed full of men watching a giant farm boy pummel his opponent to the floor.

Cavill was among the spectators.

"Jack, I thought you were fighting," Duffy said.

"I just lost five dollars on that dope," Cavill said. "That's three fights that dumb farm boy just won."

"That farm boy is the size of Mount Washington," Duffy

said. "Why are you betting against him?"

"Because after two more fights, you're going to bet a hundred bucks on me to win," Cavill said.

"I'll do no such thing," Duffy said. "We're on Mr. Porter's time and . . ."

"Not until we reach Billings," Cavill said. "And I'll split the winnings with you right down the middle."

Duffy looked at the massive farm boy as he knocked his next opponent to the floor. "Can you beat him?" he said.

"Can you count to ten?" Cavill said.

"We use your hundred," Duffy said.

"Fine. Right after the next fight," Cavill said.

The hundred or so men in the boxcar made room for the next opponent, a husky fellow about Cavill's size. He was no match for the giant farm boy and quickly fell to the floor.

Cavill gave Duffy one hundred dollars. "Make it good," he said.

Duffy walked to the center of the boxcar. "One hundred dollars on my friend to beat this giant of a lad," he said.

While eager bettors put up their money, Cavill removed his jacket and shirt and then stepped forward.

A small man standing next to the farm boy whispered something, and the farm boy bent at the knees to listen. Then the small man stepped forward.

"No bets," the small man said. "That man is a ringer. He's Jack Cavill, and I saw him fight in Peoria just last week."

Cavill stepped forward. "You said any man willing. I'm willing."

"I'm not going to allow you to hurt my son just so you can prove your point," the man said. "No more fights for today."

The farm boy said, "I can beat him, Pa."

"No you can't," the man said. "I've seen him fight, and he'll tear you to ribbons, son. That's enough for today."

"Put your shirt on, Jack, the party is over," Duffy said.

Duffy and Cavill were having dinner at a table in the dining car when the father of the farm boy approached their table.

"May I join you for a moment?" he said.

"Why not?" Cavill said.

The man took a chair at the table.

"My son is considered a giant and he's no coward, but he doesn't have the skill for the likes of you, Jack Cavill," the man said. "I know. I promoted the fighter you flattened in Peoria last week. You could have taken my man any time you felt like it."

"You must have lost a bundle," Cavill said.

"Let's just say I've had better days," the man said. "Do you have a promoter?"

Cavill, chewing on steak, shook his head no.

"Do you have plans for the future?" the man said.

Cavill washed down the steak with a sip of beer. "One day I will fight John L. Sullivan," he said.

"Not without a promoter," the man said. "Sullivan can't be reached without a promoter and the offer of big money."

"And that's where you come in," Cavill said.

"I promote fights," the man said. "I'm on my way to South Dakota to promote Fred Robinson. If he wins, he gets a shot at Sullivan later in the year."

"Tell you what," Cavill said. "My partner and I are traveling to Montana on business. How do I reach you when we're done?"

In his sleeping car, Duffy sat at a small table and read his law book by the light of a lantern.

There was a soft knock on the door and Cavill said, "Hey, Jim, are you awake?"

"I am," Duffy said.

The door opened and Cavill entered.

"Law book again, huh?" Cavill said.

Duffy closed the book.

"I've been thinking," Cavill said.

"Did it hurt?"

"Only for a few minutes."

"What's on your mind, Jack?"

"I need a manager," Cavill said.

"Talk to that fellow, the one who promotes fights."

"He's a promoter, not a manager," Cavill said. "I'd like you to be my manager, Jimmy."

"Oh for . . . tell you what, Jack. Let's finish the job at hand, and when we get back to Springfield, I'll consider it."

"Fair enough," Cavill said.

"I'm going to bed," Duffy said. "I'll see you for breakfast."

"By the way, you never returned my hundred dollars," Cavill said.

"Consider it advance payment for my future services as your potential manager," Duffy said. "Good night, Jack."

Cavill went to the door, paused, and looked back. "That doesn't make any sense," he said.

"Does to me. I've got your hundred dollars," Duffy said.

CHAPTER FOUR

As Duffy and Cavill walked their horses from the railroad station to the muddy streets of Billings, Montana, Cavill said, "What a shithole of a town, if you could even call it that."

Founded just a few years before, Billings had a population of just six hundred residents, many of whom worked for the railroad.

"Jack, it's a railroad town," Duffy said. "They're expanding the railroad west, and Billings is their home base."

"Let's see if this dump has a hotel and a decent place to eat," Cavill said.

They led the horses through the muddy streets and found a hotel on an unnamed street.

"Streets don't even have names," Cavill said.

"I don't see a livery. Did you see a . . ." Duffy said.

"Boys, you have to report to the railroad employment office before you do anything else," Railroad Police Chief Atwood said as he walked up to Duffy and Cavill.

"I'm sorry, what?" Duffy said.

"You're new employees of the railroad, ain't you?" Atwood said.

"Naw, cowboys on our way to a job," Cavill said.

"Cowboys?" Atwood said.

"A ranch near Miles City," Duffy said. "Is this the only hotel in town?"

"The only one without bedbugs," Atwood said.

21

"We need a livery stable and a steak," Cavill said.

"Follow me, boys," Atwood said. "Livery is around the corner. We got us a decent restaurant just two blocks from here."

At the livery, they checked their horses and took their saddlebags and rifles with them as they returned to the hotel and checked into a double room.

"Now about that steak," Cavill said to Atwood.

The restaurant was one block west of the hotel. It wasn't much to look at, but their beef was supplied by the railroad and prime. Atwood joined them.

"In my younger days—I'm in my fifties now—I gave cowboying a try, but I just couldn't cotton to it," Atwood said.

"It's not a life for everybody, but it suits us for now," Duffy said.

"Well, if you ask me, you boys look the type could make fine railroad police," Atwood said.

"Maybe when we're done with our cowboy job, we'll stop back and talk about it," Duffy said.

"You boys do that," Atwood said.

"Anyplace in town serve a decent whiskey?" Cavill said.

"Crown Saloon has a passable rye," Atwood said.

"Join us for a drink, Chief Atwood," Cavill said.

"Be delighted, boys," Atwood said.

The Crown Saloon was merely four walls with a plank nailed to two pickle barrels for a bar; it had just twelve tables with four chairs to each and served fifty-cents-a-shot rye whiskey.

"Three whiskies, and let me have three of those cigars you got there in that jar behind the bar," Cavill said.

At a table, they lit the cigars and sipped the rye whiskey.

"Your town has the makings of growing into a fine place," Duffy said.

"Maybe once they connect one end of Montana to the other, she'll grow a bit more," Atwood said.

"That reminds me, we have a long ride ahead of us tomorrow," Duffy said. "We'll need supplies."

"One thing this one-horse town has is a decent general store," Atwood said. "Well, boys, I have to make my rounds."

"The only good thing about this room is it has two beds," Cavill said.

On his bed, Duffy studied a map. "We have a three-hundred-mile ride east to Miles City," he said. "We'll need supplies to last us at least ten days."

Cavill opened a bottle of bourbon he kept in his saddlebags, filled two shot glasses, and gave one to Duffy. "That rye rotgut damn near burned a hole in my stomach," Cavill said.

"We could make Miles City in six days if we push it," Duffy said.

"If you want to kill our horses," Cavill said.

"Seven days then," Duffy said. "After breakfast, I'll wire Mr. Porter we're on our way to Miles City."

Cavill tossed back his shot of whiskey, poured another, and watched as Duffy folded the map and opened his law book.

"How much longer before you become a lawyer?" Cavill said.

"Oh, maybe two years," Duffy said.

"Then what?"

"Maybe private practice. I haven't decided. What about you, Jack? Given any thought to what you want to do besides fight John L. Sullivan?"

"Being the bare knuckles heavyweight champion of the world isn't enough of a goal for you?" Cavill said.

Duffy tossed back his shot and Cavill refilled his glass. "When I was a kid growing up, my grandfather once said to me that we're all an adult once and a child twice."

"What the hell does that mean?" Cavill said.

"You think on it. Quietly, so I can study my book," Duffy said.

In the middle of the night, Cavill awoke and sat up in bed. He struck a match and lit the oil lantern on the table beside the bed.

Duffy, in the other bed, was sound asleep.

"Jim," Cavill said.

Duffy didn't move an inch.

"Hey, Jimmy, wake up," Cavill said loudly.

Duffy opened one eye. "The room better be on fire, Jack."

"It means what do I do with my life after I'm too old to fight?" Cavill said.

"And?"

"I don't know."

"You're not going to figure that part out tonight, Jack. You can think about it on the next three hundred miles," Duffy said.

CHAPTER FIVE

"I see you boys are early risers," Atwood said as he approached Duffy and Cavill in front of the general store.

Duffy and Cavill were loading a hundred dollars' worth of supplies into large saddlebags on their horses.

"We have a long ride ahead of us to our next job," Duffy said.

"Have you had breakfast yet?" Atwood said.

"Actually, no," Duffy said.

"Long ride or not, it seems longer on an empty stomach," Atwood said. "Walk your horses over to the restaurant and we'll have us some flapjacks."

"Not a bad idea," Cavill said.

As they cut into stacks of pancakes, Atwood said, "You boys should give some serious consideration to what I said about working as railroad police. Pay to start is seventy-five a month and you get a pension after twenty years. It ain't a bad life, boys."

"We gave our word we'd do this cowboy job, but when we're done, we'll come back and talk to you," Duffy said.

"That suits me fine, boys," Atwood said. "I like a man that's true to his word."

"Why did you tell Atwood we'd be back?" Cavill said as he and Duffy rode northeast toward Miles City. "Neither of us is interested in a railroad police job, especially at seventy-five a month. Well, hell, we make fifty a day when on assignment, plus expenses."

"Unless you want to ride back to Springfield, we have to return to Billings to take the train home," Duffy said.

"Maybe so, but you led him on," Cavill said.

Duffy looked up at the sun as it rose in the sky. "I didn't figure it to be so hot this early in the year," he said. "And I didn't lead him on. We will go back at some point and I expect we will talk to him. In the meantime, we have to make twenty-five miles before we noon."

They broke for lunch beside a shallow creek and gave the horses one hour of rest. The horses were hot, so the men didn't allow them to drink until they cooled down a bit.

They ate cans of peaches with hunks of cornbread and water. Duffy and Cavill were experienced at riding long distances, and they knew a heavy lunch could make a fellow feel sluggish in the saddle, something they couldn't afford on a long ride.

Once the horses were cooled off enough to drink, they rode until sunset and made camp for the night.

Duffy built a fire while Cavill groomed and fed the horses. Supper was fresh steaks with crusty bread and a pot of coffee. Each had a can of peaches for dessert.

"This Montana is some open country for sure," Cavill said. "We rode thirty or more miles today and didn't see so much as one soul."

"And we're east, where most of the people live," Duffy said. "Imagine how easy it would be to rustle cattle out west where you can really get lost."

"I expect that's where we'll be headed," Cavill said.

"I expect so," Duffy said.

Cavill added wood to the fire, and Duffy read his law book

for a while. Cavill lit one of the cigars he bought in the general store. For a while, the only sound was the crackling of the fire.

"How good are you, Jack?" Duffy said, breaking the silence.

"You mean at boxing?"

"No, your culinary skills in the kitchen," Duffy said. "Of course, boxing."

"I can beat him. I can beat John L."

"Maybe we can work something out when we get home," Duffy said.

"You mean you'll manage me?" Cavill said.

"Well I'm not going to fight you, you big dunce," Duffy said. "But I figure I can get through law school and take the bar exam quicker if I'm not off on assignment for months on end. Do you still have the promoter's address?"

"In my pocket."

"Don't lose it. We'll talk more about this later. Right now I'm going to sleep."

"I can beat him, Jim," Cahill said. "I can beat John L."

"But can you shut up long enough for me to get some sleep?" Duffy said.

On the afternoon of the third day on their ride to Miles City, as they rode down the side of a grassy hill, they paused to watch a herd of bison grazing in a field.

"I thought old Buffalo Bill cleared them all out," Cavill said.

"He retired after he started that Wild West show of his," Duffy said.

"They look peaceful enough," Cavill said.

"Until you aggravate them," Duffy said. "Once roused, they won't back down to nothing. Come on, let's go."

On the fifth day out, they stopped for lunch beside a road carved into the grass by heavy wagon wheels.

Duffy checked his map. "I figure we're less than a hundred miles from Miles City," he said.

Looking down the road, Cavill said, "I see someone coming. Maybe we can ask him."

Duffy stood, removed binoculars from a saddlebag, and looked down the road. "It's a freight wagon," he said. "A driver and a shotgun rider."

Duffy replaced the binoculars and took out two spare coffee cups.

Five or so minutes later, the freight wagon arrived. The driver stopped the wagon and said, "You boys lost or something?"

"On our way to Miles City," Duffy said. "Our map shows it's about a hundred miles north on this road."

"More like ninety as the crow flies," the driver said.

"Care for some coffee?" Duffy said.

"Ain't had none since breakfast," the driver said.

Cavill filled the two spare cups and gave one to the driver and the other to the shotgun rider.

"Obliged," the driver said.

"You boys have the look of cowboys," the shotgun rider said. "Headed to Miles City looking for work?"

"Got a job on a ranch," Duffy said. "You hauling freight to Billings?"

"Every week. Provisions mostly," the driver said. "It ain't much of a town yet, but the railroad has plans."

"Expansion clear to California," the shotgun rider said. "With Billings as a hub for layovers and such."

"Thanks for the coffee, boys. We got a schedule to keep," the driver said. "And good luck with your job."

After the wagon left, Duffy said, "Let's pack up and get going."

After supper, Duffy and Cavill sat in front of the campfire and drank coffee.

"How much money do you think you can make fighting?" Duffy said.

"I made a thousand on side bets in Peoria, and that was on a barge in the river," Cavill said.

"I read in the newspaper that Sullivan has earned a half a million dollars fighting," Duffy said.

"And the man ain't done yet," Cavill said. "Not by a long shot."

"How many times in a year can you fight?"

"Once a month if the money, odds, and side bets are worth it," Cavill said. "That's where you come in."

"And if I do the arranging and promoting with that man we met on the train and take care of the side bets, what's the split?"

"Straight up fifty-fifty."

Duffy nodded. "I could take the bar exam in two years instead of four," he said.

"So you'll do it?"

"One condition," Duffy said. "I manage your money. You get what you need to live on and train, and the rest goes into a bank for your retirement. I don't want you penniless, brainless, and drunk in some back alley when you're past it. Agreed?"

Cavill extended his right hand. "Agreed."

They shook.

"Now let's get some sleep," Duffy said. "We want to be in Miles City by late afternoon."

CHAPTER SIX

Miles City was a bustling cowboy town of about a thousand residents. Stock pens lined the outskirts of town where an auction hall was located.

A dozen saloons and several brothels filled the streets of the downtown section.

The streets were muddy from a heavy, recent rain when Duffy and Cavill rode into town on Main Street around five in the afternoon.

"Let's find the telegraph office and wire Mr. Porter we're in Miles City," Duffy said. "Then we'll find a hotel and grab a shave and a bath."

"And a place to eat," Cavill said.

"Right," Duffy said. "Lest we forget your stomach."

Dressed in clean clothing after dropping off their dirty clothes at the Chinese laundry a block from the hotel, Duffy and Cavill found a restaurant on Main Street and ordered steaks.

"In the morning we'll ride over to the Trent ranch and see Mr. Trent," Duffy said.

"In the morning," Cavill said. "Tonight I want to find us a decent saloon."

"I'm tired, Jack. I'm going to bed," Duffy said.

"Well, leave the lantern on for me," Cavill said.

"That would be just like you to get in all kinds of trouble

when we're on assignment," Duffy said. "I better go with you, but it's still going to be an early night."

"The Devil's Whiskey Saloon," Cavill said. "How can you not love a saloon with a name like that?"

The Devil's Whiskey Saloon was large and loud, with a long bar, twenty-four tables, and a piano. Two bartenders worked behind the bar, and six saloon girls worked the tables.

"Must be a brothel on the second floor," Duffy said.

"Not a bad way to pass the time," Cavill said and looked at the stairs to the second floor.

"And spend the rest of our assignment with your bean dripping and you complaining about it?" Duffy said.

Cavill looked at Duffy. "You really know how to deflate a party," he said. "Let's get a drink."

They found an open spot at the bar and ordered shots of bourbon. Cavill had a cigar holder tucked into his right boot and pulled it out to light a cigar with a wood match.

They sipped their drinks and watched the crowd. Every table was full, and most had card games going. A man at a table suddenly jumped to his feet, drew his revolver, and shouted, "No man cheats me at cards and walks around still breathing with my money in his pocket."

The man was drunk and slurred his words. He cocked his revolver and fired a shot at the man seated at the table directly in front of him. The shot went wild, whizzed by Duffy's right ear, and shattered the mirror behind the bar.

"Stand up and fight, ya stinking coward," the drunken man said.

Duffy removed his heavy Smith & Wesson revolver from the holster, held it in his right hand, walked directly to the drunken man, and clubbed him across the jaw with six pounds of iron. The drunken man fell, unconscious, to the wood floor.

Duffy holstered his revolver, returned to the bar, picked up his drink, and took a sip.

The saloon, including the piano, was silent.

Cavill tossed back his shot, set the glass on the bar, and pointed at the bartender.

The swinging doors pushed inward and the town sheriff and two deputies entered. The deputies carried shotguns.

"Who did the shooting?" the sheriff said.

"That drunk on the floor accused someone at his table of cheating, and he drew his gun and fired," the bartender said. "He missed and shot my mirror. This young fellow here walked up to him and buffaloed him before he could fire another shot."

The sheriff looked at Duffy and Cavill. "You don't say. Give me a coffee, would you," he said and went to the bar.

"You boys passing through?" the sheriff said.

"More or less," Duffy said. "We have jobs at the Trent ranch waiting on us. We understand it's about thirty miles north of town."

"Sounds about right," the sheriff said.

"Sheriff, what do you want us to do with him?" a deputy said and pointed to the unconscious man on the floor.

"Toss his ass in jail," the sheriff said. "If he can't pay for the mirror, he'll serve ten days doing labor."

The deputies lifted the unconscious man and, with the help of two other men, they carried him off to jail.

The sheriff sipped his coffee. "You boys must be pretty good at moving cows," he said. "Trent only hires the best, from what I hear."

"We're fair," Cavill said.

"Well, good luck to you boys, and thanks for stopping a killing," the sheriff said.

"No problem, Sheriff," Duffy said.

"Of course, you boys are aware of the problem the ranchers

are having in these parts?" the sheriff said.

"What problem is that?" Duffy said.

"Rustling," the sheriff said. "Some boys have been killed trying to stop it. If you ask me, if you don't own them, they ain't worth dying over."

"Sound advice, Sheriff," Cavill said.

"I'll send a wire to Mr. Porter that we'll meet with Trent in the morning," Duffy said.

"That drunk tonight, he could have shot you," Cavill said.

"He was so drunk he couldn't have hit a bull standing in front of him," Duffy said.

"Even still, if you get yourself killed, I'm out a manager," Cavill said.

"I'll keep that in mind," Duffy said.

Cavill removed his shirt and tossed it on the chair in their hotel room. "How about a nightcap?" he said.

"Make it small," Duffy said.

Cavill opened his flask, filled the two shot glasses on the nightstand, and gave one to Duffy.

"You know, if you're serious about fighting, you'll have to quit whiskey," Duffy said. "It ruins your wind and makes you sweat too much."

"Sullivan drinks a mixture of tea and Irish whiskey between rounds," Cavill said.

"Good. When you fight him, you'll have the advantage," Duffy said and tossed back his shot.

CHAPTER SEVEN

Duffy and Cavill left Miles City after breakfast and rode thirty miles north until they reached the Trent ranch. A well-worn dirt road led directly to the ranch, and a large gateway with a sign that read *Trent Ranch* took them directly to a ranch house, bunkhouse, corral, and barn.

A few cowboys were at the corral, watching the bronc rider break in a mustang when Cavill and Duffy arrived at the ranch house and dismounted.

A cowboy sat on the porch with a cup of coffee. He stood when Cavill and Duffy dismounted.

"Can I help you boys?"

"We're here to see Mr. Trent," Duffy said.

"I'm ranch foreman. Name is O'Day. You looking for jobs, we're full until fall," O'Day said.

The front door opened and Trent stepped out. "It's all right, O'Day. I was expecting these boys," he said. "Come on in, lunch is just about ready."

Lunch was served in the backyard by Trent's cook, who wore a white apron and hat. He served thick, hot roast beef sandwiches with roasted potatoes. Trent always drank milk with lunch, and there were two pitchers of it chilled in buckets of ice.

"Here is the situation, boys," Trent said. "Since my visit to your office a few weeks ago, at least a hundred head have been reported stolen throughout the state by ranchers."

34

"In less than two weeks?" Duffy said.

"It's a dire situation, boys," Trent said. "Some of the ranchers are talking about hiring professional gunmen to take care of their herds."

"That's not an answer," Duffy said. "You had a big problem with wolves in Montana at one time. Wolfers were brought in to kill them all, and that's what you'd have to do with this bunch. You'd have to kill them all because, just like the wolf, this bunch has tasted free meat. Are your people prepared for that kind of bloodshed?"

"I expect when you come right down to it, we're cattlemen, not gunmen," Trent said. "We're having a meeting tonight at the Foster ranch about ten miles west of here. We'll discuss our options as group, and you boys can tell us what your plan of action is. In the meantime, I have two rooms where you can freshen up a bit and grab a nap if you're so inclined. I have to check my stock on the north range, but I'll be back in plenty of time. We'll leave here at six. Oh, my daughter, Sylvia, will be going with us."

Duffy stepped out on the porch with a cup of coffee at four-thirty in the afternoon and was surprised to see a beautiful young woman seated in a rocking chair.

She looked at Duffy and smiled. She had piercing green eyes and hair so dark it reminded Duffy of coal.

"Which one are you?" she said. "My father said there were two cowboys in the house."

"I'm James Duffy," Duffy said. "My partner is Jack Cavill."

"You look more like a banker than a cowboy," Sylvia said.

Duffy sipped coffee as he looked at Sylvia. "I can't help the way I look, miss," he said.

"I overheard my father talking to Mr. O'Day. He said you and Mr. Cavill are here to help with the rustling problem. Is that true, Mr. Duffy?"

"It is."

"Are you hired guns?"

"Detectives, Miss Trent."

"Detectives? Like in a dime novel? Guns blazing, women at your feet?"

"I don't know. I've never read a dime novel," Duffy said.

"But you can read?" Sylvia said.

"I read all the time," Duffy said.

"Really? What do you read?"

"Law books, mostly."

Sylvia stared at Duffy. "You're a funny one," she said. "Do you dance, Mr. Duffy?"

"If there is music and a partner," Duffy said.

Sylvia grinned and stood up. "I need to change for the festivities," she said. "If you're so inclined, you may ask me for a dance."

After she entered the house, Duffy said, "Damn."

Duffy and Cavill rode their horses beside the carriage Mr. Trent and Sylvia occupied. Trent worked the reins. Behind the wagon, a dozen or more of Trent's hands followed.

They reached the Foster ranch by seven o'clock. A hundred or so people were scattered throughout the front side of a large ranch house, most seated at a dozen tables. Two cooks roasted a side of beef large enough to feed a small army. On the porch, a band consisting of a fiddle player, a man playing a guitar, and another with an accordion provided music. The guitar player sang the words to several pieces of music.

Trent stopped the carriage beside the corral.

"You boys put your horses in the corral," Trent said.

By the time Duffy and Cavill and Trent's hands put their horses inside the corral, Trent and Sylvia had made their way to the head table where Foster stood with a drink.

Duffy and Cavill made their way through the crowd to Trent.

"Boys, this is Sam Foster," Trent said. "Sam, James Duffy and Jack Cavill, the men I told you about."

Foster shook hands with Duffy and Cavill.

"We have much to talk about after we eat," Foster said. "For now, enjoy the festivities."

"Thank you, sir. We will," Duffy said.

"Excuse us, boys," Trent said. "I need a word with Sam."

Trent and Foster walked to the house. Duffy and Cavill looked around for a few minutes until Sylvia approached Duffy.

"I believe you promised me a dance," she said.

"I believe you said if I was inclined," Duffy said.

"And are you?" Sylvia said.

"I'd be a fool not to," Duffy said.

They linked arms and walked to the flat piece of lawn where other couples were dancing. They stopped, bowed slightly, and then came together for a slow waltz. The dance lasted about three minutes.

When it ended, Sylvia said, "Why, you're red in the face, Mr. Duffy. I hope I haven't exhausted you."

The next song started and Duffy said, "Do you two-step?"

"Yes."

Duffy took Sylvia by the hand, and they danced a lively two-step for about two minutes until the song ended and the band took a break.

"Come with me to get some punch," Sylvia said.

They linked arms and walked to the table where punch bowls were located. Each took a cup.

"You dance very well," Sylvia said. "For a detective."

"Hopefully, I will finish law school in the next two years, and my detective days will be behind me," Duffy said.

"I could tell you were more than the ordinary cowboy," Sylvia said.

"Being a cowboy is no easy task," Duffy said.

"I know. I've been around cowboys all my life," Sylvia said. "Most are foul-mouthed, dirty men who can't read and need a bath. Most remind me of your partner, Mr. Cavill."

"Don't let Jack's appearance fool you. He's as smart as they come," Duffy said. "I know he is, because we've been partners for years."

"May I ask you a personal question, Mr. Duffy?" Sylvia said.

"Start by calling me James or Jim," Duffy said.

"All right, James. Are you married?" Sylvia said.

"That's a rather forward question, isn't it?"

"Only if you are."

"No, I'm not married."

"Engaged?"

"I don't even have a steady lady friend."

"Why is that?"

"When I'm not working, which takes me away from home quite a bit, I'm attending law school and studying for the bar exam," Duffy said. "Now, let me ask you a question. Why do you want to know?"

"I'm twenty-three-years-old," Sylvia said. "Out here I'm considered a spinster. I went to college in Boston and graduated two years ago. Here in Montana, my prospects for a husband are next to none."

Duffy stared at Sylvia for several seconds as he tried to figure out if she was serious or joking.

"Did I frighten you again?" Sylvia asked.

"No. I'm just trying to figure out if you're pulling my leg," Duffy said.

"I assure you I'm not," Sylvia said.

38

"I'm not sure I understand exactly what you're saying," Duffy said.

"I'm saying: Would you be interested in my hand as your wife?" Sylvia said.

Duffy stared at her, speechless.

"Oh, I assure you my virtue is fully intact," Sylvia said. "I'm highly educated, have a good sense of humor, have excellent birthing hips, and am not hard to look at. All good qualities in a wife."

Despite himself, Duffy glanced at her hips.

Sylvia smiled. "See?"

On the porch, a cook rang the dinner bell.

"Everybody, let's eat," Foster said.

Sylvia took Duffy's arm and led him to her father's table. "We'll continue our conversation later," she said.

Once everyone was seated at the tables, Foster stood and said, "Mr. Trent will lead us in saying grace."

After dinner, when the sun was down and the music and dancing continued on the front lawn, Trent, Foster, Duffy and Cavill, and a dozen other ranchers from the territory met on the back porch of Foster's home.

One of the cooks served brandy, coffee, and cigars.

"All right, gentlemen, we all know why we're here," Trent said. "To those of you who haven't met them yet, Mr. Duffy and Mr. Cavill are from the Illinois Detective Agency on behalf of Charles Porter."

A man close to eighty years old stood. "I know Charles Porter from the old days," he said. "He was the best stock detective ever to ride the ranges in Montana. The way Charles would have handled this is to smoke the rustlers out and kill them where they stand. How do you plan to tackle this problem?"

"Our plan is simple, Mr. . . . ?" Duffy said.

"Able. Joshua Able."

"Mr. Able, your situation is different than twenty or thirty years ago," Duffy said. "Thousands of head of cattle have been stolen and transported to places unknown. That requires organization and planning skills, knowledge of the cattle business, topography, and geography, and men, lots of men."

"I'm not sure I know what you're talking about," Able said.

"My partner means this bunch is smart," Cavill said. "Very smart and organized. They're not clipping off the drags from a herd. They're rustling significant numbers statewide and transporting them to a specified location. By the time they reach that location, the entire herd has been re-branded and ready to sell at auction."

Foster stood. "I can see why Mr. Porter employs you two. All right, what is your plan?"

"To locate the source and stop it from there," Duffy said.

Able nodded. "Cut off the head of the snake, so to speak," he said.

"What we need to find out is exactly how long this snake is," Duffy said.

"Long enough to rustle nearly two thousand head statewide during the past twelve months," Foster said. "Close to forty thousand dollars in stolen beef."

"So, young fellow, how do you propose to find this snake's head?" Able said.

"Sometimes to catch a snake you have to become a snake," Duffy said. "In order to catch this one, I believe our best course of action will be to infiltrate and become part of the snake."

"Once we are part of their organization, we can locate its source," Cavill said.

"No easy task," Foster said. "This bunch has avoided detection for close to a year now."

"Which is why the Stock Growers Association has hired us," Duffy said.

"Looking back, we should have done that sooner," Trent said.

"When will you get started?" Foster said.

"First light," Cavill said.

"Now that we've settled that, let's return to the festivities," Trent said.

Duffy, Cavill, and Trent had glasses of beer in their hands as they stood and chatted with other members of the Stock Growers Association on the front lawn.

Sylvia appeared by Trent's side.

"Father, it is the final song of the night," she said. "I would like to dance with Mr. Duffy."

"Why tell me? Ask him," Trent said.

Sylvia faced Duffy. "Mr. Duffy?"

Duffy set his beer on a table, linked arms with Sylvia, and they walked to the grass where other couples were dancing to a slow waltz.

They bowed slightly, came together, and Duffy led Sylvia over the lawn in time to the music.

"Have you thought about our conversation earlier?" Sylvia said.

"Your father wouldn't approve," Duffy said.

"My father doesn't make my decisions anymore," Sylvia said. "Can we compromise?"

"How?"

"When this job is finished, I'll come back and we'll talk about it."

"If you don't come back, I'll hunt you down," Sylvia said.

"Fair enough," Duffy said.

Duffy and Cavill were given separate rooms on the second floor

41

of the very large Trent ranch house.

Duffy was asleep when the slight creaking of his bedroom door woke him. He thought it was Cavill until, holding a candle, Sylvia quietly walked in and slowly closed the door.

"What in God's name are you doing?" Duffy said, softly.

"I've come to show you something," Sylvia whispered as she set the candle on the dresser.

"What?"

Sylvia opened her robe and it fell to the floor to expose her naked body. "This," she whispered, "is yours when we are married."

Duffy stared at her as Sylvia picked up the robe, put it on, took the candle, and walked to the door.

"Good night, Mr. Duffy," she said and left the room.

"Jesus." Duffy sighed.

CHAPTER EIGHT

At breakfast, Sylvia barely looked at Duffy and, except to say good morning, didn't speak to him.

"Where are you going to start, boys?" Trent said.

"Foster's range, since he was a recent victim," Duffy said. "From there, we'll see if we can track where the cattle were taken to."

"My cook has loaded the supplies you requested onto your horses," Trent said. "They're saddled and ready to go. We'll see you off."

Trent and Sylvia walked to the porch with Duffy and Cavill.

"We'll be in touch," Duffy said.

As he and Cavill rode away, Duffy glanced back at Sylvia, but her face showed nothing, and she turned away before eye contact was made.

They reached the Foster ranch in forty-five minutes and dismounted at the house. Foster came out before they reached the porch.

"Morning, boys," Foster said.

"Good morning, Mister Foster," Duffy said.

"I'm surprised to see you again so soon. Would you like a cup of coffee?"

"That would be fine," Duffy said.

"Come up to the porch."

A few minutes later, Foster, Duffy, and Cavill sat in chairs on the porch and drank coffee.

"We'd like to see the range where your cattle disappeared from," Duffy said.

"I can ride you over there myself," Foster said. "My men are all out on the ranges."

"I have nearly four thousand head spread out over four ranges," Foster said when they reached the south range. "This range is open land for several of us, including Trent. That's his herd and boys over there to the east. North a bit, those are mine. About thirteen hundred head. I've doubled my riders, just in case."

"How many did you lose last time out?" Cavill said.

"Sixty, maybe more," Foster said.

From atop their horses, Cavill and Duffy looked around. "What water is around here?" Duffy said.

"Tributaries of the Yellowstone, the Missouri, the Wolf, and a dozen others," Foster said. "Good water is all around."

"I want to see your herd," Duffy said.

They rode to Foster's cattle.

"Howdy, boys," Foster said to his men. "Anything today?"

"Quiet as a church on Monday morning," a cowboy said.

Duffy and Cavill dismounted. Duffy removed a notebook from his saddlebags and a pencil from his shirt pocket. He and Cavill inspected the brand of the cattle. Foster's brand was an ornate FS inside a circle.

"Is this your only brand?" Cavill said.

"It is. Why?" Foster said.

As Duffy sketched the brand into his notebook, Cavill said, "Some brands are easier to change than others. A top brander could change yours without much trouble at all."

"Is that why he's making a sketch?" Foster said.

Duffy showed the sketch to Foster.

"SF is easily changed to 8P," Duffy said. "Like Jack said, a top brander would have no trouble at all changing your brand."

Duffy closed the notebook and tucked it away in the saddle-bags.

"Let's check out the water," he said.

Foster led them to a large stream about thirty feet across and four feet deep at its deepest point.

"This comes off the Missouri," Foster said.

Duffy and Cavill walked along the banks for a few hundred feet with their horses in tow. Foster rode alongside them.

"No one has crossed in a while," Duffy said. "Even sixty head leaves its mark."

"Did you make a sketch of Trent's brand?" Cavill said.

"Not yet," Duffy said.

They rode to Trent's herd in the east range. Trent's foreman, O'Day, and six cowboys were guarding a herd of about fifteen hundred head of cattle.

O'Day was standing beside a fire, drinking a cup of coffee.

"Mr. Foster," O'Day said.

Foster, Duffy, and Cavill dismounted.

"Good morning," Foster said.

"What can I do for you, Mr. Foster?" O'Day said.

"I'd like to make a sketch of Mr. Trent's brand in my note-book," Duffy said.

"What for?" O'Day said.

"To help identify doctored brands," Duffy said.

"I think I better check with Mr. Trent before you do anything," O'Day said.

"I'm sure Mr. Trent won't mind," Foster said. "They sketched my brand, and brands are a matter of public records."

"I think I still better check," O'Day said.

"We don't have time for this," Cavill said and took the sketch book from Duffy.

O'Day drew his revolver and cocked it. "I said, I better check with Mr. Trent," he said.

"I don't think that's necessary," Foster said.

"You worry about your herd, Mr. Foster," O'Day said. "I'll worry about Mr. Trent's."

"We hired these men to . . ." Foster said.

Cavill smashed his right fist against O'Day's right forearm and the revolver fell to the ground. Before O'Day could react, Cavill lifted O'Day by the shirt and flung him aside.

"You cock a gun at a man, you better use it," Cavill said.

"Jack, that's enough," Duffy said. "Mr. O'Day, send a rider for Mr. Trent. We'll wait."

O'Day looked up at Cavill.

"You heard him," Cavill said. "We'll wait."

"You kept these men waiting for two hours over a sketch in a book?" Trent said.

"As your foreman, my job is to protect your herd," O'Day said. "How do I know what they plan to use the sketch for?"

"Understood and appreciated," Trent said. "But we hired these men to locate the rustlers. If they need a sketch of the brand, I'll allow it."

"Yes, sir," O'Day said.

While Duffy made a sketch of Trent's brand, Trent, Foster, and Cavill spoke in private.

"Your brand, an ornate T inside a circle, would be a simple trick for a top brander to change undetected," Cavill said. "Maybe you and Mr. Foster should think about changing your brands in the future."

"It's too late to change six thousand head," Trent said. "The cost and loss of time would set us back months."

"After the next drive," Foster said.

"Mr. Trent, as head of the local Stock Growers Association, maybe you could hold a meeting with all the local ranchers and talk about changing brands," Duffy said.

"We'll ride over to the Yellowstone and see if we can pick up any tracks," Duffy said.

"How many men you got on night watch?" Cavill said.

"Six," Trent said.

"Same," Foster.

"Have them spread out along the herd and have three fires going all night," Duffy said. "It gives the appearance to anyone hanging about that you have more men on night watch."

"We'll be in touch," Cavill said.

Duffy and Cavill mounted their horses and rode toward the Yellowstone River.

"We've been following the Yellowstone for two hours now and haven't seen a thing," Cavill said.

"Let's give the horses a breather," Duffy said.

"I'll make coffee," Cavill said.

A little while later, while they drank coffee and ate a few biscuits, Duffy and Cavill studied a map of Montana.

"If we follow the Yellowstone for a few days, we'll be back in Billings," Duffy said.

"I doubt they'd rustle cattle and head for Billings," Cavill said.

"Well, I know that," Duffy said. "Unless they have some secret place to stash the stolen herd and change the brands, where would they go, with every cowboy and lawman in Montana looking for them?"

"You just don't hide an entire herd," Cavill said. "No, these boys know the country and know how to move cattle quickly and undetected."

Duffy lifted the coffee pot and refilled the two cups.

Cavill lit a cigar.

They both looked at the maps.

"What do you think?" Cavill said.

"I think we need to find some signs of stolen cattle right quick, or you and I are just riding through some pretty country," Duffy said.

"Yeah," Cavill said.

"Jim, have a look," Cavill said and dismounted along the bank of the Yellowstone River.

Duffy, some twenty feet behind Cavill, rode to him and dismounted.

Both men knelt.

"A small herd crossed here," Duffy said.

Cavill stood and walked a bit through thick grass. "Some signs show they passed through and went south," he said.

Duffy stood. "Let's cross and see where they came from. We can always pick up the trail later."

They mounted the horses and crossed the shallow river to the north side and searched for tracks.

"Here," Duffy said. "Northwest a bit."

They rode for several miles until the tracks split. They dismounted and searched the area on foot.

"Six cattle and four horses without riders came from the east a bit and joined up with the rest," Cavill said. "Two riders guiding the lot."

"This isn't making any sense," Duffy said.

A bullet suddenly struck the ground between Duffy and Cavill.

"Either of you move, and you're both dead men," a woman's voice called out.

"I believe you," Duffy said.

"Drop the gun belts and then turn around," the woman said.

Duffy and Cavill opened their gun belts, let them fall to the ground, and then they turned and faced the woman.

She was about thirty yards away at the bottom of a soft hill.

Dressed in blue denim pants and a white blouse and wearing a wide-brim Stetson hat, she wore a Colt pistol on her right hip and held a Winchester rifle in her arms.

"Why, I recognize you from the newspapers," Duffy said. "You're Calamity Jane."

"The name is Jane Canary, and if you call me Calamity again, I'll shoot you for sure for saying it," Canary said.

"I meant no offense," Duffy said.

Canary walked closer to Duffy and Cavill, eyeing them carefully. "You're a big one," she said of Cavill. "A lot like my Bill in that regard. Now what's your business here?"

"We're detectives hired by the Stock Growers Association," Duffy said. "To find whoever is rustling cattle in Montana."

"Detectives, you say," Canary said. "Show me something that says you are what you say."

Duffy and Cavill removed their wallets and Cavill walked them to Canary.

"Open them," she said.

Cavill held open the wallets.

"Illinois Detective Agency," Canary said. She looked up at Cavill. "Yup, you're a big one, all right."

"What are you doing around here, Jane?" Duffy said.

"I got a place just north of here," Canary said. "I went hunting turkey. When I got back, my stock and horses were gone. I set out tracking them."

"How long ago?" Duffy said.

"I was gone two nights and got back late last night. I set out about two hours ago," Canary said.

"Your stock and horses joined up with a larger bunch and rode south across the Yellowstone," Duffy said.

"Let me get my horse from over the hill yonder, and I'll join up with you boys," Canary said.

Canary turned and walked up the hill.

49

Duffy and Cavill looked at each other and then picked up their gun belts.

CHAPTER NINE

They followed the tracks for several hours until the tracks turned east back to the Yellowstone River.

"They're headed back to the river," Duffy said.

"This bunch knows how to steal," Cavill said.

"And they'll know how to hang when I catch up with them," Canary said.

"We got about two hours of daylight left. Let's see where they're headed," Cavill said.

Kneeling beside the Yellowstone River, Cavill said, "By God, this bunch is in and out of the water more than a bar of soap at a bathhouse on a Saturday night."

"Best make camp before it gets dark," Duffy said.

Duffy and Cavill had fresh meat in their supplies, so they cooked a stew with beans and bacon and made a pot of coffee.

Canary dug out a bottle of Irish whiskey from her saddlebags and splashed some into the stew and the coffee.

As they ate, Duffy said, "The brand on your horse, is it the same on your cattle?"

"It is," Canary said.

"MJC," Duffy said. "What's the M for?"

"I was born Martha Jane, but hardly a soul knows that," Canary said. "Not even my Bill knew that."

"If you had the irons and the knack, it wouldn't be too much trouble to change your brand to MTO."

"I reckon so," Canary said.

"We figure they're changing brands and smuggling the cattle south out of Montana," Duffy said.

"I'll follow them until hell freezes over, this bunch," Canary said.

"Supper is ready," Duffy said and dished out three plates.

"So, Jane, what was Wild Bill really like?" Cavill said.

"He was tall and stout like you," Canary said. "He was afraid of no man or beast and was the best shot I've ever seen. He could hit the eye of a bird flying. Truth is, he was sickly when he died. He said it was glaucoma, and he was going blind."

"All the stories I've read, are they true?" Cavill said.

"Depends on what you want to believe," Canary said.

"They wrote you went after McCall with a meat cleaver after he shot Bill," Cavill said.

"I wasn't even in the saloon that night," Canary said. "If I had been, that little shit McCall probably wouldn't'a been able to come up behind Bill undetected. It was just bad luck his favorite chair with its back to the wall was occupied by some cheating card player."

Canary stared off into space for a few seconds. Then she said, "I did love Wild Bill, though."

"Fine breakfast, fellows," Canary said. "Saddle my horse while I do my privacy."

"She's a handful, all right," Cavill said as he saddled Canary's horse.

"Just don't call her Calamity," Duffy said.

"Right," Cavill said.

By midmorning, they had tracked the stolen horses and cattle to a campsite just two days old.

"This is one slow-moving bunch," Duffy said. "Didn't do more than ten miles between campsites."

52

"Still following close to the river," Cavill said. "They might be looking to fatten their herd a bit."

"Let's get another ten miles in before lunch," Canary said.

"By God," Duffy said.

Directly ahead were the remains of a covered wagon. It still smoldered from the fire that had consumed it.

A man, woman, and a child lay dead on the ground, each having died from gunshot wounds.

"This bunch stole their valuables and horses, murdered the family, and burned the wagon," Cavill said.

"Looks like the dead folks had a couple of cows, too," Cavill said.

"Nobody should die like this," Canary said. "No man or beast."

"Let's dig these poor souls a grave," Cavill said.

Close to sundown, Duffy and Canary made camp and built a fire while Cavill scouted ahead.

Cavill rode several miles and dismounted when he came across two dead men in a field. They had been shot in the back and then, for good measure, shot again in the face.

Cavill drew his Colt and fired two shots in the air.

"Keep supper hot. I might be gone a while," Duffy said.

"He might be in trouble. I should go with you," Canary said.

"Jack's fine,"Duffy said. "Two followed by two more is the signal for trouble. He just found something he wants me to look at."

"This is a bad bunch, Jack," Duffy said as he inspected the two dead men. "Maybe the worst I've ever seen."

"It's father and son, judging from the looks of them—what's

left of them," Cavill said.

"Let's get them in the ground," Duffy said.

"Thanks for keeping supper hot, Jane," Cavill said as he filled a plate with stew.

"Two more dead, and for what? Cows? Horses? I'd like to hang these bastards personally," Canary said.

"They can't be more than a day ahead of us," Duffy said. "You just might get your chance."

"Four riders, a dozen cows, and eight horses," Duffy said as he inspected the tracks. "A half day's ride ahead of us."

"Like you said, Jim, this is a slow-moving bunch," Cavill said.

Duffy mounted his horse. "I think they might be looking to pick up some more cows and horses."

"Is that why they're traveling so slow and staying close to the river?" Canary said.

"Easy water, and folks are always nearby," Cavill said.

"Well, let's catch this bunch before they kill again," Canary said.

Close to midnight, Duffy, Cavill, and Canary stood on a cliff overlooking a small box canyon where the four riders, stolen cattle, and horses were bedded down.

"Well, there they are, sleeping like babies," Cavill said. "Too stupid or sure of themselves to even post a night watch. I'll take them at dawn."

"We don't want to shoot them, Jack. They deserve a rope for what they've done," Cavill said.

"What do you mean, take them at dawn?" Canary said.

"He means kill them, but this bunch deserves hanging," Duffy said. "Let's get some sleep; we need to be up before they are."

★ ★ ★ ★ ★

Just before dawn broke, Cavill mounted his horse, drew his prized Colt Peacemaker, and rode down the hill into the outlaws' camp.

"He must be loco," Canary said.

"Naw," Duffy said. "No sorry ass bunch like those four could ever take Jack. Grab your rifle. We'll follow, but not too close."

Cavill reached flat ground, turned a corner, and rode into the sleeping outlaws' camp. The tethered stolen horses nervously snorted, but the sleeping outlaws didn't stir.

Until Cavill fired a shot into the air.

At the crack of the pistol, the four outlaws jumped from their bedrolls.

Cavill shot one outlaw in the shoulder, another in the leg, and then said, "Anyone else want to get shot reaching for their gun?"

One outlaw looked at Cavill. "We're cowboys just trying to get through the territory."

"Sure you are," Cavill said. "Jim, you got your rifle on this sorry-looking bunch?"

Duffy and Canary appeared from around the corner down the hill. Each had a Winchester aimed at the outlaws.

Cavill holstered the Colt, dismounted, and walked to the two outlaws still standing.

"Cowboys, huh?" Cavill said.

Cavill punched one outlaw so hard, the man was unconscious before he hit the ground.

The other remaining cowboy reached for his sidearm, but Cavill grabbed him and flung his back into the side of the hill.

"Cowboys who leave a trail of dead everywhere they go," Cavill said and kicked the outlaw in the stomach, face, and ribs.

"Jack, that's enough," Duffy said.

"Well, they got me riled," Cavill said.

55

"You and Jane watch them," Duffy said, then he turned his horse and rode away.

"Where's he going?" Canary said.

"To find a tree stout enough to hold the four of them," Cavill said.

The four outlaws sat atop their horses with hands tied behind their backs and with nooses around their necks. Two of them were semiconscious, having lost large amounts of blood from their gunshot wounds.

Duffy stood beside their horses, stick in hand.

"You have one chance to save your lives," Duffy said. "Tell me what you know about the cattle thefts in Montana."

One of the outlaws said, "Mister, we just come over from Utah, and we don't know shit about no Montana cattle thefts. We bought them cows and horses legal."

"Sure you did," Duffy said. "What about your friend there? What's he got to say?"

"Screw you," the other outlaw said.

"What's your name?" Duffy said.

"What's it to you?"

"I surely do appreciate you boys making it a pleasure to hang you," Duffy said.

"Screw you, you damned grim reaper, and get it over with," one of the men said.

"Go on and meet your maker," Duffy said.

He went from horse to horse, cracking each rump with the stick. One by one, each horse ran forward, leaving the outlaw to hang.

Cavill and Canary stood back and watched.

"By God," Canary said.

"God ain't nowhere around at the moment," Cavill said.

As the outlaws swung, Duffy said, "Let's get our shovels and dig these soulless bastards a grave."

Around a campfire, as they ate supper, Canary said, "You boys would have made Bill proud."

"I guess you'll be headed back now," Duffy said.

"At first light," Canary said. "I got my cows and horses. I might as well head them home."

"Take the rest with you," Cavill said. "Seeing as how they belong to nobody, you might as well keep them."

"I appreciate that, boys," Canary said.

Suddenly, Cavill stood and pulled his Colt. "Rider's coming," he said.

Duffy and Canary stood. A few minutes later a rider appeared in the dark.

"Hello to camp," the rider said.

"Identify yourself," Duffy said.

"Name is Parker. Robert Leroy Parker."

"What do you want, Parker?" Cavill said.

"A cup of coffee and a place to bed down for the night," Parker said.

"Come in slow," Cavill said.

Parker rode his horse from the darkness into the light of the campfire.

"It's just a kid," Cavill said.

"How old are you, son?" Duffy said.

"Seventeen."

"Dismount and help yourself to a cup of coffee," Duffy said.

Parker dismounted, grabbed a spare cup by the fire, and filled it with hot coffee.

"What's a kid like you doing out here alone?" Cavill said.

"I was looking for my employer," Parker said.

"Who is your employer?" Duffy said.

"His name is Cassidy," Parker said. "He owns a small spread in Utah. I work for him. He told me to meet him near the Yellowstone River in Montana to help him drive some cows and horses back to his ranch."

"Well, son, we hanged a bunch for horse and cattle theft and for murdering innocent people," Duffy said. "What's this Cassidy look like?"

"Tall, thin, has a beak-like nose," Parker said.

"He wasn't here," Duffy said.

"You hung them?" Parker said.

"It's nasty business for sure," Cavill said.

"Well, I guess I should keep looking for him," Parker said.

"He sounds a bad sort," Cavill said. "Maybe you might want to rethink your friendship with the man."

"I'd listen to him," Duffy said. "If this Cassidy is out in the country, you can be sure he's up to no good."

"Son, my name is Jane Canary. I have to drive my horses and cows to my place near Miles City," Canary said. "If you give me a hand, I'll pay you twenty-five dollars for your troubles."

"Twenty-five dollars, huh?" Parker said.

Cavill and Duffy grinned.

"Grab a plate of food," Duffy said to Parker. "A man travels better on a full stomach."

CHAPTER TEN

"Well, Jane, it's been a pleasure riding with you," Duffy said after breakfast.

"You boys would have given Bill a run for his money," Canary said.

"Who's Bill?" Parker said.

"I'm sure you and Jane will have a lot to talk about on the trip," Duffy said.

"Young Parker, do your friends call you Bob?" Cavill said.

"Butch, on account of I once worked in a butcher shop in Utah," Parker said.

"Take care of yourself, Butch," Cavill said.

"And pick better friends," Duffy said.

"Let's go, if we're going," Canary said.

Duffy and Cavill watched as Jane and Parker led her cows and horses away from camp; then they mounted up and rode in the opposite direction.

Around noon, Duffy and Cavill rested the horses for an hour and ate a cold lunch of canned fruit and water.

Duffy checked his maps.

"We're only a few hundred yards from the Yellowstone River, and just south of here is Billings," Duffy said. "We might as well ride in and check with that railroad police chief if there's been any new reports of rustling. And wire Mr. Porter while we're at it."

"A bed, a bath, and a steak sounds good about now," Cavill said.

"If we skip supper, we can reach Billings by eight tonight," Duffy said.

Drinking the syrup from the can after eating the peaches, Cavill said, "As Jane said, let's go, if we're going."

Duffy and Cavill mounted their horses.

"We'll need to see that railroad police chief. What's his name?" Cavill said.

"Atwood."

"Yeah, Atwood," Cavill said.

A little before eight in the evening, Duffy and Cavill rode onto Main Street in Billings.

"It's still a shithole," Cavill said.

They rode to the hotel, dismounted, and entered the lobby.

"I remember you boys from a few weeks ago," the clerk said.

"We'll need a room and a bath," Duffy said. "We'll be back as soon as we livery our horses and grab a steak."

The restaurant was closing shortly when they arrived, but the owner was happy to serve them steaks rather than toss them into the garbage.

"Looks like that telegram to Porter will have to wait until morning," Cavill said. "The whole town's gone to bed."

"We'll grab a shave and bath, send the wire in the morning, and see Atwood," Duffy said.

When they walked back to the hotel, the streets were dark and deserted.

"This is the deadest town I've ever been in," Cavill said.

"Every town can't be Chicago or New York," Duffy said.

"Hell, this place isn't even Peoria," Cavill said.

After breakfast, as they walked to the railroad police office, a large crowd was gathered outside, and Atwood stood on a soapbox.

"I need a dozen able-bodied men for a posse to ride with me to chase down the thieving scum that robbed the train last night of the railroad payroll," Atwood said. "No married men. The pay is twelve dollars a day. You supply your own firearms and bullets. We'll leave in one hour from the general store."

Atwood stepped down off the soapbox and entered his office.

Cavill and Duffy looked at each other. Cavill nodded.

"Aw, Jack, no," Duffy said.

"I'm bored chasing nothing," Cavill said. "Let's chase some outlaws for a few days. What could it hurt?"

"Dammit, Jack," Duffy said.

Cavill grinned. "Let's go," he said.

Atwood was at his desk, loading a Winchester rifle, when Duffy and Cavill entered the office. Atwood paused and looked at them.

"I didn't expect to see you boys back so soon," Atwood said.

"Our job fell short," Cavill said. "We heard your speech asking for a posse. We'd like to volunteer."

"I'll be damned," Atwood said. "This could be a hard ride, boys."

"We've done hard rides before," Cavill said.

"Raise your right hands so I can swear you in," Atwood said.

Duffy and Cavill held up their right hands.

"Will you obey my orders and conduct yourself according to the law as it is written?" Atwood said.

"Yes," Cavill said.

"Yes," Duffy said.

"Last night six armed men stopped the payroll train by burning the tracks," Atwood said. "They killed two guards and put the conductor in the hospital. I don't know if he'll make it. They robbed the safe. It had twelve thousand dollars in cash for the workers building the extension. I aim to get the money back and see the men who took it hang."

"They got a fair head start," Duffy said.

"I don't expect they're traveling none too fast," Atwood said. "When I said they robbed the safe, I meant they took the whole safe."

"Is that why they killed the guards?" Duffy said.

"Only the paymaster has the combination," Atwood said. "All right boys, let's go."

At the general store, each man was given five days' worth of supplies that supplemented whatever they'd brought themselves.

Atwood led the posse of twelve men east out of Billings. They rode hard for twenty miles before they reached the destroyed railroad tracks.

A group of railroad workers were replacing the ties and rails.

"Give the horses a breather, boys," Atwood said.

After everybody dismounted, Cavill and Duffy scouted the area for tracks. They found some left by six horses, dragging a safe and heading southeast.

They returned to Atwood, who was chatting with the railroad workers.

"We found tracks left by six riders dragging a safe," Duffy said.

"We're going to scout a bit. We'll be back in one hour," Cavill said.

"I'm coming with you boys," Atwood said. He turned to the posse. "Sit tight, men. I'll be back in an hour."

Atwood mounted his horse and followed Duffy and Cavill. The trail left by the six outlaws hauling a three-hundred-pound safe behind them was easy enough to follow.

"There was a good moon last night," Atwood said. "They

could have hauled that safe until morning before they stopped to open it."

"What kind of safe is it?" Duffy said.

"Wells Fargo, top of the line, made just for the railroad," Atwood said. "Airtight, two-inch-thick walls and floor, and with a three-inch-thick door. You can't shoot through it, you can't drop it off a cliff, you can't pick the lock, and it weighs three hundred pounds empty."

"They turned south here," Cavill said.

"They're headed to the Bighorn River," Duffy said.

Atwood cocked an eye at Cavill and Duffy. "You sure you boys never been in Montana before?"

"Not before we showed up a few weeks ago," Cavill said.

Duffy dismounted and studied the ground.

"Still dragging the safe," he said.

"They'll drag it to kingdom come before they open it," Atwood said.

Duffy returned to the saddle. "My guess is they'll open it at the river."

"What makes you say that?" Atwood said.

"These boys seem pretty smart," Cavill said. "My guess is they will flip the safe upside down, drill a hole in the bottom where the steel is the thinnest, fill it with nitroglycerin, and blow it open from the bottom where the money is protected by an inside bottom shelf that is made of steel an inch thick."

"Because nitroglycerin is unstable in liquid form and needs to be kept cool, a good place to store a jar would be in cool water," Duffy said. "Like a river."

"You boys are no ordinary cowboys," Atwood said.

"Actually, we're detectives from the Illinois Detective Agency and we were hired to track down the rustlers stealing cattle in Montana," Duffy said.

"We're also fully appointed constables sworn in by the

governor of Illinois and with federal powers granted by the US marshal out of Washington," Cavill said.

"We tell you that so you know we have the power to act on our own if need be," Duffy said.

"That's about an hour," Cavill said. "I'll go back for the posse so you can rest your horses."

"Obliged," Atwood said.

While Cavill rode back, Atwood and Duffy dismounted and found a shady tree to sit under.

"You two must be highly educated fellows," Atwood said.

"We like to think of it as seasoned," Duffy said.

Atwood pulled out a tobacco pouch and paper and rolled a cigarette. "Mind a question?" he said as he struck a wood match and lit the cigarette. "If you boys are after rustlers, why did you volunteer to join my posse?"

"My partner gets bored easily," Duffy said.

"He looks like the type of man to steer clear of when he gets his blood up," Atwood said.

"For sure," Duffy said. "Now that you know who we are and why we're here, we were going to ask you if you've heard of any new rustling in these parts."

"Some news came in with the railroad two days ago," Atwood said. "The Jordan ranch posted a reward for cattle thieves. A hundred head or more were stolen off an open range."

"How far to Helena?" Duffy said.

"Three hundred miles as the crow flies."

"I think I'll make a pot of coffee for the boys when they get here," Duffy said.

Atwood leaned against his saddle, puffed on a cigarette, sipped coffee, and said, "You make a damn fine cup of coffee."

"When you live alone, you learn how to cook," Duffy said.

"Not married then?" Atwood said.

"No time," Duffy said. "When I'm not working, I attend classes at law school."

"Law school, huh?" Atwood said. "You know, my daughter is about the right age for marrying. She's at school in Baltimore at the moment."

"I'm sure she's a lovely girl," Duffy said.

"Actually, she's as homely as a girl can get," Atwood said. "Like her mother, but she has a good, sweet, heart."

Leaning against his saddle, Duffy put his cup on the ground and stood up. "Did you hear that?" he said.

"What? I didn't hear anything," Atwood said.

"There it is again," Duffy said. "Twigs snapping."

Atwood listened carefully. "I heard it."

"About a hundred feet to the left," Duffy said.

Duffy removed his Winchester from the saddle. "I'm going to check it out," he said.

Atwood grabbed his Winchester. "I'm going with you."

"Follow me and move quietly," Duffy said.

Duffy took the lead, and they moved as quietly as possible through a thick, wooded area. After about a hundred feet, Duffy held up his right hand and they paused to listen.

"This map doesn't make a lick of sense," a man muttered.

Duffy motioned forward, and he and Atwood walked toward the man. After twenty feet or so, they stopped and peered through a clearing.

The man, dressed in buckskin, wearing round spectacles, sat on the ground and studied a map. Tethered to a tree were a horse and pack mule.

"Where in the hell am I?" the man muttered.

"Mister, we mean you no harm, so don't get jumpy," Duffy said.

The man sighed. "If you're looking to rob me, go right ahead," he said. "I have nothing of value, and I'm lost and

65

figure to die out here of starvation or lose my scalp to an Indian, anyway."

"Mister, we're the law," Duffy said. "Nobody is going to rob you."

"The law?"

"We're coming in, so don't get jumpy," Duffy said.

Duffy and Atwood approached the man, and he turned around and looked at them.

"I'm Theodore Roosevelt," he said. "My friends call me Ted."

"What the hell are you doing alone out here?" Atwood said.

"I purchased a ranch in Medora, North Dakota," Roosevelt said. "I'm traveling north to explore all this new country."

"If this don't beat all," Atwood said.

"Would you gentlemen happen to know where I am?" Roosevelt said. "I seem to be . . . well, lost."

"You're less than a mile from the Bighorn River, is where you are," Atwood said. "About four hundred miles west of Medora give or take."

"Mister Roosevelt, you better come with us," Duffy said.

"Why?" Roosevelt said. "If my destination is east."

"As you can see by this badge on my shirt, I am a federal police officer for the railroad," Atwood said. "There is a bad bunch of murdering scum loose on the river somewhere and until we catch them, it ain't safe for a tenderfoot like you to be out here alone."

"You'll be safe with us, Mr. Roosevelt," Duffy said.

"Well, let me pack up my mule then," Roosevelt said.

When Cavill returned with the posse, he dismounted and looked at Roosevelt. "Who—or should I say what—is that?" he said.

"This is Mr. Theodore Roosevelt, and he's lost," Atwood said. "I figured he better stay with us until we catch up to those outlaws."

"Lost?" Cavill said.

"Let's pick up the trail again and see if we can find a discarded safe," Duffy said.

An hour before dark, Duffy and Cavill led Atwood and the posse to the discarded safe on the banks of the Bighorn River. It was upside down, with a gaping hole in its bottom.

"Looks like you boys were right. They blew the bottom off," Atwood said. "Well, let's make camp and get a fresh start in the morning."

"We're going to scout ahead," Duffy said. "Be back in about an hour."

"They crossed here at this shallow point," Cavill said as he knelt before six sets of tracks.

"Let's cross and pick up their trail," Duffy suggested.

Cavill mounted his horse. "Right."

They crossed the Bighorn River in water barely four feet deep and emerged onto a shallow bank that led to a field of tall grass.

The tracks led southeast and were easy enough to follow.

They dismounted for a few minutes to give the horses a breather.

"There's something familiar about that Roosevelt fellow," Duffy said. "Like I've seen him someplace before."

"I doubt we ever met him before," Cavill said. "I'd remember a guy who dresses like that."

"He's a dude, for sure," Duffy said. "Sounds like New Jersey or New York, the way he talks."

"Let's go back before it gets dark," Cavill said.

Supper was cooking in several large pans when Duffy and Cavill returned to camp.

"They crossed and headed southeast," Cavill said as he dismounted.

"Southeast, huh?" Atwood said. "They could be headed almost anywhere."

"They're barely twelve hours ahead of us," Duffy said. "The safe slowed them down considerably."

Roosevelt carried two cups of coffee to Duffy and Cavill.

"Thank you," Duffy said. "Mr. Roosevelt, have we ever met before?"

"Not that I'm aware of," Roosevelt said.

"Your face is very familiar," Duffy said.

"I'm thinking that very thing," Atwood said.

"You were in the newspaper, weren't you?" Duffy said.

"Say, you ain't wanted, are you?" Atwood said.

"No, he's not wanted. At least by the law," Duffy said. "You gave a speech at the Republican Convention a while ago, didn't you?"

"I read that myself," Atwood said. "In the newspapers."

"A bad experience for me, I'm afraid," Roosevelt said. "The loss of the man I nominated has left a bad taste in my mouth for politics."

"That's why you're out here? To get away from it all?" Duffy said.

"More or less," Roosevelt said. "I purchased a ranch in Medora where my family can live in peace."

"Boys, I'm starved," Atwood said. "Let's eat."

As Duffy removed the saddle from his horse, he looked at Cavill. "I don't think we've seen the last of Mr. Roosevelt."

CHAPTER ELEVEN

Duffy and Cavill tracked the outlaws southeast ahead of Atwood and the posse. Midafternoon, they dismounted and made a pot of coffee to allow the posse to catch up to them.

"They're just a few hours ahead of us and traveling in no hurry," Duffy said when Atwood and the posse arrived.

"They must figure they're in the free and clear by now," Atwood said.

"Let's get reasonably close and make camp," Duffy said.

They rode until an hour before sunset.

"Make camp," Duffy said. "Jack and I will be back directly."

"I should go with you," Atwood said.

"No offense, Atwood, but you'd just slow us down," Cavill said.

Atwood watched as Duffy and Cavill rode off.

"If this don't beat all," Atwood said. "All right men, make camp."

"Smell that?" Cavill said.

"Yeah. Campfire," Duffy said.

They dismounted, tethered their horses to a narrow tree, and followed the scent across a narrow stretch of open ground to a box canyon where they could see the campfire about a hundred yards below.

"Why do these assholes always think a box canyon protects

them?" Cavill said softly.

"Let's go," Duffy whispered. "And be grateful they're stupid."

As he ladled stew onto a tin plate, Cavill said, "Jimmy and I will grab some sleep and head back around midnight. Then I'll kill them all for you, Atwood."

"What? What? No," Atwood said.

Duffy grinned as he ate a spoonful of stew. "Afraid when Jack makes up his mind to kill outlaws, they're as good as dead," he said.

"Boys, I don't want them dead," Atwood said. "I want them to stand trial for their crimes and be hanged properly, in accordance with the law."

Cavill filled a cup with coffee. "You sure take the fun out of being a lawman, Atwood," he said.

"Fun? You consider this fun?" Atwood said.

"May I make a suggestion?" Roosevelt said. "Take alive those who are willing to go, and those who put up a fight, if you have to, you kill."

"You'll make a politician yet, Mr. Roosevelt," Duffy said.

"That's how we'll handle her then," Atwood said. "Finish supper, grab some sleep, and be ready to ride at midnight."

"They're sleeping," Roosevelt said.

"They feel secure in the knowledge they made it away clean," Atwood said.

"I've had a tougher time shooting paper ducks at the state fair," Cavill said. "Atwood, have your posse close the back and front door to the canyon after Jimmy and I go down and subdue these idiots."

"Give us five minutes," Duffy said.

"No killing if it can be helped," Atwood said.

"Sure, whatever," Cavill said.

Duffy and Cavill quietly made their way down the side of the hill into the canyon. They waited for the posse to close off the canyon and then walked directly into the sleeping outlaws' camp.

"You want to wake these sleeping beauties or should I?" Cavill said.

Duffy drew his Smith & Wesson .44, cocked it, and fired one shot into the ground.

The six outlaws woke with a start. As they reached for their guns, Cavill shot one in the arm and another in the shoulder.

"Hold on! Now you just hold on," an outlaw said. "We're cowboys looking for work, just trying to get through the territory."

"And I'm your fairy godmother," Cavill said. He waved his deadly Colt. "And this is my magic wand."

"Atwood, bring your people out," Duffy shouted.

Within seconds, Atwood and the posse had surrounded the outlaws.

"That was fine police work," Atwood said. "I'll make sure the railroad knows about you two when we get back to Billings."

"Just so long as we get back there quick," Cavill said. "We still have a long road ahead of us."

The entire town of Billings turned out to witness Atwood and the posse ride the six outlaws down Main Street shortly before sunset.

They dismounted at Atwood's office.

"All you boys come back in an hour to get paid," Atwood said. "Someone send for the doc to patch up the two who're shot."

"We're going for a steak," Cavill said. "Join us for a drink later. We still need information on that cattle theft near Helena."

"I'll buy," Atwood said.

After stabling the horses, Duffy and Cavill checked into the hotel and found themselves in the same room they'd had before.

"I remember you boys from a few weeks ago," the clerk at the desk said.

"I hope you changed the linen," Cavill said.

"Every week, whether it needs it or not," the clerk said.

Duffy and Cavill locked their Winchester rifles and saddlebags in the room and then walked over to the restaurant. Most of the men who rode in the posse were having steaks. Duffy and Cavill joined them.

"You men did a fine job of being a posse," Cavill said. "Me and my partner would like to buy you all a drink at the saloon."

"Actually, Jack, I could use some sleep," Duffy said.

"One drink. What's it going to hurt?" Cavill said.

"One drink," Duffy said.

The saloon was packed, with every table occupied. Cavill, Duffy, and the men from the posse had to find spots at the bar.

Cavill placed a twenty-dollar gold piece on the bar and said, "Barkeep, a drink for the brave men who rode on the posse."

"And Police Chief Atwood and Mr. Roosevelt," Duffy said as Atwood and Roosevelt entered the saloon.

The bartender set up fifteen shot glasses and filled them with rye whiskey.

Atwood lifted his glass. "Boys, a toast," he said. "To brave posses everywhere."

"And stupid outlaws who make the job fun," Cavill added.

Shots were downed, and a second round was poured.

"Hey, tenderfoot, watch what you're doing," a huge railroad worker next to Roosevelt said.

"I beg your pardon?" Roosevelt said.

"You spilled whiskey on me," the railroad worker said.

"I beg to disagree with you, sir, but I did no such thing," Roosevelt said.

Atwood stepped forward. "I'm afraid I have to agree with Mr. Roosevelt, Clarence. He was nowhere near you," he said.

"And I say he was," Clarence said.

"Listen, calm down and have another drink on me," Atwood said.

"No, on him," Clarence said and pointed to Roosevelt. "Right after he apologizes."

"I'll gladly buy you a drink, but I won't apologize for something I didn't do," Roosevelt said.

"Are you calling me a liar?" Clarence said.

"Here we go," Cavill said.

"I've called you nothing, sir," Roosevelt said.

"No man calls me a liar," Clarence said.

Cavill stepped forward. "Well, you big blowhard, that is exactly what you are, a liar."

"Here we go," Duffy said.

"Maybe you'd like to settle this outside?" Clarence said to Cavill.

"No, but I would," Roosevelt said.

"What?" Cavill said.

"What?" Duffy said.

"This man is obviously attempting to pick a fight with me, so I shall accommodate him," Roosevelt said.

"He's got fifty pounds on you," Duffy said. "Let Jack handle this."

Roosevelt looked up at Clarence. "I warn you, sir. I am an expert at pugilism."

"I don't care what your religion is. No man calls me a liar," Clarence said.

Duffy turned to Atwood. "Are you going to allow this?"

"No, I'm not," Atwood said. "Clarence, I'm plumb tired of you picking fights every time you get paid and drunk. This time I'm going to lock you up."

"No," Roosevelt said. "I accept his challenge."

"Let's go outside then," Clarence said.

Clarence and his friends left the saloon and went to the street.

"Mr. Roosevelt, are you sure you know what you're doing?" Duffy said.

"I'll be perfectly fine," Roosevelt said.

"Boys, carry out some lanterns," Atwood said.

A few minutes later, Roosevelt and Clarence stood inside a circle of patrons from the bar. A dozen handheld lanterns provided light.

"Mr. Roosevelt, are you sure about this?" Duffy said. "The man has fifty or more pounds on you."

Roosevelt did some deep knee bends. "Quite sure."

"Quit stalling, tenderfoot. I ain't got all night," Clarence said.

"Let's get this over with," Atwood said. "But afterwards you're going to jail, Clarence."

Roosevelt faced Clarence. As soon as Clarence put up his fists, Roosevelt assumed the classic Marquess of Queensberry boxing stance.

Clarence threw the first punch, which Roosevelt easily avoided and answered with three stiff jabs to Clarence's face, followed by a powerful right hook to the jaw.

"Holy shit," Cavill said.

"Why, you little son of a bitch," Clarence snarled.

Try as he might, Clarence couldn't lay a fist on Roosevelt as Roosevelt tore Clarence's face to ribbons with repeated jabs and hooks.

"You best quit while you still got some blood left," Atwood advised.

"How about it?" Roosevelt said and extended his right hand to Clarence.

Clarence sighed and took Roosevelt's hand.

"Well I'll be damned," Cavill said.

"All right, boys, the next round of drinks is on me," Atwood said.

An hour later, Roosevelt and Clarence were somewhat drunk and singing together at the bar.

Atwood, Cavill, and Duffy occupied a table and nursed beers.

"Boys, I would say we've had us a successful day," Atwood said.

CHAPTER TWELVE

After stocking up on supplies, Cavill and Duffy shook hands with Atwood in front of Atwood's office.

"We have a long way to go to reach the Jordan ranch in Helena," Duffy said.

"Boys, it's been a pleasure riding with you," Atwood said.

"Hey, Jack, look," Duffy said.

Riding toward them were Roosevelt and Clarence.

"Going somewhere, Clarence?" Atwood said.

"Clarence has agreed to guide me north to Medora," Roosevelt said.

"I'm from there," Clarence said. "I decided to head north with my friend Theodore and work on the railroad expansion north."

"If this don't beat all," Atwood said.

"We'll head north a bit to the Missouri River and cross the Breaks to Helena," Duffy said. "Maybe by then there will be more information on the Jordan ranch."

"Well, between here and Helena is three hundred miles of nothing," Cavill said.

"It's pretty country though," Duffy said.

"Pretty empty," Cavill said. "I read somewhere Montana is a cattleman's paradise. It's more like a rustler's and outlaw's paradise."

"You're just mad you didn't get to beat up Clarence," Duffy said.

"Roosevelt handled him well enough, although he's too small to knock out so big a man as Clarence," Cavill said.

"I have the feeling we haven't heard the last of Theodore Roosevelt," Duffy said.

"Since we missed breakfast to get an early start, what say we find a shady spot to noon?" Cavill said.

"Good idea," Duffy agreed.

As they ate plates of beans and bacon with cornbread and coffee, Duffy studied maps of the territory.

"There's talk from the governor of Montana that they want statehood," Duffy said. "They won't get it unless the population increases, and they won't get *that* unless ranchers feel safe to start spreads this far north."

"There isn't forty thousand people in the whole territory," Cavill said. "That's one neighborhood in Chicago."

"We're not in Chicago." Duffy looked up from the map. "We should hit the Missouri River in six days or so. The Jordan ranch has to be south of the Breaks, but I'm sure we can get directions in Helena."

"Do you know anything about Helena?" Cavill said.

"I know it's about four thousand feet above sea level and that people have been looking for gold in the Last Chance Gulch for fifteen years or so," Duffy said.

"People are looking for gold everywhere," Cavill said.

"Yeah, but they actually found some near Helena," Duffy said as he folded the map and tucked it into his shirt pocket.

"We got seven hours of daylight left. Let's see if we can get forty miles out of that nag you're riding," Cavill said.

"I'll put Bull up against Blue any day of the week," Duffy said.

"We should be coming up to the place they call Three Forks in the next thirty-six hours," Duffy said.

"I think I've heard of that," Cavill said.

"It's where the Jefferson, Madison, and Gallatin Rivers come together to form the Missouri," Duffy said.

"Sounds like cattle country," Cavill said.

"Another hour should put us right in the middle of it," Duffy said.

"Hold up a second," Cavill said. "I think Blue picked up a stone."

Cavill dismounted and checked the right front shoe of his horse, removed his field knife, and dug out a small stone.

"Jack," Duffy said.

"Riders. I hear them," Cavill said.

Duffy dismounted and stood beside his horse.

"They'll be here in a minute," Cavill said.

Duffy removed his Winchester rifle from the saddle. Cavill unlashed his Colt revolver.

A minute or so, sixteen riders surrounded Duffy and Cavill.

"It ain't them," county sheriff George Goode said.

"We ain't who?" Cavill said.

"Charles Allen," Goode said. "He robbed and murdered several families in Virginia City, and we've been tracking him for a week. We're going to hang the sumbitch on sight."

"And you are?" Cavill said.

"Sheriff George Goode. It happened in my county, and I'll get him if it's the last thing I ever do on this earth," Goode said. "Now who are you boys?"

"Name is Cavill. My partner is James Duffy. We're detectives hired by the Stock Growers Association to stop the cattle rustling," Cavill said.

"We're headed to Helena to see a rancher," Duffy said.

"That's the general direction this scum was last seen headed," Goode said. "You boys can ride along with us."

"There's been a fair amount of rustling all across Montana the past year or so," Goode said. "Before that, it was minor, a bit here and there."

"What's changed?" Duffy said.

"How do you mean?" Goode said.

"In the territory," Cavill said. "What's changed that rustling has increased?"

"Montana has become a cattleman's paradise," Goode said. "More ranchers means more cattle, and more cattle means more rustlers."

"How is it these rustlers are able to function undetected?" Duffy said. "Montana is a huge territory for sure, but it's no easy task hiding hundreds of stolen cattle."

"I expect it ain't, but I'm just a small-time county sheriff, and right now my concern is catching up with Charles Allen," Goode said. "It's getting late, boys. Let's make camp."

"Sheriff, we're going to scout ahead for an hour," Duffy said. "Join us."

"Get a fire and supper going, boys," Goode said. "We'll be back directly."

"Somebody passed this way less than two days ago," Cavill said as he knelt before deep impressions in the earth.

"That's him no doubt," Goode said. "We'll run him to ground before we reach Helena."

"From the looks of this busted shoe, it will be before then," Cavill said.

"If his horse goes lame, he'll kill anybody crossing his path to

79

get a new one," Goode said.

"Let's go a little further," Duffy said.

They rode for about a mile, and Duffy dismounted to inspect the tracks. "He'll be afoot come morning," he said.

"Let's head back and see what we got cooking for grub," Goode said.

"This is excellent beef stew," Duffy said.

"Poe was a cook at some fancy restaurant in Boston before he came west and took a job at the Ladder Eight ranch," Goode said.

"My compliments, Poe," Duffy said.

"So what do you boys do as detectives?" Goode said.

"We work for the Illinois Detective Agency," Duffy said. "We handle various assignments such as cattle theft, bank robbery, undercover work, and many other such jobs."

"The Illinois Detective Agency. That wouldn't be old Charles Porter, would it?" Goode said.

"You know him?" Cavill said.

"Of him, but everybody in cattle country knows of Charles Porter," Goode said.

"I expect so," Cavill said.

Over by the fire, Poe suddenly blew a bugle.

"That means there's plenty of seconds if you fellows want any," Goode said.

"I'd be a fool not to," Cavill said. "Jim?"

Duffy handed Cavill his empty plate.

"This Charles Allen, what exactly did he do?" Duffy said.

"He robbed and killed seven people up in my county," Goode said. "He's the worst sort. Kills for a quarter or a thousand. It makes no difference to him."

"Any rustling up your way?" Duffy said.

"Not many ranches in that part," Goode said. "Except for

the Ladder Eight, folks are still trying to strike it rich panning for gold."

Cavill returned with two plates of stew and gave one to Duffy.

"Well, boys, I'm turning in," Goode said. "I'd like to be in the saddle before dawn."

After Goode left them, Cavill said, "We should check and see if anybody in the posse is riding a Ladder Eight brand for our sketch book."

"Good idea. We'll check in the morning," Duffy said.

"That's some book of drawings you fellows got there," Goode said as Duffy drew sketches of the posse's brands.

"A good brander can change any brand easily enough," Duffy said. "If we know what the original brand looks like, we can often pick out the re-brand."

"Well, boys, let's ride," Goode said.

Close to noon, Duffy inspected a set of tracks in the soft dirt and said, "He cut his horse loose, and he's walking."

"He didn't shoot his horse?" Goode said.

"A shot could be heard for miles out here," Cavill said. "He didn't want to alert anybody who might be about, especially if he's looking to steal a new horse."

"Give the horses a breather," Goode said. "We'll catch him by nightfall."

Close to sunset, Duffy and Cavill scouted ahead while Goode and the posse rested their horses.

They rode for a half mile and stopped when they caught the aroma of food cooking over a fire.

They dismounted and walked to within a hundred feet of Charles Allen. He had carried his saddle and was resting against it as food cooked in a pan.

"I'll sit with this son of a bitch while you go back for Goode,"

Cavill whispered.

"Do not kill him," Duffy whispered.

After Duffy left, Cavill went around Allen and came up behind him. He drew his Colt and cocked it. The click immediately alerted Allen, who jumped to his feet and reached for his sidearm.

Cavill cracked Allen across the jaw, knocking him senseless.

By the time Duffy, Goode, and the posse arrived, Allen was tied up, and Cavill was smoking a cigar and drinking a cup of Allen's coffee.

"Well, I'll be a son of a bitch," Goode said.

"You bastards are all cowards, or you'd a fight me fair," Allen said.

Goode kicked Allen in the face with his boot. "Shut your pie-hole, you back-shooting murderer," he said. "Poe, get supper going while we hang this sumbitch."

Goode turned and walked away.

"That's it, you coward. Walk away," Allen said.

"He's not walking away, stupid," Cavill said. "He's going to pick out a nice tree to hang you from."

"I ain't done nothing to cause no hanging," Allen said.

"I don't think the sheriff is quite convinced of your innocence," Cavill said.

Allen looked over at Poe, who was building a campfire. "Hang me and sit down to supper. Is that it, you cowards?" he said.

Goode returned. "Get him on my horse," he said.

A few minutes later, Allen sat atop Goode's horse with a noose around his neck and his hands tied behind his back.

"Do you want some words said over you?" Duffy said.

"Screw you," Allen said. "Screw all of you."

"Mister, you're the type of man I wish I could hang twice," Goode said and smacked the horse on the rump.

The horse ran forward, Allen's neck cracked, and he swayed

back and forth several times.

"All right, Poe, what's for supper?" Goode said.

"Helena is a good three days' ride from here, boys. Just across the Three Forks," Goode said. "I'd ride with you, but I have my duties back home, and most of the boys in the posse got families waiting on them."

"I'm going to miss your cook," Cavill said.

"What about Allen?" Duffy said.

"We'll cut him down and bury him in the morning," Goode said.

Poe blew his bugle.

Cavill stood up. "He's playing my song."

CHAPTER THIRTEEN

After burying Allen's body, Cavill and Duffy shook hands with Goode.

"Well, boys, you ever find yourself up north, stop in and pay me a visit," Atwood said. "I'd be proud to buy you both a drink."

"We'll do that," Cavill said.

Duffy and Cavill mounted their horses and rode at a steady pace for several hours until they reached the banks of the Three Forks River.

"You ever see anything so pretty?" Duffy said.

"This gal I knew back in Kansas City," Cavill said.

"Well, we're not in Kansas City," Duffy said. "Let's find a place to cross."

They rode north along the Three Forks River until they located a river crossing station. Six riders were waiting for crossing. The fee was a dollar fifty a person and two dollars per horse.

Duffy paid the fare, and they waited with the others for the raft to arrive from the opposite shore.

Duffy used the time to study his maps.

"We can make Helena in thirty-six hours," Duffy said.

"Are you fellows riding to Helena?" a man nearby said.

Duffy looked at the man. He was in his sixties and a bit stooped over at the waist.

"Are you alone?" Duffy said.

"Alone and looking to reach Helena without getting scalped

or robbed or both," the man said.

"My name is James Duffy," Duffy said. "This is my partner, Jack Cavill."

"Henry Toole," Toole said as he shook hands with Duffy and Cavill.

"Do you live in Helena?" Duffy said.

"Never been," Toole said. "I raised my sons down Arizona way. My wife died and my sons moved back east. Keeping the ranch didn't seem worth it anymore, especially after losing half my herd to thieves."

"Rustlers?" Duffy said.

"Stole half of my three hundred head right from under my nose," Toole said. "Sold the rest and the ranch and thought I'd get in on the gold strike up in Last Chance at the gulch."

"Mr. Toole, we've been hired to investigate the cattle rustling taking place in Montana, which is why we're going to Helena," Duffy said. "Would your brand on your horse be the same on your cattle?"

"It is, why?" Toole said.

"One way to sell stolen cattle at auction is to change the brand immediately upon stealing them," Duffy said. "A good brander can do that easily enough. Would you mind if I took a look at your brand on your horse?"

"Go right ahead," Toole said.

Toole's brand was a simple large TH inside a half circle.

"Wouldn't be much trouble to alter your brand and sell your herd at auction," Duffy said.

"Well, it's someone else's headache now," Toole said. "I'll be spending my remaining days working a claim."

"Were there many other incidents of rustling in Arizona?" Duffy said.

"Several that I'm aware of," Toole said. "The law hasn't been able to get a handle on the rustlers as far as I know. Even old

Henry Hooker doubled his cowboys to keep watch."

The ferry arrived and everybody was quickly loaded.

As the ferry crew pulled the large raft across five hundred feet of water, Duffy said, "Mr. Toole, my partner and I would be glad for your company."

After crossing the river, Cavill, Duffy, and Toole rode northwest toward Helena.

"You say you fellows have been hired to look into the rustling," Toole said. "By who may I ask?"

"The Stock Growers Association," Duffy said.

"I complained to them. In writing. They said they was looking into the matter," Toole said. "I guess they are if they sent you fellows."

"Let's give the horses an hour of rest and fix some lunch," Duffy suggested.

Over a hot lunch, Duffy checked his maps and Toole spoke about his past.

"I came out here in fifty-three when Arizona was wilderness, and Indians ruled the day," Toole said. "With the help of the army, we survived and tamed the damned territory so a man could build a ranch and a home. The last ten years I became friends with many of the Comanche. I gave them a parting gift of a dozen head of longhorns and six horses."

"Things have a way of coming around," Duffy said.

"Mr. Toole, did you ever see these rustlers on your property?" Cavill said.

"Never did. Damned ghosts," Toole said.

"We've found rustlers work best at night if guards aren't posted," Duffy said.

"It's amazing what men can do working by the light of a full moon out on a prairie," Cavill said.

"I can't dispute that, since they cleaned me out," Toole said.

"Well, let's get back to work," Cavill said. "We might make Helena by nightfall tomorrow."

After dark, they made camp and tended to the horses while supper cooked over a crackling campfire.

Supper was beans, bacon, cornbread, and coffee. Dessert was a can of peaches for each man.

"Fine supper, boys, but I'm going to turn in," Toole said. "My sixty-three-year-old back ain't what it used to be."

After Toole turned in, Cavill lit a cigar and refilled the coffee cups. "Are you thinking this cattle theft might be bigger than just Montana?" he said.

"I've thought that since we left Billings," Duffy said.

"We'll send a wire to Porter and ask for any new information in Montana, Arizona, and New Mexico," Cavill said.

"It's possible we might need some backup if we uncover anything vital," Duffy said. "We can't be everywhere at once."

"Mention it, but don't insist," Cavill said. "We don't want the old man thinking we're going soft."

"We are soft," Duffy said. "In the head, to be out here in the middle of nowhere looking for cattle rustlers that probably aren't even in the state anymore."

"Our deal still stands?" Cavill said.

"About fighting?"

"Unless I've gone really soft in the head, it's the only deal we made," Cavill said.

"When we get home, you go into serious training," Duffy said. "Maybe we can rent a small warehouse and set it up as a training camp."

"That promoter fellow we met, he can get fights," Cavill said.

"Let's get to Helena first before we go scheduling any matches," Duffy said.

"Right," Cavill agreed.

"Might as well follow the old man's advice and grab some sleep," Duffy said.

Duffy stirred the fire and said, "Jack, coffee is ready. Go wake the old man."

Cavill went to Toole's bedroll. "Mr. Toole, it's morning. Coffee's ready."

Toole didn't stir. Cavill knelt beside him and gently shook Toole's shoulder.

"Hey, Jim?" Cavill said.

While Cavill dug a grave, Duffy went through Toole's possessions.

"Letters with his two sons' address back east," Duffy said. "And a bank draft from the Denver National Bank for ten thousand dollars. He also had four hundred in cash on him. When we get to Helena, we'll wire his sons."

"How come I'm the only one digging?" Cavill said.

"Consider it part of your training," Duffy said.

"Training?"

"We should take his horse to Helena," Duffy said. "His sons can decide what to do with it."

"That's deep enough. Help me get him in the ground," Cavill said.

They rode into Helena shortly before nine in the evening. A boomtown with a swollen population of four thousand, the streets were illuminated with oil lamps every thirty feet.

Music echoed from a dozen saloons, and the streets were so crowded it might as well have been high noon.

A deputy equipped with a sidearm and a Winchester stood on every street corner. As Duffy and Cavill rode along Main

Street with Toole's horse in tow, a deputy stepped out to greet them.

"Evening, gents," the deputy said. "Kindly stop off at the sheriff's office at the end of this street and check your firearms. We have an ordinance against carrying firearms in Helena."

"End of the street?" Duffy said.

The deputy pointed. "Straight ahead.

Duffy and Cavill rode to the end of the street and dismounted. They tethered the three horses to the hitching post, then entered the sheriff's office.

Sheriff Charles Kelly sat behind his desk. A deputy with a rifle stood beside him.

"Evening, gentlemen. Come to check your guns?" Kelly said.

Duffy and Cavill set their wallets on the desk.

"My name is James Duffy and this is my partner, Jack Cavill," Duffy said. "We work for the Illinois Detective Agency, and we've been hired to investigate cattle theft in Montana."

Kelly looked at the wallets. "Hired by who?" he said.

"Stock Growers Association," Duffy said.

"As you can imagine, with the gold fever in these parts, ranches are almost unheard of these days," Kelly said.

"We heard about the Jordan ranch losing cattle. We'd like to see Mr. Jordan come morning. Do you know him?" Duffy said.

"Everybody around here knows Joe Jordan," Kelly said.

"What can you tell us about the cattle thefts?" Duffy said.

"Not as much as Marshal Titus," Kelly said. "He's investigated the complaints. My jurisdiction is limited to town and the mines."

"Where can we find the marshal?" Duffy said.

"He's out serving warrants, but I expect him back by morning," Kelly said.

"Can you point us to a hotel and a place to eat?" Duffy said.

"The Helena Hotel is the best in town," Kelly said. "Serves a decent steak, too."

"Best take your wallets and explain to my deputies you're allowed to walk around heeled," Kelly said.

"Care for a late bite to eat?" Duffy said.

"I got a prisoner back here," Kelly said. "I'll meet you at the restaurant."

The Helena Hotel was the most expensive hotel in town and had its own private stables with twenty-four-hour service. Most of the guests were investors and bankers from back east and wealthy miners and new arrivals to the town struck with gold fever.

After stabling their horses and checking into a room on the top floor, Duffy and Cavill met Sheriff Kelly in the restaurant.

"How large is the Jordan ranch?" Duffy said.

"Last year they drove four thousand head to market," Kelly said. "I expect them to do the same this year, or better."

"Any idea how many they've lost?" Cavill said.

"Two hundred is what they told the marshal," Kelly said. "No one even realized it for weeks, the loss was so subtle."

"Is there an army post in the territory?" Duffy said.

"Keogh is a piece from here," Kelly said. "The army has outposts closer, in Wyoming and Idaho, if the need arises."

"Most folks around here are into gold," Cavill said. "So stealing cattle from an open range wouldn't be much of a chore."

"I expect not," Kelly said.

A woman of about twenty-five approached the table.

"Sheriff Kelly, I need to talk to you," she said.

"Now Amanda, we've been over this again and again," Kelly said.

"You know my husband didn't kill that man," Amanda said.

"The jury said otherwise," Kelly said. "It doesn't matter what I think."

"I don't care what the jury said. I know my husband," Amanda said. "My husband would never shoot anybody over a pouch of gold."

"Amanda, please," Kelly said.

"They're going to take him to Miles City and hang him for a crime he didn't commit, and you sit there drinking coffee," Amanda said.

"Amanda, he had his day in court," Kelly said. "Do like I said and make an appeal to the court."

"What good would that do? The circuit judge isn't due back for a month, and you're going to hang him in two weeks," Amanda said.

"I'm sorry, Amanda, but it's the law," Kelly said.

"The law," Amanda said, then she turned and walked away.

"The prisoner in your jail?" Duffy said.

Kelly nodded. "I've known him since he was fifteen," he said. "Moved here with his family in seventy-one to work a claim. I never thought he was the type to commit murder over a sack of gold dust."

"Did he?" Duffy said.

"The jury said so," Kelly said.

"But did he?" Cavill said.

Kelly sighed. "I have doubts," he said. "Serious doubts."

"Because?" Duffy said.

"If you had a successful claim of your own, would you murder a man for eight ounces of dust?" Kelly said. "Mark, Amanda's husband, claimed he was riding into town to exchange his dust at the bank when he found the body already shot on the road. The man's partners swore in court they witnessed Mark shoot and rob the man for his sack of gold, and Mark had a sack on him when he rode into town."

"That's circumstantial at best," Duffy said. "You can't hang a man on that."

"The trial lasted three days, and the man's partners both testified," Kelly said. "Mark had a sack of dust on him and no alibi that could clear him of the crime."

"He shot the man twice?" Cavill said.

Kelly nodded.

"Were the bullets recovered?" Duffy said.

"By the town doctor. Why?" Kelly said.

"Where is this doctor?" Cavill said.

"Most likely in his office over on Ash Street," Kelly said.

Cavill and Duffy exchanged glances.

"What?" Kelly said.

"What in hell are you getting me out of bed for?" Doctor Stone said when he opened the door to his home.

"Calm down, Doc," Kelly said. "We just need a minute."

Stone looked at Duffy and Cavill. "Who are you two?" he said.

"Do you have the bullets recovered from the man murdered by Mark Urban?" Kelly said.

"You woke me up for that?" Stone said.

"Just get them, Doc. Please," Kelly said.

Stone sighed. "Follow me," he said.

In his office, Stone opened a desk drawer and produced the two bullets.

"They're .38 Long Colt, both still intact," Duffy said. "Can we use your microscope?"

"Aw, what the hell, go ahead," Stone said. "I'm awake now, so you might as well entertain me."

Duffy placed the two bullets under the microscope and compared them to each other. "Take a look, Sheriff," he said.

Kelly looked through the eyepiece. "What am I looking at?" he said.

"Do you see those grooves and markings on the bullets?" Duffy said.

"What of them?" Kelly said.

"Every gun makes it own mark on a bullet from the rifling inside the barrel," Duffy said. "No two are alike anywhere in the world."

"Where is Urban's gun?" Cavill said.

"Locked up in my office," Kelly said.

"This is a fine Walker Colt," Cavill said as he expertly twirled the weapon.

"Have a gunsmith in town?" Duffy said.

"As every miner is armed to the teeth, we couldn't exist without one," Kelly said.

"Let's load this Colt and run a test," Cavill said.

As they walked the several blocks to the gunsmith shop, Duffy said, "Were two rounds fired when he was arrested?"

"The gun was fully loaded, but as the prosecutor pointed out at the trial, he had plenty of time to reload on the way to town," Kelly said.

They reached the gunsmith shop, and Kelly knocked several times on the door until a light from inside the shop came on.

"Who is it?" the gunsmith demanded.

"Sheriff Kelly," Kelly said.

"It's midnight, Sheriff," the gunsmith said.

"I know what time it is. Open up," Kelly said.

Behind the gunsmith shop was a fenced-in target range for testing guns. Cavill loaded the Walker Colt and fired six bullets into a large, hanging sandbag. He reloaded and fired six more.

"Now what?" Kelly said.

"We dig out the twelve bullets and take them to the doctor," Cavill said.

"You again," Stone said.

"We'll only be a moment," Duffy said. "We want to use . . ."

"The microscope," Stone said. "Go ahead, and then leave me get some sleep."

Under the microscope, Duffy compared the dozen bullets fired from the Walker Colt. He asked Kelly to do the same.

"No doubt the markings are all identical," Duffy said. "Now let's compare the recovered bullets to the ones we just fired."

Kelly inspected the bullets under the microscope. "They're not even close," he said.

"There is no way Urban killed that man with this Walker Colt," Duffy said.

"Then who did?" Kelly said.

"In the morning, let's visit the man's two partners and check their guns," Cavill said.

United States Marshal Edward Titus, convinced by the newfound evidence, rode out to the camp of the dead man and spoke to his two surviving partners.

Duffy and Cavill rode with him.

"I read something not long ago in the *Police Gazette* about something called forensic evidence and ballistics," Titus said. "How in the future it will play a big part in police work."

"Not just the future, Marshal," Duffy said.

"I never did believe Urban shot that man, not with a successful claim of his own," Titus said. "It just didn't make sense to me a man with a claim producing gold would kill a man for a small sack of it."

"Where is their claim?" Duffy said.

"About a mile ahead," Titus said.

Along the creek in the area known as Last Chance Gulch, the Harper brothers, Bill and Tom, had their claim staked out along with a hundred others.

At the Harper brothers' tent, Titus, Cavill, and Duffy dismounted.

Having breakfast at a table, the Harper brothers didn't bother to stand.

"Morning, Marshal, have some coffee with us?" Bill said.

"I'm afraid I'm here on business, boys," Titus said. "I'll need you to come into town with me."

"What for?" Tom said.

"I think you killed your partner and framed Urban for your crime," Titus said.

"A jury said Urban did it," Bill said.

"Well, I think they got it wrong," Titus said. "I think you did it."

Bill and Tom grinned at Titus. "Prove it," Bill said.

In the blink of an eye, Cavill was off his horse with his Colt in hand and smacked the brothers in the jaw with the heavy barrel.

"Jim, help me get these clowns on their horses," Cavill said.

After test-firing the revolvers belonging to the Harper brothers, Duffy, Cavill, Titus, and Kelly compared the results at the doctor's office.

"There is no doubt the bullets that killed the victim came from the gun worn by Tom Harper," Duffy said. "Urban couldn't have killed anybody unless he was using Harper's gun to do it."

"I'll be damned," Titus said.

"Marshal, let me buy you lunch, and you can fill us in on the Jordan ranch," Duffy said.

CHAPTER FOURTEEN

Duffy, Cavill, Marshal Titus, and Sheriff Kelly sat at a window table in the Helena Hotel dining room and ordered baked chicken for lunch.

"You boys are a lot more than just stock detectives," Titus said. "Urban would have been hanged, and the Harper brothers would have gotten away with murder if you hadn't ridden into town. Solving a murder the way you did is decades away from being accepted police work, even by the *Police Gazette.*"

"We didn't just happen to ride in," Duffy said. "Like we told you this morning, we were hired to investigate the cattle rustling going on in Montana. We're headed out to the Jordan ranch, so anything you can tell us could be useful."

"Over the last three months, Joe Jordan has reported a hundred head missing," Titus said. "The Jordan ranch covers more than forty thousand acres of prime grazing land twenty miles west of town. It's difficult to patrol and stop rustlers from picking off drags and stragglers. Joe last reported a dozen head missing from the south range just two weeks ago."

"How many cowboys does Jordan employ?" Duffy asked.

"During drive season, twenty," Titus said. "Right now it's probably twelve."

"Twelve to cover forty thousand acres is nowhere near enough to stop rustling, especially if the crooks have been successful the first few tries," Cavill said.

"We have a telegram to send to our office back in Illinois,

96

and then we'll ride over and see Joe Jordan," Duffy said.

"Boys, I'd appreciate it if you could see your way clear to waiting until morning to see Jordan," Titus said. "I need to wire the territorial governor about Urban, and I'd like you to write a detailed report on your findings. We got a justice of the peace in town who can witness your statements."

"Jack?" Duffy said.

"I hate paperwork," Cavill said.

"I'll write it, you sign it," Duffy said.

"Amanda," Kelly said as Amanda approached the table.

"Good evening, Marshal, Sheriff Kelly," Amanda said. "I wanted to thank you for what you did to save my husband's life today."

"You can thank these boys for that, Amanda," Titus said. "Mr. Duffy and Mr. Cavill. They proved your husband's innocence today, or I'd've been forced to take him to Miles City."

"I remember you gentlemen from yesterday," Amanda said. "My husband and I are deeply indebted to you both."

"Our pleasure, Mrs. Urban," Duffy said.

"Sheriff, would it be all right with you if I brought my husband a steak?" Amanda said.

"You go right ahead, Amanda," Kelly said.

Amanda looked at Duffy and Cavill. "Thank you again," she said.

After Amanda left, Titus said, "Well, boys, let's head over to my office."

Duffy wrote a five-page report, which he and Cavill signed. Titus sent for the justice of the peace, who witnessed and signed each page.

"I'll wire the governor this afternoon," Titus said.

"Speaking of which, we need to telegram our office," Duffy said. "We'll see you later, Marshal."

Duffy and Cavill walked several blocks from the marshal's office to River Street, where the telegraph office was located. Duffy sent a telegram to Porter informing him of their location and progress.

They waited outside for Porter's response. Cavill smoked a cigar as they waited. After thirty minutes, the operator brought out the reply.

"Proceed to Jordan ranch, assess and report back to me. May have new reports of rustling farther south and west. Porter," Duffy read aloud.

"We have to come back here to report?" Cavill said. "That will slow us down."

"Only if we have someplace to go," Duffy said. "So far, all we've done is ride around and get involved in everything except rustling."

"Let's go get a drink," Cavill said.

"Jack, I need a bath and, standing downwind from you, I'd say you need the same," Duffy said.

"I suppose a shave and a bath wouldn't hurt none," Cavill said. "But then we'll get a drink."

Before soaking in tubs in the hotel bathhouse, Duffy and Cavill visited the hotel barbershop for shaves.

"This bathwater smells funny," Cavill said.

"I think that's us, Jack," Duffy said.

Cavill sniffed the air. "I think you're right."

As they soaked in hot, soapy water, Cavill lit a cigar. Earlier they requested coffee with the bath and a waiter from the restaurant carried in a tray with two cups.

"This is how we'd be living if I was fighting for a living instead of chasing rustlers across the prairie," Cavill said. "Hot baths and room service."

"Jack, let me ask you a question," Duffy said. "You ever give thought to marriage?"

"No, never."

"You never want to settle down with a woman and have some children?"

"Maybe when I'm sixty I'll find some woman half my age and have a couple of heirs to leave my millions to," Cavill said.

"Well, what happens if you meet some woman who sweeps you off your feet?" Duffy said.

"You're serious?" Cavill said. "Don't tell me you're thinking of getting married, Jim? You haven't finished law school yet. We have our plans for fighting. You can't back out of our deal over some woman."

"Relax, Jack," Duffy said. "It was just a question."

"And a damn fool one if you ask me," Cavill said. "Let's get out of here and go get a drink."

The Red Dog Saloon was the most expensive saloon in town. Housed in a brick and wood, two-story structure, it featured a forty-foot-long mahogany bar, a mirror the length of the bar, tables with actual tablecloths, a kitchen that served food, and the entire second floor was reserved for gambling.

Firearms were not permitted except by law enforcement officers. A coatroom was set up to check all handguns and rifles.

Two burly men were employed to keep the peace on both floors.

Duffy and Cavill had to settle for a small table near the kitchen. They ordered drinks from a waitress, who asked them if they wanted food.

"Might as well. We're here," Cavill said.

"The beef stew is excellent and the bread is fresh," the waitress said.

"Make it two and bring us each a cold beer," Duffy said.

"So who caught your fancy?" Cavill said.

"I didn't say anybody did," Duffy said. "And I thought we closed the subject."

"I reopened it," Cavill said. "Your future is also mine, in case you forgot. And besides, we've been partners too long for you to pull the wool over my eyes. So who is she?"

"It's just a thought, Jack," Duffy said.

"What's the thought's name?" Cavill said.

"If I tell you, will you leave it alone?"

"I've been looking all over for you boys," Marshal Titus said as he approached the table.

"Pull up a chair, Marshal," Cavill said. "Want a beer?"

Titus took a chair and removed a folded telegram from a pocket. "From the territorial governor," he said. "Urban will be released tomorrow and allowed to return home with all charges dropped."

"That's good news, Marshal," Duffy said.

"It's because of you two," Titus said. "I know you're moving on tomorrow, but if you ever get back here, I know Urban would like to thank you personally."

"We'll only be gone a day or two," Duffy said. "Our office wants a report on the Jordan ranch. Then we'll be back to wire for instructions."

"I doubt Urban will be here for weeks," Titus said.

"Then you can tell him he's welcome from us," Duffy said.

Titus stood up. "I'll do just that. See you when you return."

After Titus left the table, the waitress arrived with the stew and beer. "Fresh apple pie for dessert if you're so inclined," she said.

After the waitress left, Duffy said, "We should leave at first light, and maybe we could be back here by dark and wire Porter."

"What were we talking about?" Cavill said.

"I don't remember," Duffy said.

"It couldn't have been important," Cavill said.

"Probably not," Duffy said.

"I remember now," Cavill said and sat up in bed. "Hey, Jim, I remember what we were talking about at supper."

When Duffy didn't respond, Cavill reached for a match on the nightstand between the beds and lit the lantern.

Duffy was sound asleep.

And as sound a sleeper as there ever was.

"It will keep," Cavill said and blew out the lantern.

CHAPTER FIFTEEN

Duffy and Cavill rode west out of Helena shortly after breakfast. Somewhat of a road had been carved into the prairie over the years by heavy wagons. They followed the road for about ten miles and encountered a wagon with two cowboys in it headed to town.

As they approached the wagon, the cowboy riding shotgun, who was cradling a shotgun, cocked both hammers and aimed it loosely at Duffy and Cavill.

"Morning, fellows. No need for that shotgun," Duffy said.

"I'll decide the need," the cowboy with the shotgun said.

"Mister, I don't like shotguns pointed at me," Cavill said. "So I'd uncock it and put it aside and leave us pass."

"We're on our way to see Joe Jordan," Duffy said. "We've been hired by the Stock Growers Association to look into the cattle thefts in Montana."

"Got something that says so?" the driver of the wagon said.

Duffy reached into his vest inside pocket for his wallet and tossed it to the driver.

"James Duffy, detective, the Illinois Detective Agency," the driver said.

"This is my partner, Jack Cavill," Duffy said.

The driver tossed the wallet back to Duffy.

"We heard the Jordan ranch lost some cattle," Duffy said.

"A hundred head the last three months," the driver said. "We've been fencing in the ranges the past month. We're going into Helena to pick up more wire and supplies."

"Well, we'll see you at the ranch later on," Duffy said.

As the wagon rolled forward, Duffy and Cavill continued along the road.

"Fencing in an open range is never a good idea," Cavill said.

"Remember Wyoming a few years back?" Duffy said. "Range war over water rights."

"That was a bloodbath," Cavill said.

"Since Jordan's is the only large ranch in these parts, I doubt that will happen," Duffy said. "And even if it does happen, it isn't our assignment."

"Seems like this trip, we've been doing everything but our assignment," Cavill said.

The road ended where the Jordan ranch began. A tall archway with a sign read *The Jordan Ranch.* Duffy and Cavill rode under the arch and followed the path to a large ranch house, corral, barn, and bunkhouse.

Two cowboys were in the corral tending to a horse. One cowboy stood outside the corral, watching.

The cowboy outside the corral turned and looked at Duffy and Cavill as they dismounted.

"You're late, boys, and I don't like it," he said.

"Late for what?" Cavill said.

"When I hire new men, I expect them to be on time," the cowboy said.

"Who do you think we are?" Cavill said.

"Turley and Hobbs, the new men I hired."

"And who are you?" Cavill said.

"Tom Jenkins, foreman of the Jordan ranch."

"Well, Tom, I'm not Turley," Cavill said.

Jenkins looked at Duffy. "And you're not Turley?"

"No, I'm not Hobbs," Duffy said.

"Well, Goddammit, where are they?" Jenkins said.

"My guess is not here," Cavill said.

"If you ain't Turley and Hobbs, then who the hell are you?" Jenkins said.

"James Duffy, and this is Jack Cavill," Duffy said. "We've been hired by the Stock Growers Association to investigate the cattle thefts in Montana."

"What are you, some kind of police?" Jenkins said.

Duffy removed his wallet and showed his identification to Jenkins.

"Follow me to the house, boys," Jenkins said.

Duffy and Cavill followed Jenkins to the house. On the porch, Jenkins said, "Wait here, boys," and went inside.

Jenkins was gone for about thirty seconds and returned with a stunning redhead who wore dungaree pants, a white blouse, and boots. She looked at Duffy and Cavill.

"My foreman tells me you're from the Illinois Detective Agency and have been hired by the Stock Growers Association," she said.

"That's correct, miss," Duffy said. "My name is James Duffy. This is my partner, Jack Cavill."

Cavill stared at the woman as if transfixed.

"Does he speak?" the woman said.

"Jack?" Duffy said.

"Yes, hello," Cavill said.

Duffy looked at Cavill, then said, "We'd like to see Mr. Jordan, if we may."

"My father passed away about a year ago. I'm his daughter, Joe Jordan."

"Joe?" Duffy said.

"Josephine."

"I see. What shall we call you, Miss Jordan?" Duffy said.

"Joey will do fine. Mr. Jenkins, tell Cookie there will be two guests for lunch."

"That's very kind of you," Duffy said. "Can we talk about your cattle theft?"

Joey, who stood a foot shorter than Cavill, even in her boots, looked up at him and said, "Is something wrong with him, Mr. Duffy? Did a horse kick him in the head or something?"

"He's shy sometimes around women," Duffy said.

"Well, let's have a seat on the porch and talk," Joey said. "Mr. Jenkins, ask Cookie to bring us some fresh coffee."

Jenkins went inside while Joey, Duffy, and Cavill took chairs.

"I've lost one hundred head the past three months," Joey said. "My men are fencing in the ranges, even though my father swore he'd never do that. But I have no choice. I can't allow these rustlers to steal me blind."

"When was the last theft?" Duffy said.

"Not a week ago," Joey said. "Six disappeared from the south range overnight. I know it was six, because I asked the men to do an accurate count before sundown and again in the morning. The count was six short."

"It was close to a full moon a week ago," Duffy said. "It wouldn't be that difficult to snare six head at night under a full moon."

"Apparently not," Joey said.

"Would it be possible to see the south range?" Duffy said. "Maybe your foreman could ride us over?"

"Mr. Jenkins has things to do around here," Joey said. "I'll ride you over myself."

Cavill stared at Joey, who looked back at him.

"Right after lunch," Joey said.

The south range was the farthest from the house and took about an hour to reach. The area was about eight thousand acres of grazing land, and the cowboys moved the cattle every morning so the grass could replenish itself.

"How many head on this range?" Duffy asked.

"Last count was eleven hundred," Joey said. "The other ranges have twice to three times that number. These are the youngest."

"What water is nearby?" Duffy said.

"A mile south or so is the Bitterroot River," Joey said. "After that is the Missouri, the Big Hole, and so on. My father selected this area for its access to so much water."

"Most likely those who stole your cattle followed the water south," Duffy said.

"To where?" Joey said.

"Good question," Duffy said. "Your brand, a simple J&J, is easy enough to change in the right hands. My guess is they are changing the brand and selling re-branded cattle at auction."

"Where?" Joey said.

"Another good question," Duffy said.

"What are your plans?" Joey said.

"Head south and see if we can pick up a trail," Duffy said. "First we have to return to Helena and wire our office and let them know our plans."

"But you'll stop here in the morning?" Joey said.

"With your permission," Duffy said.

"You'll need supplies," Joey said.

"We'll pick up enough in town," Duffy said.

"I'll have my cook cut up enough fresh meat to last you a week," Joey said.

"Thank you, Joey," Duffy said. "Ready, Jack?"

Jack nodded.

"We'll escort you back to the house and see you in the morning," Duffy said.

As they rode back to Helena, Duffy said, "What was wrong with

106

you back there?"

"Nothing," Cavill said.

"I've never seen you tongue-tied around a woman before," Duffy said.

"What are you talking about?" Cavill said.

"Joey Jordan is one attractive woman, isn't she?" Duffy said.

"I didn't notice," Cavill said.

"Not much." Duffy grinned. "Let's get back to town," he said.

"Well, I didn't notice. What are you saying?" Cavill demanded.

"I'm saying that Joey Jordan is an attractive woman," Duffy said.

"Like I said, I didn't notice," Cavill said. "And let's not talk about it anymore."

"Whatever you say," Duffy said with a grin.

Duffy and Cavill waited in chairs outside the telegraph office in Helena for a response from Porter.

Cavill smoked a cigar. Duffy read a newspaper.

"Howdy, boys," Sheriff Kelly said as he approached the telegraph office.

"Afternoon, Sheriff," Duffy said.

"How did it go at the Jordan ranch?" Kelly said.

"They have a definite problem. Why didn't you tell us Joe Jordan is a woman?" Duffy said.

"I assumed you knew," Kelly said. "So what are your plans?"

"That's what we're waiting to find out," Duffy said.

The telegraph operator opened the door and said, "Got a reply for you," and handed a paper to Cavill.

Cavill read it and then handed it to Duffy.

"I guess we'll stay in town tonight," Duffy said. "Join us for supper later, Sheriff."

"Sure, why not."

"If you see him, ask the marshal to join us," Duffy said.

As he changed into a clean shirt, Cavill said, "I wonder why Porter thinks they might come back for more cattle?"

"Probably because it was easy, and we have no other leads to go on at this point," Duffy said. "And if we get lucky and they get stupid, it might lead to something."

Cavill tucked his shirt in and reached for his hat. "Come on, I'm starved," he said.

"I'm glad we kept the room for another night," Duffy said. "It might be our last bed for a while."

"Ever give any thought to becoming a US marshal?" Titus said. "Men like you two are always welcome."

They were having coffee after dinner in the Helena Hotel dining room.

"I'm actually studying for the bar exam," Duffy said.

"Lawyer, huh?" Titus said. He looked at Cavill. "And you?"

"Ever hear of John L. Sullivan?" Cavill said.

"The heavyweight champion?" Kelly said.

"When we're not doing this, Jack is a fighter," Duffy said. "And a damned good one, at that."

"He looks it," Titus said.

"I read that Sullivan is on tour," Kelly said. "North Dakota, I believe."

"First things first," Duffy said. "Right now we have a job to do."

"Well, good luck, boys," Titus said. "If you do find any rustlers on the Jordan ranch, come back to town and I'll arrest them, but I suspect it isn't going to be that easy."

"I expect you're right," Duffy said.

"I need to get back to the office," Kelly said.

"Same here," Titus said.

"This one is on us," Duffy said. "If we make it back here, you can buy us a drink."

After Titus and Kelly left the table, Duffy and Cavill had another cup of coffee.

"Jim, how long have we been partners?" Cavill said.

"Almost six years now. Since we joined the agency. Why?"

"When you brought up you were thinking of getting married the other day, I was wondering why," Cavill said. "You were going to tell me, remember?"

"I get the feeling this is more about you than me," Duffy said.

"Come on, Jim," Cavill said.

Duffy sipped some coffee and then set the cup down. "Do you remember Sylvia Trent at the Trent ranch?" he said.

"Trent's daughter," Cavill said. "She's a stargazer, all right. It's her, isn't it?"

"I don't know. Maybe."

"Did it just hit you like a fist to the chest?" Cavill said. "Like, all of a sudden you couldn't breathe?"

"Joey Jordan," Duffy said. "That's why you couldn't talk when she was around. I'll be damned."

"Damned or not, does it go away?" Cavill said.

"Not if it's real," Duffy said.

"How do you know if it's real?"

"I don't know, but when this job is done, I plan to see Sylvia Trent and find out," Duffy said. "Maybe you should do the same?"

"Yeah, but I'll be seeing her tomorrow," Cavill said.

"Then you have the chance to talk to her," Duffy said.

"And say what?" Cavill said.

"What do men say to women?" Duffy said.

"I'll sleep on it," Cavill said.

CHAPTER SIXTEEN

Joey Jordan read Porter's telegram and then returned it to Duffy. They were on the porch of her ranch house. Each had a cup of coffee.

"I have no objection to you patrolling my ranges, but do you think they will strike again so soon?" she said.

"They might if they think no one is watching for them," Duffy said. "We'll ride south and then find a place to camp and take up a position for night watch."

"How long will you stay?" Joey said.

"A week should do," Duffy said. "Make sure your people know we've left the ranch and headed south."

"I'll have my cook cut you out enough fresh meat to last a week," Joey said. "Do you need any other supplies?"

"We loaded up on everything but meat," Duffy said.

"I'll tell my cook to prepare the meat," Joey said, then she stood and entered the house.

Duffy looked at Cavill. "You didn't say one word, Jack."

"I know it," Cavill said. "I can't think of anything to say."

Joey returned to the porch. "My cook will meet you at the kitchen door behind the house with your supplies," she said.

Duffy and Cavill stood up. "Thank you, Miss Jordan," Duffy said. "We'll do our best to stop any more theft."

"Miss Jordan?" Cavill said.

Joey looked up at the lumbering Cavill.

"Yes?" she said.

"Uh . . . thank you," Cavill said. "For the meat."

"You're welcome," Joey said.

After they rode south with fifty pounds of fresh beef in their saddlebags, Duffy said, " 'Thank you for the meat' was the best you could do?"

"I couldn't think of anything else," Cavill said.

"Well, you're going to get a second chance," Duffy said. "Look behind us."

Cavill turned and spotted Joey riding her horse directly at them.

"Hold up," Duffy said.

They stopped their horses and waited for Joey to arrive.

"Is something wrong?" Duffy said.

"No, but I need to see my foreman, and he's on the south range. I thought I'd ride with you until we reach the range and tell the men you're leaving," Joey said. "You can ride south and then circle back later."

Joey rode between them.

"This is some beautiful country out here," Duffy said.

"It is that," Joey said. "My father knew what he was doing when he selected this place, for sure."

"Your father must have been one hell of a rancher to carve this out of what was a wilderness," Duffy said.

"He was that and more," Joey said.

"It must have been hard on you, growing up here back then," Duffy said.

"I never knew another life," Joey said. "My mother was a schoolteacher before my father moved us here. She saw to it I received a proper education. My father saw to it I learned everything there is to know about a ranch. What about you, Mr. Duffy?"

"I plan to take the bar exam and be a lawyer," Duffy said.

111

"And you, Mr. Cavill?" Joey said.

"And me what?" Cavill said.

"Plans for the future?" Joey said.

"I'm not sure at the moment," Cavill said.

"I see my men," Joey said.

They rode about a thousand feet where Jenkins and several others were digging postholes for a fence. Scattered about were a thousand head of cattle, peacefully grazing.

"Well, Mr. Duffy, Mr. Cavill, have a safe journey," Joey said.

"Bye, ma'am," Duffy said.

While Joey dismounted, Duffy and Cavill continued to ride south. They rode past some tall hills overlooking the south range and herd.

"The high ground is a good place to observe the range," Cavill said. "And keep a fire hidden."

They chose a hill with an elevation of around five hundred feet. Even without binoculars, they could see the herd and the cowboys on duty.

"Half-moon tonight, no clouds. It would be a good night to rustle off a few head," Duffy said. "After tonight, we'd have to wait weeks for another good night."

"Put on some coffee while I scout around," Cavill said.

"Don't get lost and forget to come back," Duffy said.

Cavill rode south in the high ground that overlooked the lush valley below. He saw no signs of stolen cattle or even horses, but no rustler would take cattle to a high elevation to avoid detection.

He'd want a quick escape, undetected, and would travel a preplanned route to his destination.

Not with just six cows, though. Six wasn't enough to risk a rope.

After a few miles, Cavill dismounted, found a shady tree, lit a cigar, and thought.

He was never a man to waste thoughts on fancy and romance. He wasn't sure he even believed in love, so why did he have this feeling in the pit of his stomach like he just ate raw Mexican chili peppers?

Joey Jordan was a beautiful woman, for sure, but he'd seen lots of beautiful women in his life, and not one of them caused him to go mute in her presence.

What did Jim say? "Like a fist to the chest?"

Cavill smoked and looked at the wide, blue sky overhead. She'd barely noticed him, if at all. She probably had no use for a man like him in her life. Most of her callers were probably wealthy miners from Helena, men with sacks of gold ready to be placed at her feet.

There was no use even thinking about it. It was best to put such thoughts out of his mind and do what he came out here to do, which was put a stop to the cattle theft.

Cavill returned to the saddle and rode back to Duffy.

Duffy had coffee and lunch cooking on a fire. One pan was full of beans and bacon while two cuts of beef cooked in another.

"See anything?" Duffy said.

"A lot of pretty country," Cavill said as he dismounted. "And that's about it."

Cavill grabbed a cup and filled it with coffee. "I was thinking six cows aren't worth the risk of a rope," he said.

"I thought that very thing," Duffy said. "Statewide it's a thousand or more head that have gone missing. We may be looking at something far more organized than we first thought."

"What's the price for cattle these days? Eighteen, nineteen, maybe even twenty a head? Put together a big enough herd and you're a rich man," Cavill said.

"Or small enough to go unnoticed?" Duffy said.

"Like six at a time?"

"Exactly," Duffy said. "Move small amounts to a designated

place until brands are changed and you have enough cattle to sell at auction."

"What place?" Cavill said. "And how much is enough?"

"I guess we'll find out if they return for more cattle," Duffy said.

"Let's eat and grab some sleep if we're going to be up all night," Cavill said.

The moon rose shortly after eight in the evening. By nine, Duffy and Cavill had a clear view of the range below the cliff, and they could see the herd and a campfire.

Waiting was a difficult task, especially if what you were waiting for might never happen.

Their campfire was set far back enough so it couldn't be seen from below, and they kept a pot of coffee warming beside the fire.

Cattle were restless, even when they slept. Duffy and Cavill heard the nighttime noises the herd produced, but it was nothing out of the ordinary.

Around eleven in the evening, Cavill squinted into the darkness and said softly, "Jim, do you see something in the rear of the herd?"

Duffy trained his eyes toward the back of the herd.

"Shadows moving," Duffy said.

Cavill watched the moonlight just above the horizon and saw cattle and men moving away from the rear of the herd. "They're walking the cattle," he said.

"Let's go down, close the rear door, and give them a welcome," Duffy said.

Duffy and Cavill mounted their horses, raced down the far side of the hill, and rode in a wide arc behind the south range. When they picked up sign of the stolen cattle, they slowed their pace and finally stopped about a hundred yards in front of them.

Two men wearing white hoods walked the cattle forward. The necks of the cattle, ten in all, were connected by rope so as to make it easier to keep them moving.

Duffy and Cavill dismounted, walked their horses to safety, and removed their Winchester rifles from their saddles.

"Let them come to us," Duffy whispered.

They stood aside in darkness and waited for the cattle and men to arrive. Then, from the darkness, Duffy and Cavill cocked the levers of their Winchesters.

"One twitch, and you're dead men," Cavill said.

The two men guiding the stolen cattle froze in place.

"Go ahead and move, and you'll never move again," Cavill said.

One of the men reached for his sidearm. Cavill shot him dead on the spot and immediately cocked the lever on the Winchester again. "Apparently your friend was hard of hearing. Are you?" Cavill said.

"No, mister, I ain't," the second hooded man said.

"Toss your gun," Duffy said.

The man slowly removed the gun from his holster and tossed it to the ground.

Duffy walked to the man.

"The hood," Duffy said.

The man removed the hood and looked at Duffy.

"Hey, Jack, have a look at this," Duffy said.

Cavill walked to Duffy and looked at the man.

"Jenkins. Son of a bitch," Cavill said.

Wearing a thin robe over a long nightshirt, Joey looked at Jenkins and said, "Why, Mr. Jenkins? After all these years, why?"

Seated in a chair between Duffy and Cavill, who stood,

Jenkins glared at Joey.

"When I first came to work for your father, you were just a kid," Jenkins said. "This place was a wilderness. We battled Indians, bandits, and freezing winters. The winter that took your mother damn near killed me as well."

"I'm aware of all the hardships all of us endured," Joey said. "What does any of that have to do with you stealing my cattle?"

"*Your* cattle?" Jenkins said. "I'm the one who was shot twice and took an arrow for them, not you. I'm the one who damn near froze to death guarding them in winter and baked in the summer sun. Not you."

"Nonetheless, the cattle are my property and I believe I have the right to know why you decided to steal from me," Joey said.

"Fifty dollars a month," Jenkins said.

"What?" Joey said.

"That's what I make as your foreman."

"I don't see the . . ."

"That's what I made as your foreman five years ago," Jenkins said.

"If you wanted a raise, all you had to do is ask," Joey said. "I would have doubled your salary."

"Crawl to a woman for money?" Jenkins said.

"It beats crawling to a rope," Cavill said.

"I'll tell you what, Jenkins," Duffy said. "You tell us how you got involved in this and everything you know, and we'll see to it you don't swing."

"Yeah, sure. Like this bitch would agree to—" Jenkins said.

Cavill grabbed Jenkins by the shirt, yanked him to his feet, and tossed him over the porch railing to the ground.

In an instant, Cavill was off the porch. He grabbed Jenkins, lifted him up, slapped him five or six times, and then threw him against the porch stairs.

"Forget going to the marshal, I'll hang you right now," Cavill said. He grabbed Jenkins and dragged him across the ground to his horse.

"Stop him!" Jenkins yelled. "Help! Get him off me!"

"Jack, that's enough," Duffy said.

Cavill picked Jenkins up like a doll and shook him violently.

"Jack. Enough," Duffy said.

Cavill released Jenkins and he slumped to the ground.

"Bring him back to the porch," Duffy said.

Cavill lifted Jenkins and tossed him over the porch railing.

Joey looked at Duffy. "I get the feeling you're the only one he'll listen to," she said.

Cavill returned to the porch, removed his cigar case from the right boot, removed a cigar, and lit it with a wood match.

Duffy helped Jenkins back into a chair.

"Mr. Jenkins, do you wish to hang?" Duffy said.

Bleeding, battered, Jenkins looked up at Duffy. "Of course not, no," he said. "Who in their right mind wants to hang?"

"Tell us everything you know, and we'll talk to the marshal on your behalf," Duffy said.

"That isn't good enough," Jenkins said.

"I could just beat it out of him," Cavill said. "And hang him anyway."

"Jack," Duffy said.

"No, he's right. That isn't good enough," Joey said.

"What are you saying?" Duffy said.

"Mr. Jenkins, how many of my cattle have you stolen?" Joey said.

Jenkins looked at Joey, but remained quiet.

"Mr. Jenkins, I am the only one who can save you from the noose," Joey said. "Do you understand that?"

"Why would you want to save me?" Jenkins said.

"Because I want my cattle returned, and I want the information you have. In return you get to walk away free," Joey said.

"Free?" Jenkins said. "No charges?"

"None, but you have to tell us everything you know and take us to my cattle. Then I will set you free," Joey said. "You have my word."

Jenkins nodded. "All right, but I get to keep my gear and the money I have saved in my mattress."

"Deal," Joey said.

"So talk, Mr. Jenkins," Duffy said.

"Can I roll a cigarette?" Jenkins said.

"Yes," Duffy said.

Jenkins pulled a pouch of tobacco and papers from his shirt pocket and rolled a cigarette. "During the spring thaw when I was checking the ranges, a group of four men rode up to me," he said as he struck a match and lit the cigarette. "The one fellow, he said would I be interested in taking part in a territory-wide event. He used that word, 'event.' He said they recruited men from ranches all across Montana to siphon off small amounts of cattle and deliver them to a designated spot. He said a hundred per ranch would do. He said the owners would never even miss a hundred spread out over a year. I'd get paid two dollars for every head I brought in."

"Counting tonight?" Duffy said.

"Would have made me two hundred," Jenkins said.

"Is two hundred dollars worth your life?" Duffy said.

"As foreman, I make six hundred a year," Jenkins said. "An extra two hundred goes a long way."

"Who is the man who approached you, and where are the cattle?" Duffy said.

"Man's name is Cassidy," Jenkins said. "And the cattle are forty miles south of here in a little box canyon, but you'll never find it without me."

"Lucky for us we have you," Duffy said. "What was the plan for tonight? Drive them away from the herd and ride them to the box canyon in the morning?"

"Ride forty miles and back in one day? No," Jenkins said. "Ten miles south two cowboys from the box canyon were waiting to pick them up. They ride them the rest of the way."

"This is going on statewide?" Duffy said.

"What I know of it, yeah," Jenkins said.

"Relay stations set up along a route to this box canyon," Duffy said. "A clever way to avoid detection and move the stolen cattle quickly."

"If you say so," Jenkins said.

"From the box canyon, where are the cattle moved to?" Duffy said.

"I wasn't told, and I didn't ask," Jenkins said.

"Did you see a brander at this relay place?" Duffy said.

"Two of them."

"And how many other men?"

"Six at most."

Duffy looked at Joey. "Is there a room where we can secure Mr. Jenkins in for the night?"

"The root cellar," Joey said.

"I'll ride for the marshal at first light," Duffy said. "I think it'd be best if Jack stays behind in case Jenkins has a change of heart."

Cavill smiled at Jenkins. "Please do," he said. "Have a change of heart."

Jenkins looked at Cavill. "I don't think so," he said.

Duffy and Cavill were offered a guest room on the second floor that had two beds.

"I'm not sure how long it will take to return," Duffy said as he got into his bed. "The marshal might want to put together a posse."

"If there are large numbers of stolen cattle at this box canyon, a dozen drovers might be better," Cavill said.

"I'll mention that, and maybe Joey can free up a few of hers for the trip," Duffy said.

"Let's get some sleep," Cavill said. "We need to be up in four hours."

CHAPTER SEVENTEEN

Duffy and Cavill retrieved Jenkins from the root cellar and escorted him to the breakfast table in the ranch house.

Joey, already seated, wore dungaree pants, a blue denim shirt, and riding boots.

The cook served scrambled eggs, bacon, potatoes, toast, and coffee.

"Two of my men have agreed to ride with us," Joey said. "I'm afraid I need the rest out on the ranges."

"You're not going with us," Duffy said.

"Of course I am," Joey said. "They are my cattle, my responsibility."

"If there is any shooting you'll . . ." Duffy said.

"I'll stay out of the way," Joey said.

Duffy stood up from the table. "I should be back by noon," he said.

After Duffy left, Cavill said, "Finish your breakfast, Jenkins, so I can put you back in the root cellar."

After Jenkins was safely returned to the root cellar, Cavill took a cup of coffee to the porch, sat, and lit a cigar.

Joey exited the house with a cup of coffee and took the chair next to Cavill.

"I don't think it's a good idea for you to ride with us," Cavill said.

"I can take care of myself," Joey said.

"It's not a good idea," Cavill said.

Joey sipped coffee and then looked at Cavill. "Twenty years ago, when I was just nine, we came under attack from a group of angry Sioux. My father handed me a Henry rifle, put me at a window, and told me to shoot anything that came into my vision. It wasn't a good idea on my father's part, but it was necessary. Sometimes necessary outweighs a bad idea."

Cavill nodded. "All right," he said. "But if trouble starts, you do as I say when I say it, or you don't go."

Joey stared at Cavill for a moment. "You think you can stop me?"

"Do you want to test me?"

Joey grinned. "After the way I saw you handle Mr. Jenkins, I think not," she said.

"Good."

"Why did you get so angry with Mr. Jenkins last night?" Joey said.

"I didn't like the way he spoke to you."

"You mean when he called me a bitch?"

"Yeah, yes."

Joey grinned again, and Cavill felt his head would explode just from looking at her.

"Are you one of those men who always comes to a woman's rescue?" Joey said.

"I don't . . . I'm not sure I understand you," Cavill said.

"Us helpless little women," Joey said and mock-fluttered her eyelashes.

Cavill laughed at her gesture. "I just didn't like his language, is all," he said.

"Are you referring to his use of the word *bitch*?"

"Yeah."

"It's what men with little to no power and money usually call a woman who has both, and I have both," Joey said.

"That doesn't mean I have to like to hear him call you one," Cavill said.

"Maybe not, but you acted as if you took it personally," Joey said. "Did you?"

Cavill looked at Joey.

"Are you a married man, Mr. Cavill?" Joey said.

"No."

"Have a steady woman?"

Cavill shook his head.

"Would you object to courting me when you're finished with this job?" Joey said.

"Courting?" Cavill said.

"Yes, courting. It means . . ."

"I know what it means," Cavill said.

"Well, what's your answer?"

"I expect that with a wiggle of your little finger, you could have any available man in the entire Montana territory," Cavill said. "Men with packs of gold lined up at your feet."

"Flattering, but not an answer," Joey said.

"I wouldn't object to it," Cavill said. "You're about the handsomest woman I have ever seen, but I don't think you'd like what I want."

"And what do you want?"

"To fight John L. Sullivan for the heavyweight title of the world," Cavill said.

"Are you talking about prizefighting?"

"I am."

"I don't see what one has to do with the other," Joey said. "I don't see why a man can't court a woman and still prize-fight. Who is John L. Sullivan, anyway?"

"Like I said, he's the heavyweight champion of the world."

"Can you beat him?"

"I think so."

"So it's agreed then that you'll officially court me," Joey said.

"I agreed to that?"

"I think you agreed to that the moment you rode in here and were tongue-tied like a schoolboy," Joey said.

"What about Jim? He's my manager," Cavill said.

"I thought he wants to be a lawyer."

"He does, but he's still my manager."

"I don't see why that has to change. What does a manager do?"

"Arranges my fights and works with a promoter."

"Like I said, I don't see why that has to change," Joey said. "It's settled then. You may court me when this assignment has concluded."

"One question," Cavill said. "How long does a man court a woman?"

"Well, I'm not sure," Joey said. "I guess it will take as long as it takes. I've never really had a man court me before. I've never had the time or the inclination."

"I never have either," Cavill said.

"I guess this is new water for both of us," Joey said. "Would you like to take a ride? I need to check the west range."

"Sheriff Kelly, I'd like to deputize you and one deputy as a federal posse to ride with us," Marshal Titus said.

"We'll need supplies for at least four days," Kelly said.

"My department will pay for them," Titus said.

"We'll need at least two more men," Duffy said. "Miss Jordan is lending us two of her drovers, but they're not gun hands."

"I'll have the blacksmith and gunsmith close their shops," Titus said. "I've used both before, and both men are cool under fire."

"Should be enough," Duffy said.

"We'll meet in front of my office in one hour," Titus said.

"I'll supply the ammunition."

"Marshal, Miss Jordan insists on going along," Duffy said.

"What? Why?" Titus said.

"It's her cattle," Duffy said. "And she wouldn't take no for an answer."

Titus sighed. "All right, but we'll have to watch her close if there's any trouble."

"I wouldn't worry," Duffy said. "I have the feeling my partner has that covered."

"How many?" Cavill said as he looked at the herd on the west range.

"At last count, a thousand," Joey said.

"Altogether?"

"Close to five thousand, I expect."

"At twenty a head, you really are a wealthy woman," Cavill said.

"Does that bother you?" Joey said.

"No, I plan on having some wealth of my own," Cavill said. "It's just I don't want you thinking I agreed to court you for your money."

Joey laughed a bit and said, "I seem to recall it was me who suggested it. Would I have brought it up if I was worried you might be after my money?"

"No, I suppose not," Cavill said.

"Let's sit for a minute under that tall tree there," Joey said and dismounted her horse.

"Jim should be back soon with the marshal," Cavill said.

"Just for a few minutes," Joey said.

Cavill dismounted and they walked to the tree and sat in the shade.

"You may kiss me if you'd like," Joey said.

"I'm not going to want to stop with a kiss," Cavill said.

"Don't worry. I'll stop you," Joey said.

Cavill and Joey reached the ranch house a few minutes before Duffy returned with Titus and the posse.

Joey dismounted and dashed onto the porch. "I can't let them see my hair like this," she said.

"I thought you said you'd stop me," Cavill said.

"We'll talk about that later," Joey said as she ran inside.

"Women," Cavill said as he waited beside his horse for Duffy to arrive.

While the cook packed fresh meat into the saddlebags on the horses, Duffy, Cavill, Titus, Kelly, and the posse met with Joey on the porch.

Joey served coffee.

"I'd feel a whole lot better if you stayed behind, Miss Jordan," Titus said.

"Nonsense, Marshal," Joey said. "Now two of my men are coming with me to wrangle whatever stolen cattle we find. I am more than able to drive my own cows."

"All right, but if—" Titus said.

"Shooting starts, I stay out of the way. Yes, I know," Joey said.

"Well, get Jenkins and let's get started," Titus said.

Chapter Eighteen

"They broke camp and left," Titus said when they reached the relay area.

"What did you expect them to do when I didn't show?" Jenkins said.

Cavill inspected the ashes in the campfire. "Looks like they gave up after two nights," he said.

"Sure, not enough moon to wait," Jenkins said.

"Just two riders," Cavill said.

"I already told you that," Jenkins said.

"Let's go," Titus said. "We need to make twenty miles before dark."

Around a campfire, as they ate supper, Duffy said, "Mr. Jenkins, are there any other relay stations you're aware of?"

"I'm sure there are, but my concern was just the one," Jenkins said.

"Where is this canyon where the cattle are being held?" Titus said.

"Bridger Mountains, and that's all I'm going to tell you until we get there," Jenkins said. "Lest you change your mind about hanging me."

"I gave you my word," Joey said.

Jenkins looked at Cavill. "You didn't give his," he said.

"My partner and I have been hired to stop the cattle theft in Montana and elsewhere," Cavill said. "If letting you go means we accomplish that, then that's what will happen."

"Satisfied?" Joey said.

"I'll be satisfied when I'm free of him," Jenkins said and looked at Cavill.

"Enough talk, Jenkins," Titus said. "If you lead us astray tomorrow morning, I'll noose you up myself."

"I'm not crazy," Jenkins said. "I have no desire to die from a rope—or any other way, for that matter, except old age."

"Finish eating so I can put the irons on you for the night," Titus said.

"Mr. Jenkins, how well do you know this box canyon?" Duffy said.

"Well enough. Why?" Jenkins said.

"I want to make sure we don't ride into a trap," Duffy said.

"How? Nobody knows we're coming," Jenkins said.

"Enough talk, Jenkins," Titus said. "Let's get you tucked in for the night."

Away from the campfire, Cavill and Joey sat together on a fallen log. The night air had a chill to it, and Joey wore a jacket. Each held a cup of coffee.

"So what now?" Cavill said.

"That's up to you," Joey said. "Generally, when a man samples the milk for free, he doesn't buy the cow."

"Well, doesn't this just screw up the works," Cavill said.

"Does that mean you'll come back and court me?" Joey said. "Yes."

"Good. Let's get some sleep then."

"But I'm not giving up prizefighting."

"Nobody asked you to."

"I'm just stating it for the record."

"State it all you want. Nobody asked you to."

"Good," Cavill said.

"Good," Joey said. "Maybe now we can get some sleep."

Jenkins led the way through the Bridger Mountains to a sheer cliff that overlooked a box canyon some two thousand feet below.

Even without binoculars, they could see the herd of close to one thousand cattle in the green valley below.

Titus, Kelly, Cavill, and Duffy had binoculars and zoomed in on the operation.

"I count two branders and six cowboys," Duffy said.

"They probably won't move out until all the cattle have been re-branded," Cavill said. "Several days, at least."

Titus turned to Jenkins. "There is a pass to the north and one to the south. What is the way down?" he said.

"To the west from here to flat ground, and then turn north or south," Jenkins said. "About a mile each way."

"Let's fix some lunch and discuss a plan," Duffy said.

Joey was more than a decent cook over a campfire. She prepared beef stew with thick slices of crusty bread.

Duffy drew a map in the dirt with a stick. "After dark, Jack and I will enter the canyon from the south. Marshal, you and the rest come in from the north. It's unlikely this bunch will post guards, so if we go in after midnight, we should have no trouble getting the drop on them. Jack, we want them all alive for questioning."

"Sure," Cavill said.

Joey looked at Cavill. He was, for sure, a fearless warrior of a man, but it was more than that. It was as if the thought of being shot or killed never entered his mind.

Cavill looked at Joey, and she smiled and nodded at him.

"Just the two of you?" Titus said.

"Hell, Marshal, Jack could do it himself," Duffy said. "I'm

going with him to make sure he doesn't kill anybody."

"All right, but I want them all alive for questioning," Titus said. "They'll hang soon enough in Miles City. Joey, you ride with us, but you stay to the rear at all times. Understood?"

Joey nodded. "We can drive this herd to my place, contact the ranchers with stolen cattle, and ask them to come identify them."

"About what I figured," Titus said.

"Might as well rest up while we can," Duffy said. "I don't figure we'll be doing much sleeping tonight."

"What about me?" Jenkins said. "If this bunch sees me, there'll be a bounty on my head for sure."

Titus looked at Joey. "What do you want to do, Joey?"

"Just before we head down tonight, cut him loose," Joey said. "Give him his rifle, sidearm, gear, and supplies."

"Best post a few lookouts until dark," Duffy said.

"I'll go," Cavill said.

From two thousand feet away, Cavill sat behind a large rock and watched the branders go about their work. He used binoculars and was impressed by how efficient they were at roping and branding the cattle.

The other cowboys kept the herd from wandering and brought fresh cows to the branders.

Joey approached Cavill from behind with two cups of coffee.

"That's quite a sight down there," Joey said as she sat beside Cavill.

"About eight or nine hundred head, as near as I can figure," Cavill said. "My guess is they're waiting on an even thousand before moving them out."

"To where?"

"My guess is we'll find out tonight."

Joey sipped from her cup and then looked at Cavill. "I've

never really had a man before," she said. "Not seriously. There was always so much to do, even when my father was alive, that I never had the time or the need. Then along you come and change that. What I want to know is, are you really coming back for me, or are you just talking the way men do to get what they want?"

"I thought we already settled that," Cavill said.

"But is it just talk?"

"No, it's not just talk," Cavill said. "I had no thoughts of marriage or settling down until we rode to your ranch, and you popped out the door. Jim says it just hits you, and when it does, you'll know it. Well, you hit me, and I know it, and when we're done, I'll be back."

"What about your job with the detective agency?"

"Jim and I both agreed this would be our last job with the agency," Cavill said. "He's going to finish law school and manage my boxing career. I don't see how that has to change at all."

"It changes if you get yourself killed," Joey said.

"Getting killed is not in my immediate plans," Cavill said. "Besides, a man could get killed branding a cow or a horse just as easily as getting shot, so it never enters my mind."

"It occurs to me that when your job is done, we have a lot of getting to know each other in store," Joey said.

"I'm a man of bad habits," Cavill said. "You should know that up front. I've made a good amount of money working for the agency and saved very little. I enjoy the work because I'm good at it, which is the same reason I enjoy prizefighting. I'm sloppy and, except for Jim, I never put much stock in the opinions of others."

"My whole life has been spent as a rancher," Joey said. "I know cattle and I know land and not much else. I always figured I would die a rich old maid. I'm stubborn and opinionated, just like my father, and I never took men seriously. So we have some work to do when you return."

"That's part of the fun, isn't it?" Cavill said.

"How about a kiss?" Joey said.

"Can they see us?"

"No, but who cares if they do?"

Duffy watched as the last of the campfires went out in the box canyon. Then he walked back to camp to wake the others.

"It's midnight, and they're all asleep," Duffy said as he shook Cavill awake.

Coffee was keeping hot in a large pot over a fire. Once everyone was awake and had a cup, Titus said, "Everybody stick to the plan, and we'll have no shooting. The goal is to take everybody back alive, but if they insist on shooting, shoot to kill."

"Give Jack and me a full minute to wake this bunch before you ride in and surround them. Remember, we'll be on foot," Duffy said.

"Are you sure you boys know what you're doing?" Titus said.

"Hell, Marshal, I'll kill the whole bunch if you want me to," Cavill said.

"That's exactly what we don't want, Jack," Duffy said. "And we especially want this Cassidy fellow alive, if he's in there."

"He's there," Jenkins said. "Tall, rangy fellow of about forty or so."

"All right, Jenkins. Get on your horse and ride," Titus said. "I don't care where you go, just so long as it's out of Montana."

Once Jenkins was gone, Duffy and Cavill mounted their horses. "Give us a full minute before you ride in," Duffy said.

Joey walked to Cavill's horse and looked up at him. "Don't do anything stupid," she said.

Cavill nodded, and he and Duffy rode down the side of the hill to the south passage leading to the box canyon.

"Well, you two certainly seem to have hit it off," Duffy said.

"We'll talk about it later," Cavill said.

The quarter moon provided just enough light to navigate the hilly terrain, and they slowly worked their way to the canyon.

"She's a striking-looking woman, Miss Jordan," Duffy said. "A man could do far worse."

"Keep your mind on the job," Cavill said.

"I am. Are you?" Duffy said.

"Aw, hell, Jim," Cavill said. "You know better than that."

At the entrance to the south pass, they paused to remove their torches, which they'd made from sticks and cloth that they'd wetted with whiskey. They struck matches and lit the torches.

"We'll go in a hundred yards and then walk," Duffy said.

At the north pass, Titus gave the signal to light the torches. Once all were lit, Titus led the way into the north pass. They rode until the pass ended at the entrance to the canyon.

The stolen herd was nearby, mostly asleep, a few grazing, but none of them bothered by the posse.

Joey stopped beside Titus. She watched, fascinated, as Duffy and Cavill, torches in hand, simply walked into the outlaws' camp as if they were out for a midnight stroll. When they reached the extinguished campfire, they tossed the torches onto the embers.

Duffy carried a Winchester rifle, and he fired a shot into the dirt.

The sleeping rustlers snapped awake, but before they could react, Cavill fired a shot into the night.

"Any man who reaches for his gun is a dead man," Cavill said.

"There are a dozen rifles on you right now, and if you do something stupid, you'll be cut to ribbons," Duffy said. "Marshal Titus, come ahead."

Titus and the posses rode to Duffy and Cavill.

"Howdy, boys. Did we disturb your slumber?" Titus said.

"Which one of you scum is Cassidy?" Cavill said.

None of the rustlers moved or spoke up.

"I'll ask again, and then I'll start shooting until Cassidy speaks up," Cavill said and cocked his Colt.

"I'm Cassidy," a tall man in the rear said.

Joey realized she had been holding her breath and exhaled a long sigh of relief.

Once all the rustlers were roped together around a campfire, Titus spoke directly to Cassidy.

"Who is the head man?" Titus said.

"I have no idea," Cassidy said.

"Well, who do you work for?" Titus said.

"What's it worth to you?" Cassidy said.

"Prison instead of a noose," Titus said. "It's your neck."

"Can I have a cup of that coffee?" Cassidy said.

Joey was pouring coffee from a large pot. She handed a cup to Cavill and looked at Titus, who nodded.

Joey filled a cup and handed it to Cassidy, who had to take it in two hands, as his wrists were bound with rope.

"I'll tell you what I know in exchange for your word I don't swing," Cassidy said.

Titus nodded. "Go ahead," he said.

"We ride the herd down to a secret place in the Bighorn Mountains," Cassidy said. "It's a week or more ride from here. Bill Parsons runs things, but not for himself. For somebody else."

"Who?" Duffy said.

"You'd have to ask Parsons that," Cassidy said. "He plays it close to the vest. All I know is I got a small spread in Utah that amounts to nothing but dirt. Parsons rode by one day looking

134

for hands to help with this big plan to rustle thousands of cattle. He said I could make two dollars a head, plus he'd allow me to keep twenty-five head for myself. The cattle are driven to the secret location, and when the herd is large enough, Parsons and his boys move them."

"To where?" Duffy said.

"You'd have to ask Parsons that," Cassidy said.

"Where do the re-brands come from?" Duffy said.

"You'd have to ask Parsons that, too. He supplies the irons."

"Look at this, Jim," Cavill said as he hefted a large sack of branding irons. "An iron for every brand."

Duffy removed a few irons. "Specially made to change any brand," he said. "How about it, Cassidy?"

"I don't know where Parsons gets them from," Cassidy said. "And that's the truth."

"You got a kid works for you back in Utah," Duffy said. "We met him on the trail. What's his name? You got one chance to answer correctly."

"You must mean young Robert Parker," Cassidy said. "Where is he?"

"At the moment, we don't know," Duffy said. "The last we saw of him, he was riding with Jane Canary."

Joey handed a cup of coffee to Cavill and Duffy. "Can you tell which iron they used on mine?" she said.

"In daylight maybe," Cavill said.

"Speaking of which, there's not much we can do until daybreak," Titus said. "Two men keep watch while we get some sleep. We'll rotate the two men every hour."

"Jack and I will take first watch," Duffy said.

As the posse settled in to sleep, Joey took Cavill aside. "I was frightened half to death watching you walk in here the way you did," she said.

"It's nothing Jim and I haven't done a dozen times before,"

Cavill said. "Now why don't you get some sleep before the sun comes up."

"All right, but when you're through with your watch, come sleep beside me," Joey said.

"I will. Now go on and rest," Cavill said.

After Joey went to her bedroll, Cavill joined Duffy at the fire.

"You're going to marry that girl, aren't you?" Duffy said.

"I never thought I'd hear myself say this, but I believe so," Cavill said.

Duffy handed Cavill a fresh cup of coffee. Cavill lit a cigar.

"You know what we have to do in the morning, right?" Duffy said.

Cavill blew a large smoke ring. "Yeah," he said.

CHAPTER NINETEEN

After breakfast, while Joey and others checked the herd for brands, Duffy and Cavill spoke privately with Titus and Kelly.

"We need to take Cassidy with us," Duffy said. "He knows where this secret place is in the Bighorns."

"Otherwise we could be roaming around those mountains for a month," Cavill said.

"You're not seriously going after this bunch alone?" Kelly said.

"I don't see as how we have a choice," Duffy said.

"Every day we put it off, this Parsons fellow steals more cattle and might even move them out before he's stopped," Cavill said.

"Time is a factor here," Duffy said.

"And Cassidy?" Titus said.

"We'll decide that when the time comes," Duffy said.

"Most likely we'll cut him loose like we did Jenkins," Cavill said.

Titus sighed and looked at Kelly. "What do you think?" he said.

"I have to agree with them," Kelly said. "Time is a factor, and Cassidy knows the location of the herd."

"All right, but if possible, bring Cassidy to the marshal in the town of Cody," Titus said. "It's about twenty miles northeast of the Bighorns. The army outpost in Sheridan has two hundred men you can call upon if need be."

"We best get started," Duffy said.

"Give me a few minutes," Cavill said. He walked to the stolen herd where Joey was checking the cattle.

She smiled broadly at him and said, "I've identified about fifty of mine. We'll drive the herd to my place and wire all the ranchers to come identify theirs. Some of the brands were altered to a P and a B and a few marked Q, but half are untouched. I guess we'll see what kind of a wrangler you are on the—"

"Jim and I are leaving for the Bighorn Mountains and taking Cassidy with us," Cavill said.

Joey stared at Cavill for several seconds. "I thought you would help drive the cattle back to my ranch," she said.

"You have plenty of men here for that," Cavill said. "Right now we have Cassidy in custody, and he knows where the stolen herds are being kept. We have to take advantage of the situation while we can. It will take two days or more to get this herd to your place. If we go with you, by the time Jim and I return to where we are right now, we'd have lost almost a week. You see that, don't you, Joey?"

"I see it. I don't like it, but I see it," Joey said. "What am I supposed to do? Wait and worry you might get killed out there in the mountains?"

"Jim and I aren't so easy to kill," Cavill said. "Have a little faith, and I'll be back before you know it."

"The men can see us, so I won't make a fuss," Joey said. "Send me a telegram when you can."

"You sure are beautiful in the morning," Cavill said.

Joey turned away so Cavill couldn't see the mist forming in her eyes. "Go, if you're going," she said.

Cavill sighed and returned to Duffy, who had Cassidy mounted on his horse. Cassidy's legs were shackled together under his horse and his wrists were shackled together in front of him.

"Let's go," Cavill said.

After riding southeast for twenty miles, they broke for an hour to rest the horses and fix a hot lunch.

Duffy studied his maps as they ate plates of beef with beans and coffee.

"We can make twenty more miles by dark and cross into Wyoming by midday tomorrow," Duffy said. He turned to Cassidy. "How far to reach this secret location?"

"About twenty miles west of Cody is the way into the Bighorns," Cassidy said. "From there, it's a full day's ride to the pass."

"Keep in mind that if you cross us, I'll hang you on the spot," Cavill said.

"I know that, and I won't cross you," Cassidy said. "Like I said, I ain't stupid."

"I hope not," Cavill said. "For your sake."

"All right, let's herd them together for the night," Joey said.

"We have an hour of daylight left, Joey," Titus said.

"Once we stop, it will take them an hour to settle down," Joey said. "I'd rather them settle when I can still see them and send my men back for the drags."

"All right. Boys, you heard the lady. Let's make camp," Titus said.

Around a campfire, as they ate beef stew, Duffy studied his maps. "We'll be in Wyoming by noon," he said. "Cassidy, are you wanted in Wyoming?"

"Not as far as I know. Why?" Cassidy said.

"What about Utah?" Duffy said.

"Again, no. Again, why?"

"I wouldn't like to have to fight off bounty hunters for reward money before we get where we're going," Duffy said.

"Well, I ain't wanted, so relax," Cassidy said.

Cavill filled three cups with coffee and passed a cup to Duffy and Cassidy. "They have a telegraph office in Cody?" Cavill said.

"They do," Cassidy said. "It's a small town, but it's on the line to the army post in Sheridan."

"What do you think, Jim? Wire Porter with our plans?" Cavill said.

Duffy nodded. "I'll go. You wait outside of town with Cassidy in case he lied to us about being wanted."

"I didn't lie," Cassidy said.

"And you didn't steal cattle, either," Cavill said.

"If you don't mind, I'm going to sleep," Cassidy said.

Joey stretched out in her bedroll beside the campfire and watched the stars overhead. Montana was so far north, the stars seemed limitless as they stretched across the night horizon.

She didn't want to, but she found herself thinking about Jack. Was he stretched out as she was and thinking about her?

She was never a woman taken to thoughts of fancy. She started working on the ranch when she was but ten years old. By the time she was twelve, she could ride, wrangle, rope, and shoot. When she was eighteen, the age when women generally start to think of marriage, she was accompanying her father on cattle drives to Miles City.

Her suitors were miners or clerks who worked in the stores in Helena, and both were poor choices. As the years rolled by and the ranch grew more and more successful, she put all thoughts of marriage out of her mind.

After her father died, she found herself a wealthy woman

consumed by the workload of running a successful ranch.

Then along came Jack Cavill, and he swept her off her feet. And thoughts of cattle turned to thoughts of fancy.

Maybe he should have gone with Joey to drive the herd back to her place? Isn't that what a man does, look after his woman?

His woman.

The words sounded so strange to Cavill.

He wondered if she was awake and thinking of him.

The job could take several more weeks, even months, to complete. He wondered if Joey would feel the same when it was over and he returned to her.

Out of the corner of his eye, Cavill caught a glimpse of Duffy, who was writing on a piece of paper. Drafting the telegram to Porter, most likely.

Cavill looked up at the millions of stars overhead, and they made him think of Joey.

"That's Cody there, about a mile in the distance," Cassidy said.

"All right, Jack, you wait here with Cassidy," Duffy said. "I won't be long."

"Pick up some extra supplies," Cavill said.

Duffy nodded and rode west toward Cody.

"All right, Cassidy, we might as well get comfortable," Cavill said.

Duffy rode into the small town of Cody, which had a population of under a thousand. The telegraph office was on Main Street, wedged between the barbershop and sheriff's office.

Duffy tied his horse to the hitching post outside the telegraph office, went in, and paid the operator to send the lengthy report to Porter. The cost of sending such a long telegram was two dollars and eighty cents.

Duffy asked for and got a receipt.

Outside the telegraph office, Duffy looked around for a post office, didn't see one, and entered the sheriff's office.

Sheriff Pratt, a man of about sixty, sat behind a small desk and looked at Duffy as he entered the office.

"Help you, young fellow?" Pratt said.

"I was wondering where I could post a letter," Duffy said.

"The general store at the end of the block handles the mail," Pratt said. "The stage from Sheridan stops twice a week."

"Thanks," Duffy said.

"Just passing through, are you?" Pratt said.

"Headed south," Duffy said. "Pick up some supplies, mail a letter, and I'll be on my way."

"You aren't wanted for anything, are you?" Pratt said.

"No. No, I'm not," Duffy said.

Pratt lifted the revolver off his lap and set it on the desk. "Good," he said. "I didn't feel like shooting you anyway."

"I'm obliged for that," Duffy said. "Well, I'll see you, Sheriff."

Duffy exited the sheriff's office and walked his horse to the general store. "Ten pounds of beans, bacon, coffee, jerky, sugar, and flour. Also some lard, a few cans of condensed milk, and, if you got them, some canned peaches."

"Is that it?" the man behind the counter said.

"And I need to mail this," Duffy said and set the letter on the counter.

"Come back in a half hour," the man said.

Duffy walked to the barbershop and had a shave. When he returned to the general store, his supplies were ready. The cost was twenty-three dollars. Duffy paid in folding money rather than coin.

Cavill and Cassidy were seated against a tree in the shade when Duffy returned to them.

"I see you took a shave in town," Cavill said.

"I needed to kill some time while waiting for the supplies,"

Duffy said. "Cassidy, how far to the entrance to the Bighorns?"

"Be there by nightfall," Cassidy said.

With the sun about to set, Cassidy said, "Right here just over this hill is the secret passage."

"And after that?" Cavill said.

"If we leave at sunup, we'll be there by late afternoon," Cassidy said.

"Keep this in mind," Cavill said. "If we ride into a trap, even if it's not your doing, you die first. No matter who else should die, me, my partner, whoever, you die first."

"I told you already, I don't wish to die," Cassidy said. "By hanging or any other way."

"Then we understand each other," Cavill said.

"Let's make camp," Duffy said.

An hour later, Duffy filled three bowls with thick beef stew and cut up large hunks of crusty bread for dipping.

"I'm going to miss your cooking," Cassidy said.

"Let me ask you something," Cavill said. "You don't really seem the violent type. How did you get into rustling cattle?"

"Like I told you, Parsons asked me if I was interested in earning some quick, easy money," Cassidy said.

"I know that, but most men aren't so willing to risk their neck for two dollars a head," Cavill said.

"You ever worked a patch of dirt that just wouldn't produce a damn thing?" Cassidy said. "Sunup to sundown, breaking your back, and for nothing. Two dollars a head and twenty-five of my own seemed like all the money in the world."

"Maybe so, but the only reason your neck won't be stretched along with the others is because you have knowledge we need," Cavill said.

"You ain't going back on your word, are you?" Cassidy said.

"No, we're not," Duffy said.

"Just remember what I said about riding into a trap: you die first," Cavill said.

"I picked up some canned peaches in town," Duffy said. "Anybody want some peaches?"

CHAPTER TWENTY

"This is it. This is the entrance to the secret pass," Cassidy said.

Duffy and Cavill looked up at the hill on the side of a mountain in the Bighorn range.

"It looks like just another hill," Cavill said.

"That's why it's stayed hidden so long," Cassidy said. He glanced up at the setting sun. "We got just enough time to make the other side."

"Lead the way," Duffy said.

Cassidy rode up the side of the gently rolling hill, followed by Duffy and then Cavill. At around a thousand feet in altitude, the hill leveled off and Cassidy rode west along a flat stretch of ground.

"The way in is about a quarter mile from here," Cassidy said.

"It'll be dark in fifteen minutes," Duffy said.

"Just enough time," Cassidy said.

They reached the entrance to the pass just as the sun set.

"Through this pass leads to the secret outlaw camp," Cassidy said.

"We'll camp here the night," Duffy said. "From here, how far to the outlaw camp?"

"Twenty miles as the crow flies," Cassidy said.

"How is it a bunch of outlaws know where this place is, and no one else does?" Duffy said.

"All I know is what I heard from Parsons and some of the boys," Cassidy said. "They heard of it from some drunken

Ethan J. Wolfe

Indians who traded the secret for a case of whiskey."

"That sounds like total horseshit," Cavill said.

"Maybe it does, but I can't say it isn't true," Cassidy said.

"I'm going to make a fire," Duffy said. "Jack, you see to the horses."

Duffy and Cavill waited until Cassidy was asleep. Then they walked far enough away so their voices wouldn't wake him.

"What do you want to do about Cassidy?" Cavill said.

"I have an idea," Duffy said. "But it depends on what we find."

"There. Look there," Cassidy said.

They rode all morning, the pass taking them through winding mazes, flat ground, steep hills, and finally to lush prairie land nestled between rolling hills.

Cassidy took them atop a tall hill that overlooked the outlaw camp about a quarter mile away.

Using their binoculars, Duffy and Cavill zoomed in on the camp. There were three cabins, a barn and a corral, and a large water trough beside a pump.

"I see only one horse in the corral," Duffy said.

"Where would the herd be located?" Cavill said.

"About a mile south of the cabins," Cassidy said. "The men could be with the herd."

"Let's go find out," Cavill said.

They rode to the cabins, where Duffy and Cavill dismounted with their Winchester rifles in hand.

"Wait. I know that horse in the corral," Cassidy said. "Robert Parker, are you in there? It's Mike Cassidy. Come on out."

Duffy and Cavill cocked their Winchesters and aimed them at the front door of the cabin and waited. The door opened, and Robert Parker meekly steeped outside to the porch.

"Howdy, Mike," Parker said.

"It's just that kid Parker," Cavill said.

"I was just making some coffee, Mike," Parker said. He looked at Duffy and Cavill. "How did you guys find this place?"

At the small table in the main room of the cabin, Parker filled four cups with coffee and then sat next to Cassidy.

"All right, let's start from the beginning," Duffy said.

"Young Robert here works for me sometimes, like I told you," Cassidy said. "I asked him to meet me here to help drive my twenty-five head back to Utah. I didn't know he would set out looking for me."

"That's the truth, mister," Parker said. "Mike wrote me instructions on how to get here and when. When I showed up two days ago, no one was here."

"Why didn't you tell us that back in Montana?" Duffy said.

"I didn't want to get Mike in trouble," Parker said.

"How old are you, kid?" Cavill said.

"Seventeen, like I told you."

"Are you really from Utah, too?" Cavill said.

"The Great Salt Lake," Parker said. "My folks are Mormons. My friends call me Butch, on account I used to work in a butcher shop in Salt Lake."

"Nobody was here, no cattle, no nothing?" Duffy said.

"No, sir, nobody," Parker said.

"Saddle your horse, kid," Duffy said.

They rode south to the range where the cattle had been located.

"From the looks of this prairie, I'd say about two thousand cows grazed here for quite a spell," Cavill said.

"Do you know where they went?" Duffy said to Cassidy.

"That's something only Parsons knows," Cassidy said.

Duffy and Cavill exchanged looks.

147

"How hard could it be to track two thousand cows?" Cavill said.

"Parker, get off your horse," Duffy said. "You too, Cassidy."

Parker and Cassidy dismounted.

"Spend the night at the cabin," Duffy said. "You'll find your horses twenty miles south of here. I advise the both of you to head back to Utah and keep your noses clean. The chance you get, Cassidy, won't happen twice."

Duffy took the reins on Cassidy's horse.

"Parker, stay on the right side," Cavill said. "You don't want the life of an outlaw."

"Yes, sir," Parker said.

Cavill took the reins on Parker's horse.

"Get walking back to the cabin," Cavill said.

Close to dark Duffy and Cavill made camp after following the path of the herd for close to twenty miles.

"We'll cut their horses loose in the morning," Duffy said.

"How long ago did they leave you figure, ten days?" Cavill said.

"About, judging from the growth of the grass," Duffy said.

"Once we get off these mountains, they could be anywhere," Cavill said.

"We know they were changing brands to P, B, and Q," Duffy said. "Maybe they're headed to an auction house?"

"In Wyoming, where would that be?" Cavill said.

"Cheyenne," Duffy said. "Where the auction houses are."

"For a time, didn't the Stock Growers Association act as a local government for the territory?" Cavill said.

"Right after the railroad came through in sixty-seven."

"We could head straight for Cheyenne?" Cavill said. "Even with a ten-day lead we could nearly beat them there if we push it."

"If that's where they're headed," Duffy said.

"I guess we'll find out when we get out of these mountains," Cavill said.

Duffy stirred the stew in the pot. "Supper is ready," he said. "Grab a couple of biscuits from the sack."

Once the trail reached a canyon wide enough to fit four horses across, they knew they had reached the way out of the secret pass.

"Must have been hell, getting cattle through here," Cavill said.

"It's what's on the other side that interests me," Duffy said.

The canyon, after a mile or so, fed into flat prairie.

"Let's see where they're going and then rest our horses," Duffy said.

They rode for a few miles and reached the spot where the stolen cattle had feasted on sweet grass for several days.

"Might as well make camp and get a fresh start in the morning," Duffy said.

"Why here?" Cavill said. "Why pick here to rest the herd?"

"I'll make camp," Duffy said. "Why don't you scout ahead for a bit?"

Cavill rode west for about a mile and dismounted to check for tracks. He mounted up and rode another two miles and dismounted to check again.

"Huh, son of a bitch," he said.

Duffy had food cooking in several pans and coffee ready when Cavill returned to camp. After he dismounted and filled a cup with coffee, Cavill sat beside Duffy and said, "How many riders have we been tracking?"

"Eight."

"Make it twelve," Cavill said. "Four riders from the east joined up a few miles east of here."

"Twelve wranglers? What do you think?"

"I think they might be splitting the herd," Cavill said.

"To what end?"

"If we track them long enough, I guess we'll find out," Cavill said. "Is that stew ready?"

CHAPTER TWENTY-ONE

"Well, here is where they divided up the herd," Duffy said. "Half went south, the other half southeast toward Cheyenne."

"Cheyenne to sell the cattle they branded with brands that could pass as legitimate at auction, and south into old Mexico where they can get thirty dollars a head, no questions asked," Cavill said.

"I agree, but why not just sell the whole lot in Mexico for thirty a head instead of eighteen or twenty?" Duffy said.

As they inspected the tracks of the riders, Cavill said, "Maybe too many stolen cattle at auction would alert the Stock Growers Association, so they divided it up."

"Still, why not just drive the entire herd into Mexico?" Duffy said.

"Supply and demand?" Cavill said.

"Of course," Duffy said. "Too many cattle drives the price down. Keep the flow even, and the price stays even."

"The man behind all this isn't stupid," Cavill said.

"Not by a long shot," Duffy said.

"So we'll ride to Cheyenne then," Cavill said.

"Looks like," Duffy said.

"Nothing like a week in the saddle to make a man homesick for his own bed," Cavill said.

"We got plenty of supplies, and besides, absence makes the heart grow fonder, don't you know?" Duffy said.

"Are you talking about Joey or the Trent girl you never really told me about?" Cavill said.

"Let's mount up and get going," Duffy said. "We got about three hundred miles to Cheyenne."

They mounted their horses and rode southeast.

"So what about this Sylvia Trent?" Cavill said.

"What about her?" Duffy said.

"You've been playing it close to the vest," Cavill said. "You haven't said more than two words about her like it's some secret or something."

"It's no secret, Jack," Duffy said. "I'm just not sure yet if it's a passing fancy on her part or it's real."

"So what happened?"

"Nothing happened. She just wanted to talk."

Cavill grinned. "Talk?"

"Yes, talk," Duffy said. "If you say otherwise, I'll bust you one in the nose."

"Go ahead. I've had worse bee stings," Cavill said.

From a distance of about a mile away, a rifle shot suddenly sounded. It echoed for two or three seconds and faded away.

"Somebody hunting?" Cavill said.

A second shot sounded.

"That was from a different gun," Duffy said.

"Let's go see who is shooting at who," Cavill said as several more shots rang out.

They rode in the direction of the gunshots, and the path took them to the far side of a steep hill.

The shooting continued at a more rapid pace as Cavill and Duffy dismounted.

"Somebody on this hill is being shot at by somebody on a higher hill," Cavill said.

"Let's have a look," Duffy said.

They took their Winchester rifles with them as they ascended the five-hundred-foot-high hill. Once on top, they got down on

152

their stomachs and observed a lone man about fifty feet below them. He was hiding behind a large rock and fending off three men shooting at him from a slightly higher hill opposite him.

"We'll kill you, you son of a bitch," one of the three men shouted and then fired his rifle.

"Goddamn bounty hunter," another of the three men shouted.

"Well, you shouldn't have raped no woman and kilt that bank clerk," the man below Duffy and Cavill shouted.

"That was his fault," one of the three men shouted. "All we wanted was the money. He wouldn't give it to us. We had no choice."

"What do you think?" Cavill said.

"I think we should give this fellow a hand," Duffy said.

"Let's do it," Cavill said.

"You three, this is the law," Duffy shouted. "Throw down your weapons and surrender, and we won't have to kill you."

"Who's up there?" the lone man shouted.

Shots rang out and bullets struck the rock the man hid behind.

"You up there! Are you really the law?" the man shouted.

"Are you going to surrender, or what?" Cavill shouted.

"You go to hell," one of the three men shouted.

"Well, hell," Cavill said.

Duffy and Cavill rapid-fired their Winchesters at the three men.

"You three, we don't want to kill you, but we will and lose no sleep over it if we do," Cavill shouted. "Decide if you want to die here and now or ride on."

"Those are wanted men," the man below shouted.

"They have you in a crossfire," Duffy shouted. "Even if we do kill these three, they will probably kill you in the process. It's best to let them go and capture them another time."

"Well, shit," the man said.

"I share your sentiments, but tomorrow is another day," Cavill said.

"Go on and go, you bushwhackers, before I change my mind," the man shouted.

"Son, they've already gone," Duffy said. "Might as well come up here."

"Name is Tom Horn, and I guess I owe you my life."

Horn was as tall as Duffy and thin, with a chiseled face and drooping mustache. His eyes were dark and friendly.

"How did you get caught in a crossfire like that?" Duffy said.

"I've been after those men since they raped a woman and kilt a bank clerk down in New Mexico," Horn said. "I'm not a bounty hunter. I'm a scout for the army. I'm attached to Fort Bowie, although I took it upon myself to pursue those men."

"I hope you're a better scout than bounty hunter," Cavill said.

"Oh, they got the drop on me all right, but it was an accident," Horn said. "I lost them and figured I might get a better vantage point on the hill, which just happened to be where they were hiding. Before I knew it I was pinned down. If you hadn't come along, I figure they would have waited me out and killed me for sure."

"Happy to help, Mr. Horn," Duffy said.

"I expect I'll let them go and return to my duties," Horn said. "I'm being assigned to Lieutenant Gatewood to help with the Geronimo wars."

"Is he still at large?" Cavill said.

"Word is he's heading down to old Mexico," Horn said.

"Where is your horse, Tom?" Cavill said.

"Tied to a tree around that corner," Horn said.

★ ★ ★ ★ ★

"Where are you fellows off to?" Horn said as he mounted his horse.

"Cheyenne," Duffy said. "You?"

"Fort Bowie, where I'm to join Gatewood and scout for the capture of Geronimo," Horn said. "Although he's probably at McKinney by now."

"Well that's hell and gone from here," Cavill said. "Your best bet is to ride to Cheyenne with us, take the railroad, and save yourself weeks in the saddle."

"I believe I will do just that," Horn said. "Are you really lawmen?"

"We're investigating the cattle thefts in Montana. The trail has led us here," Duffy said.

"I've heard talk of widespread cattle theft clean into Arizona, New Mexico, and Nebraska," Horn said. "Even Kansas."

"I can't say as I disagree with that, Tom," Duffy said.

"If I may ask, what's in Cheyenne?" Horn said.

"That's what we're going there to find out," Cavill said.

"I've never been to Cheyenne," Horn said. "I've heard it was once a rough place to get stranded in."

"Before the railroad brought the cattle business there, it was as bad as or worse than Deadwood," Duffy said. "But time and money have a way of changing things."

"Hold up," Cavill said.

Cavill dismounted and looked closely at the three sets of horse tracks ahead of them. "Tom, have a look and tell me if these are the three you were after," Cavill said.

Horn dismounted, knelt down, and inspected the tracks. "It's them. I followed these tracks for two hundred miles," he said.

"Looks like they're headed for Cheyenne," Cavill said. "Imagine that."

★　★　★　★　★

"Why are you building a lean-to?" Horn said. "Ain't a drop of rain in the sky."

As Duffy pounded stakes into the ground, he said, "A fire can be seen for miles in open country. A fire can give away a man's position quicker than anything."

Cavill tossed Duffy his slicker.

"So we'll hide ours and look for theirs," Cavill said.

"I never thought of that," Horn said. "You two are no ordinary lawmen, are you?"

"We're investigators for the Illinois Detective Agency," Duffy said. "Hired by the Stock Growers Association to investigate the cattle thefts in Montana and wherever else the trail takes us."

"Right now that trail is taking us to Cheyenne," Cavill said.

"Back there, could you have really killed those three?" Horn said.

"We could have sure enough, but not without risking your neck in the process," Cavill said. "And we didn't really feel like digging four graves."

"You two have been partners for a while, haven't you?" Horn said.

"Years," Cavill said. "We have some beef we need to use up. Fancy a beef stew with some thick bread, Tom?"

"Are you kidding? I've been eating beans, jerky, and stale bread for the last eighty miles," Horn said.

"Gather up some firewood, and I'll get things going," Cavill said.

As they ate plates of beef stew, they watched the red dot of a campfire on the horizon.

"How far away is that light?" Horn said.

"Two, maybe three miles," Duffy said.

156

"Close enough to get the drop on them during the night?" Horn said.

"Sure, but why bother, when we're still three days from Cheyenne," Cavill said. "I'd rather have to babysit them just one night instead of three."

Horn looked at Cavill and Duffy. "I can learn a lot from you two," he said. "How do you plan to take them?"

"Ask us that question again two nights from now," Cavill said.

"These last three days have been an education for me," Tom Horn said. "I'll never forget the things you fellows have taught me."

"We appreciate that, Tom, but the night is young," Cavill said.

Behind the lean-to, Duffy stirred a pan of beans, bacon, and beef and said, "Cut off a hunk of bread, Tom. Supper is ready."

They ate while watching the red glow of the fire about three miles away.

"We'll wait until they go to sleep and wake them with a nightmare of our own choosing," Cavill said.

"How will you know when they go to sleep?" Horn said.

"The temperature drops twenty degrees or more after dark in these parts," Duffy said. "Last thing a man does before he turns in is build up the fire so it lasts the night."

"Tom, after we eat, me and Jim are going to take a little nap," Cavill said. "Wake us when the fire goes big, and we'll capture those outlaws for you."

By his pocket watch, the time was ten-forty-five when the fire increased in size. Horn woke Duffy and Cavill, and they both looked at the fire in the distance.

"That will do," Cavill said.

"Let's break camp and go for a nighttime stroll," Duffy said.

After packing up, they rode at a slow pace to within two hundred yards of the fire.

"Hobble the horses and grab your Winchester, Tom," Cavill whispered.

They hobbled the horses and then, Winchesters in hand, Cavill led the way to the sleeping outlaws. The fire was still burning, and they stopped ten feet from it. Cavill nodded to Duffy and stepped forward.

Horn went to join Cavill, but Duffy put his arm out and shook his head no.

Cavill cocked the lever on his Winchester and fired a shot into the dirt. The three outlaws jumped awake, but before they could react, Cavill clubbed one with the butt of the Winchester and then smacked another over the head with it.

The third outlaw simply looked at Cavill.

"I'm sorry, but did I disturb your beauty sleep?" Cavill said.

Once the outlaws were tied in a circle with rope, Horn said, "Mister Cavill, you got stones of iron."

"It doesn't take much to get the jump on a sleeping man, Tom," Cavill said. "Remember that in your future days, and you'll live a lot longer."

One of the outlaws spoke up and said, "Mister, you got the wrong men. We're just trying to—"

"Get through the territory," Cavill said. "Seems I've heard that one before."

CHAPTER TWENTY-TWO

Cheyenne was a bustling town of four thousand residents that had blossomed into existence when the railroad built a major hub in eighteen sixty-seven. During the railroad construction, Cheyenne was a lawless place that rivaled Deadwood and Dodge City in its wicked ways.

Once Cheyenne became a major stop for cattle and passengers alike, the law took control and transformed the town into a beacon of commerce and trade.

Although it was just after sunup when Duffy, Cavill, and Horn rode into town with the three prisoners, the streets were bustling with excitement.

A large banner strung across Main Street announced: *Cheyenne Rodeo Event.*

"Look at this, boys," Cavill said to the three outlaws in tow. "They must have known you were coming. They've thrown you a party."

"The sheriff's office is down the block," Duffy said. "Drop your prisoners off, but don't say a word about us. We need to blend in if we're to find the people we're looking for, and we can't do that if we're known."

"I understand," Horn said. "And I thank the both of you."

"Keep your nose clean, and you'll go far, Tom Horn," Cavill said.

Duffy and Cavill rode past the sheriff's office without looking back at Horn. They dismounted on the next block.

"Just our luck there's a rodeo in town," Duffy said. "Every hotel room is probably booked up by now."

The clerk at the third hotel they tried told them the only place in town that might have a room was Kate's Boarding House on River Street.

River Street was located on the last block in town and was just a hundred yards from Crow Creek, a tributary of the South Platte River.

Kate was seated in a rocking chair on the front porch of a very large house. She was around sixty years old and a stout woman with gray hair worn up in a bun. She was smoking a pipe and sipping whiskey from a water glass.

Duffy and Cavill dismounted at the yellow picket fence.

"Good morning. Are you Kate?" Duffy said.

Kate turned her head and looked at Duffy and Cavill. "I run a clean establishment, so if you two are looking for more than a bed and two meals a day, ride on."

"A bed and a meal is all we're looking for," Duffy said. "And maybe a bath?"

"I have one room with two beds left," Kate said. "Three dollars a night. If you want breakfast and supper it's another two dollars a day. A bath is seventy-five cents. You can livery your horse out back. That's a dollar a day for feed."

Duffy counted out ten dollars and climbed up to the porch and gave it to Kate.

"Are you drinking men?" Kate said.

"From time to time," Duffy said.

"I always have a snort after breakfast to keep my circulation moving," Kate said. "Have one with me, boys, both of you."

Duffy and Cavill took chairs on the porch, and Kate poured each man a drink. "I hope you like rye, because that's all I drink," she said.

Duffy and Cavill sampled the rye. It was sweet and had a

160

strong, fruity bite to it.

"Are you boys passing through or looking for work?" Kate said.

"Work," Cavill said.

"Cowboys?" Kate said.

"When we can get the work," Duffy said.

"Some big outfits in town right now," Kate said. "You might try the auction house. I saw one outfit ride in a thousand head a few days ago. Somebody is always looking for good men."

"That's what we figured to do as soon as we get cleaned up a bit," Duffy said.

Kate stood up. "I'll get your baths ready," she said. "Any clothes you want washed is an extra two bits."

By noon, Duffy and Cavill found a small restaurant near the stockyards and had lunch. They left the horses in Kate's livery and walked. They were surprised how expansive Cheyenne was, spread out over quite a large area.

The stockyards were close to the railroad depot.

They found where the auction house was located. Although the pens were filled with thousands of cattle, very few people were around.

They entered the auction house, where they knocked on an office door.

"Come in," a man said from behind the door.

Duffy opened the door and he and Cavill entered the office.

"Help you fellows?" the man behind a desk said.

"We're looking for work," Duffy said. "Know of any outfits hiring?"

"The big outfits came and went," the man said. "Won't be back for several months. One fellow was making inquiries a few days ago. Came through with a thousand head he wrangled in from outfits too small to drive them themselves. I think he's still in town."

"Would you know his name?" Duffy said.

"Carson. No. Parsons, I believe," the man said. "Didn't get his first name."

"What's he look like?" Cavill said.

"Not as tall as you, but tall, and thin and wiry like," the man said. "Wears a Colt with a yellow butt plate."

"Thanks," Duffy said.

"Good luck," the man said.

Back on the street, Cavill said, "Let's try the saloons. He's flush with cash, and he's probably got the itch to try his luck."

"What's the best saloon in town?" Duffy said. "We'll try there first."

The largest, most ornate saloon in Cheyenne was the Golden Dragon. It was centered on Main Street and was a full two stories high. It was founded in sixty-seven by a Chinese businessman who, at the time, was in the business of supplying Chinese labor to the railroad.

Two golden dragons hung from the ceiling. A forty-foot-long mirror highlighted the mahogany bar. A separate room served as a restaurant. The games of chance were blackjack, faro, roulette, craps, and cards.

Although prostitution was illegal in Wyoming, a dozen rooms with a dozen prostitutes occupied the second floor.

A piano player played a standup piano set against the wall beside the kitchen.

Duffy and Cavill found a vacant spot at the bar and ordered bourbon. As they sipped their drinks, Cavill lit a cigar.

They studied the tables and gamblers from the bar.

"Poker table by the window," Duffy said. "The man with his back to us has a Colt with a yellow butt plate."

They watched the table for a while until one man quit the game and left.

"Flip a coin?" Cavill said.

"Flip a coin," Duffy said.

Cavill flipped a gold coin, caught it, and slapped it on his left wrist.

"Call it," Cavill said.

"Heads I play," Duffy said.

Cavill removed his hand. The coin was heads.

"You play," Cavill said. "Don't forget to lose."

Duffy went to the table and said, "May I take the vacant seat, gentlemen?"

Bill Parsons looked up at Duffy. Parsons was, as described, a wiry man of about forty with a thick mustache. His dark eyes were emotionless, like the eyes of a snake.

"Chair's open," Parsons said.

Duffy took the chair. "What's the game?"

"Stud," Parsons said.

Duffy put fifty dollars on the table. "Let's play," he said.

From the bar, Cavill watched Duffy play and lose six consecutive hands.

"Not your lucky day, is it friend?" Parsons said.

"No, it is not," Duffy said. "My partner and I came here looking for work, only to find every large outfit has come and gone. We're down to eating money after this."

"Where's your partner?" Parsons said.

"Big fellow over there at the bar," Duffy said.

Parsons turned and looked at Cavill, who had his back to him and was smoking his cigar.

"You cowboys?" Parsons said.

"When we can get the work," Duffy said.

"Any good?"

"We're more than fair."

163

"Is he as hearty as he looks?" Parsons said.

"I wouldn't get on his wrong side," Duffy said.

"Cash out. Let's have us a drink," Parsons said.

Cavill followed Parsons and Duffy to a small vacant table against a wall. Cavill brought a bottle and three glasses.

"My name is Jim Duffy. This is my partner Jack Cavill," Duffy said.

"Bill Parsons. Pour us a drink," Parsons said.

Cavill filled three shot glasses.

"So you're looking for work?" Parsons said and tossed back his drink.

"Actually, we were looking for you," Duffy said.

Parsons stared at Duffy. "You best explain that," he said.

"Relax, friend," Cavill said. "We were brought in by Mike Cassidy in Montana. He found us working a spread near Billings. We had fifty head and were taking them to the relay spot, when Cassidy and his people got pinched by the US marshal in Helena. He and his people are in the Helena jail right about now, looking at the wrong end of a noose."

"Say I believe you," Parsons said. "Say Cassidy is in jail. That doesn't explain how you knew me and knew where to find me."

"Cassidy said we'd probably move the herd to Cheyenne after you gave the order," Duffy said. "He said if the herd was gone by the time we reached the hideout, we were to head to Cheyenne and look for Bill Parsons. He said you wore a Colt with a yellow butt plate."

"We were late bringing our fifty head, or we'd'a got pinched along with Mike. We didn't know what else to do. So we rode to your hideout, but you were gone. After that, we rode to Cheyenne," Cavill said.

"You were in our hideout?" Parsons said. "Where is it?"

"Bighorn Mountains," Cavill said. "Twenty miles or so west of Cody is a hill that leads to a narrow canyon that empties out to your secret hideout. You got cabins, a corral, and a barn."

"Cassidy told us the way in a few days before he got pinched," Duffy said. "We rode there to see for ourselves. All we found was some kid name Parker. He told us you moved the herd out a week before we got there."

"What's Parker look like?" Parsons said.

"He's a kid maybe sixteen or so," Duffy said. "Good-looking boy from Utah. He said he worked for Cassidy on Cassidy's spread. He calls himself Butch because he once worked in a butcher shop in Salt Lake.

"We told him Cassidy was in the Helena jail, so he rode back to Utah," Duffy said.

Parsons filled his shot glass and sipped the drink. "I guess you wouldn't know what you know if you weren't telling the truth," he said.

"We sold our fifty head on the way here, but all we have now is eating money," Duffy said. "And mister, we are ready to be rich."

"Yeah? What are you willing to risk in the process?" Parsons said.

"Whatever it takes," Duffy said.

"Why don't you get us another bottle," Parsons said.

"I'll get it," Cavill said.

Cavill went to the bar and ordered a bottle of bourbon. He placed a five-dollar gold piece on the bar, turned, and looked at Tom Horn, who had just walked into the saloon.

Horn grinned at Cavill, but before Horn could speak, Cavill hit Horn under the chin with a vicious right uppercut that sent Horn flying six feet across the floor where he landed, unconscious, against a table leg.

"That will teach you to step on my foot, you clumsy oaf," Cavill said.

At the table, Parsons looked at Duffy. "Like you said, don't get on his wrong side," Parsons said.

Cavill returned to the table with the bottle.

"Stupid dandy stepped on my foot," Cavill said.

"All right, you got another bottle," Duffy said. "Let's talk about the work."

"You know the drill from Cassidy," Parsons said. "We cleaned out Montana for now. The next target is Colorado and Nebraska. With Cassidy gone, I need men to drive the herds to the holding spots until the numbers are large enough. I have men to do the night work of siphoning off the cattle, but with Cassidy gone, I need a trail boss to bring the herd to the Bighorns. Are you interested?"

"Well, we already know the secret location," Duffy said. "What's the pay?"

"Same as Cassidy's. Two dollars a head," Parsons said.

"Cassidy said there were two thousand head in the Bighorns," Cavill said.

"That's right. Were," Parsons said.

"That's a lot of money," Duffy said.

"You sign on with me, you'll earn every cent," Parsons said. "If somebody needs killing, I expect you to make sure it's done."

"We got no problem with killing," Cavill said.

"One last thing," Parsons said. "I don't care how big you think you are, if you cross me, I'll kill you on the spot. Are we clear on that point?"

"Crystal," Duffy said.

"Good," Parsons said. "We'll leave for Nebraska by train tomorrow morning. I'll introduce you to the boys in the morning. Enjoy yourself tonight. Get drunk; get a whore, whatever, because come tomorrow, you won't get a day off for months. Questions?"

"What time does the train leave?" Cavill said.

CHAPTER TWENTY-THREE

On the front porch at Kate's Boarding House, Duffy wrote a letter to Porter rather than risk using a public telegraph office where a nosy operator might talk to the wrong person.

Holding two cups of coffee, Cavill exited the house and sat next to Duffy.

Duffy took the cup from Cavill and sipped.

"I feel kind of bad about clocking Horn, but he was about to give us away," Cavill said.

"A painful lesson, no doubt, but one well learned," Duffy said.

"I think I might write a letter myself," Cavill said.

Duffy grinned. "Make it quick. I already wrote mine," he said.

"What are you telling Porter?" Cavill said.

"Our progress. About Parsons and where we'll be in case we're killed," Duffy said.

"If it's all the same to you, I'll leave that part out of my letter to Joey," Cavill said.

Sylvia Trent and her father spent a quiet afternoon shopping for supplies in Miles City. While Trent and several of his men purchased wire for fencing, Sylvia browsed some of the shops and finally made a trip to the post office.

She was astonished to find a letter from James Duffy mixed in with the regular mail. Her first instinct was to tear it open right there in the post office, but she resisted the urge and went outside.

She felt anxious and tense and looked around the busy streets for a safe place to open the letter. Across the street was a small restaurant so she dashed to it, entered, and found a quiet table beside the window. A waitress approached the table, and Sylvia ordered coffee.

The she tore open the letter and read it quickly.

Sylvia, I am still on assignment and can't tell you where I will be next, for I don't know. I want to tell you that you have been in my thoughts every day since I left you. I denied what I felt for you, believing it was a passing fancy, but I have since admitted to myself that it is not.

As soon as this assignment is concluded, I plan to return to you and, hopefully, you will feel about me as I do you.

Yours,
James Duffy

Sylvia lowered the letter and tucked it back into the envelope. "I do, James, I do," she said aloud.

Duffy made it to the post office just minutes before it closed. He mailed the report to Porter, Cavill's letter to Joey, and another letter to Sylvia.

Cavill waited for Duffy at the boarding house. As a favor to Kate, he was chopping wood on the side of the house when Duffy returned.

Shirtless, sweat dripping down his massive chest, arms, and back, Cavill paused to wipe sweat from his brow and looked at Duffy.

"Mail the letters?" Cavill said.

"I did. Why are you chopping wood?" Duffy said.

"For something to do," Cavill said. "I'm not much for sitting

168

around waiting for trains, and Kate needed the wood chopped."

"Well, when you're done with your chopping, we need to figure out a strategy," Duffy said.

Cavill swung the ax into the large chopping block and split it in two. "I'm done," he said.

Cavill grabbed his shirt and put it on as he and Duffy walked to the porch. They sat, and Cavill removed his cigar holder from his right boot.

"The way it is now, we have several options," Duffy said.

Cavill struck a match and lit the cigar.

"We can arrest Parsons and take him to the local sheriff," Duffy said. "But we have no evidence. It would be his word against ours, and we'd be no closer to the top dog running the show. We'd only wind up with nothing for all this trouble."

"We didn't come this far and go to all this trouble just to lose it all," Cavill said.

"Agreed," Duffy said. "Option two is we go along with Parsons and learn all we can about the entire operation, including who is behind it all. Then we take it to the law."

"That could take months, if we even live through it," Cavill said.

"I know," Duffy said. "Which brings us to option three. Quit."

"Quit?" Cavill said. "That doesn't sound like you."

"Well, what do you want to do?" Duffy said. "We are partners, and we should both agree on a course of action."

"I hate to quit a job before it's finished," Cavill said.

"I feel the same way," Duffy said. "So, what do you want to do?"

"Nebraska, here we come," Cavill said.

"All right, but we have to be smart on this one," Duffy said. "If Parsons suspects we aren't on the level, he'll order his men to kill us, and we both have women now to think about."

Cavill blew a thick smoke ring. "So we play it his way," he

said. "Until it's time to play it ours."

"Right."

"Porter better do right by us when this is over," Cavill said.

"He always has," Duffy said. "I expect he will this time."

Cavill flicked ashes off the cigar end. "We best hide our identification in our boots," he said. "Like we did on that job in Kansas City."

"Jack, what have you got squirreled away? It must be a fair amount by now," Duffy said.

"The house, my belongings, and about twelve thousand in the bank," Cavill said.

"I have about the same," Duffy said. "Plus, we each have a twenty-five-thousand-dollar insurance policy with Porter."

"What are you driving at?" Cavill said.

"Who gets it if we're killed?" Duffy said.

"I don't know. I've no family left. You know that."

"Me, too."

"Maybe we could leave it to the women?"

"Both of them could buy and sell us a dozen times over."

"Well, who then?"

"I thought I'd do some good with mine," Duffy said. "I instructed Porter to donate mine to charity, to the orphanages around Springfield and in Chicago."

"Fine idea," Cavill said. "I should have done the same."

Duffy looked at Cavill. "You did," he said.

"When were you going to tell me? After I'm dead?" Cavill said.

Duffy smiled. "Let's see what Kate has for supper," he said. "You must be hungry after chopping all that wood."

After supper, Duffy and Cavill took cups of coffee to the porch. Cavill lit a cigar. They sat quietly as the sky darkened and night set in.

The street, far from the center of town, was still and quiet.

Footsteps in the distance alerted Duffy and Cavill. They watched the street as the footsteps grew louder.

Cavill reached for the lash on his Colt and slipped it off.

A figure appeared and walked to the porch. In the dim light of the two lanterns mounted on the wall of the house, the figure became visible.

"Howdy, boys," Parsons said.

"Evening," Duffy said.

"I had a hell of a time locating you boys," Parsons said. "When I couldn't find you at the hotels, I figured you might be here at Kate's. I've stayed here a few times myself."

"Care for some coffee?" Cavill said.

"I believe I will," Parsons said.

Cavill stood and entered the house. Parsons took the empty chair beside Duffy. A few moments later, Cavill returned with a cup of coffee and handed it to Parsons.

"I thought you'd like to know the train schedule has been changed to ten-thirty for tomorrow," Parsons said.

"Obliged to know that," Duffy said.

"How come you boys ain't at a saloon with a couple of whores?" Parsons said.

"Same reason as you," Cavill said. "We don't like starting a job hungover and with a case of the drips."

Parsons grinned as he rolled a cigarette. "Wise words, boys," he said as he struck a match.

"Mind a question or two?" Duffy said.

"You boys aren't changing your mind, are you?" Parsons said.

"Nothing like that," Duffy said. "Me and Jack have worked in Nebraska on some of the big spreads near Omaha and Lincoln, and as far west as McCook. There isn't a hill anywhere in the whole damned state. Rustling off the drags in the dead of night is easy enough, but without a canyon or a valley, where do you plan to stash the herd until it's big enough to take to the Bighorns?"

"I like men who think," Parsons said. He removed a folded paper from his shirt pocket. "Ten ranches are the target. We're going to hit all ten in a two-week span. A hundred head each, and all one thousand will be delivered to you two just over the border in Colorado where we have a place to hide the herd in the area they call the Front Range. The goal is a thousand head before you move them out to the Bighorns."

Duffy and Cavill exchanged glances.

"What?" Parsons said.

"From Cheyenne to the Bighorns with a herd is a two-week drive," Duffy said. "Why not take the thousand to where they're going?"

"We're going to fatten them up and triple the numbers in the Bighorns," Parsons said. "Then, once brands are changed and cattle are fat and happy, we'll drive them to where they're going."

"Three thousand head?" Cavill said.

"Nebraska, Colorado, and Utah are the targets, boys," Parsons said. "I'd figure on two months in the saddle, at least."

"For two dollars a head and six thousand dollars, I'll sleep in the damned saddle," Cavill said.

"It's a lot of money for sure, but you're going to have to earn it," Parsons said. "Not just by driving the cattle, but with the gun if the law happens to stop by for breakfast."

"I already told you, we got no problem with killing," Cavill said.

Parsons smiled. "Get some sleep, boys. Work starts in the morning," he said. He stood up and placed the cup on the porch railing. "Thanks for the coffee."

After Parsons left, Duffy looked at Cavill.

"Whoever the top dog is in this pack has given this a great deal of thought," Cavill said.

"Parsons may be the field boss, but he takes his orders," Duffy said. "Who from is what we need to find out."

"Maybe we should write another letter to Porter and tell him we'll be in Colorado," Cavill said.

"Good idea," Duffy said. "I'll ask Kate to mail it for us in the morning so we're not seen at the post office."

"Jim, if it comes to it, I'm not killing a lawman," Cavill said.

"If it comes to that, we surrender and ask the law to verify who we are with Porter," Duffy said.

"Agreed. Let's get some sleep," Cavill said.

CHAPTER TWENTY-FOUR

After breakfast, Duffy asked Kate to mail the letter the next time she went into town. He gave her a ten-dollar tip for her trouble.

Duffy and Cavill rode across town and met Parsons at the railroad depot at nine-fifteen in the morning.

Parsons was seated on a bench outside the ticket office, sipping coffee and smoking a cigarette when Duffy and Cavill arrived. Standing beside the bench was a large man with long black hair and eyes as dark as coal.

"Boys, this is Joe Goodluck," Parsons said as he stood up. "He's half Mexican and half Comanche and the best brander I've ever seen. He's going to handle the branding for you at the holding spot. He don't talk much unless he's got something to say."

"Well, what do we call you?" Cavill said.

"Joe," Goodluck said. "If you get on my bad side, I will kill you, remove your skin and wear it, and leave your corpse for the coyotes and buzzards."

Cavill stared at Goodluck for a moment. Besides a Smith & Wesson revolver on his right hip, Goodluck had a Bowie knife in a sheath on the left side of his belt.

"Jim?" Cavill said.

"By all means," Duffy said.

Cavill hit Goodluck in the jaw with a powerful left hook that sent Goodluck reeling to the ground.

"A man threatens me for no reason better be prepared to take his medicine," Cavill said.

Goodluck sat up and shook his head. He slowly rose to his feet and pulled the Bowie knife.

Duffy drew his revolver, cocked it, and aimed it at Goodluck. "Lose the knife and the piece," he said.

Goodluck dropped the knife.

"The piece," Duffy said.

Goodluck slowly drew his revolver and dropped it to the ground.

"Jack, toss me your Colt," Duffy said.

Cavill handed Duffy his Colt.

"Don't kill him," Duffy said. "I don't feel like branding cows for the next two months."

Unconscious in a seat in the last car, Goodluck's face was battered and bruised. Duffy and Cavill occupied the seats on the other side of the aisle. Parsons sat opposite Goodluck.

"I have to admit, Cavill, I've never seen a better man with his fists," Parsons said.

"I'm sorry to have had to do that to him, but like I said, I don't take kindly to threats, especially when they're unwarranted," Cavill said.

"Not his fault," Parsons said. "I asked him to do that."

"Why?" Cavill said.

"I like to know the men I hire can handle themselves in a corner," Parsons said.

"You let a man take a beating like that for a test?" Duffy said.

Parsons looked at Goodluck. "Well, look at it this way. Joe won't ever cross you again," he said.

"You said Nebraska," Duffy said. "Why are we on a train to Colorado, and where are the rest of your men?"

"We're going to the holding point to get you set up for branding," Parsons said. "My other boys left for Nebraska days ago to scout the ranches on my list."

"You're very organized," Duffy said. "Mind a question?"

"Depends on the question," Parsons said.

"When we left the Bighorns, we followed the trail left by the herd," Duffy said. "It split, and half went south, and the other half went to Cheyenne. We followed the half to Cheyenne hoping to meet up with you. Where did the other half go?"

"That's not your concern," Parsons said.

"It is if you ask us to drive a few thousand head into Mexico," Duffy said.

"I see your point," Parsons said as he rolled a cigarette. "All right, in all likelihood they'll go to old Mexico, where the price is thirty dollars a head. Where in old Mexico isn't your concern until the time comes. Fair?"

"Fair enough," Duffy said. "We just like to know where we might be going when the time comes."

Goodluck opened his eyes and moaned. "I've not had a beating like that since I'm a little boy," he said.

"Well, you asked for it," Cavill said.

"We got about two hours before we get off," Parsons said. "I'm going for some coffee."

"I could use some," Goodluck said.

"Aw, hell, we'll all go," Cavill said.

The dining car was the middle car in the train, and they walked through four cars to reach it. Well before lunch, just a few passengers were at tables having coffee.

They took a table beside a window where the scenery rolled by at fifty miles per hour.

The waiter approached the table and said softly, "They can ride the train, but they can't eat in here."

"Who?" Cavill said.

"You know who. The breed," the waiter said.

"We'll have four cups of coffee," Cavill said.

"Did you hear what I said?" the waiter said.

"We'll have four cups of coffee, please," Cavill said. "If I have to ask again, I will throw you out the window and get them myself."

The waiter stared at Cavill.

"Mister, you can save yourself a whole lot of trouble by bringing us the coffee," Duffy said.

The waiter sighed. "I'm just doing my job," he said.

"Do you get paid enough to get thrown off a moving train?" Cavill said.

"No."

The waiter returned to the counter.

"First you beat the hell out of him, now you come to his defense," Parsons said.

"I don't like bigots," Cavill said. "I've rode with blacks, Chinese, Mexicans, and Indians; it's all the same to me."

Parsons looked at Goodluck. "What do you say, Joe?"

"I hope the waiter remembers to bring sugar," Goodluck said.

Cavill laughed, and Duffy and Parsons joined in.

"What?" Goodluck said. "What's funny about sugar?"

By noon, Duffy, Cavill, Parsons, and Goodluck were walking their horses from the railroad station in Greeley to the center of town.

"Fort Collins is just thirty miles to the west, which is why the railroad stops at this one-horse town," Parsons said. "Let's get you supplies and ride out."

With a hundred and fifty pounds of supplies divided among three horses, Parsons led the way to the canyon hiding place in the Front Range Mountains.

"We'll make camp at dark and reach the hiding place by

noon tomorrow," Parsons said. "Remember the way in and out, because you may need to resupply in Greeley before this party is over."

"Pretty country," Duffy said.

"It is that, and I hope you come to love it because you'll be looking at it until the herd is big enough to move," Parsons said.

"How big is that?" Cavill said.

"A thousand would be the goal, but if the law is breathing down our necks, we'll settle for less," Parsons said.

"If your people do their job, the law will have no part of it," Cavill said.

"Sometimes things happen," Parsons said.

"Maybe so, but if any of your people are stupid enough to bring the law with them, I'll kill them along with the law," Cavill said. "Two dollars a head isn't worth my neck."

"I won't fault you on that," Parsons said.

"Just so long as we understand each other," Cavill said.

"Clear enough," Parsons said. "Let's find a place to make camp."

Around a campfire, as a pot of beef stew cooked, Goodluck cleaned and tested the bow and arrows he packed in his gear.

"I hope you don't plan on joining up with Geronimo," Cavill said.

"No, but I plan on eating fresh deer meat, turkey, and chicken," Goodluck said. "And guns make echoes, and echoes bring men. An arrow brings nobody."

"I can't fault that kind of thinking," Cavill said.

Stirring the pot, Duffy said, "Supper is ready. Jack, grab the bread."

After supper, Parsons sat with his back against the saddle and rolled a cigarette. Cavill smoked a cigar and Goodluck smoked a pipe.

"Tomorrow we should reach the hideout by noon," Parsons said. "I'll head back and take the railroad into Nebraska and check on my men. If everything is running smooth, you won't see me again until you're ready to move the herd to the Bighorns."

"If things don't go smooth?" Duffy said.

"I'll get word to you," Parsons said. "Get to Cheyenne and we'll regroup."

"How are you with those branding irons?" Duffy said to Goodluck.

"I branded for the army everywhere from Fort Dodge to Fort Keogh," Goodluck said. "I branded for John Chisum and Henry Hooker and the Englishman in New Mexico before he was murdered. There isn't a brand I can't change."

"The Indian speaks true," Parsons said. "He'll hold up his end, you hold up yours, and we'll all be fat and happy."

Spreading out his bedroll, Cavill said, "Fat and happy sounds real good about now."

"Remember this pass," Parsons said as he led them through a narrow gorge in the Front Range Mountains. "It's known but to a few. If you need to resupply, this is the only way out west to Greeley."

After leaving the gorge, they rode several miles to a well-protected valley between two mountains.

"Good water from a creek that runs off the Butte River," Parsons said as he dismounted.

Duffy and Cavill dismounted and looked around. "You could hide five thousand head here," Duffy said.

"A thousand is the goal," Parsons said. "Any more than that is likely to attract the attention of a lot of law."

"How long do you figure it will take to amass a thousand head?" Duffy said.

"Ten a night from four different teams, maybe a month," Parsons said. "As soon as Goodluck has them all re-branded you move them out to the Bighorns. I'll meet you there, and we'll ride to the next location."

"Let's make camp," Goodluck said as he removed his bow from his saddle. "I'll be back with a turkey or a few chickens."

"Mind some company?" Cavill said. "I need to stretch my legs a bit."

"Can you be quiet?" Goodluck said.

"Like a titmouse in church," Cavill said.

Goodluck and Cavill sat on a ledge of rock several hundred yards away from a flock of turkeys pecking at the ground in a clearing.

"Can you hit one from here?" Cavill whispered.

"Yes, but they're moving toward us," Goodluck whispered. "I'll wait."

As they pecked the ground, the turkeys slowly moved closer to the ledge. When the flock was about a hundred and fifty yards from the ledge, Goodluck slowly stood up and took aim with his bow and arrow.

His target was a plump female, as there were three times the numbers of females to males.

Goodluck's arm didn't waver as he held his aim on the female turkey.

Cavill watched as Goodluck released the arrow. In the blink of an eye, the turkey was down and the flock scattered.

"How did we ever defeat your people?" Cavill said.

"We defeated ourselves," Goodluck said. "I'll dress the turkey here and leave the gizzards for the coyotes."

★ ★ ★ ★ ★

"I'm stuffed," Cavill said.

"Same here," Duffy said. "That was quite a bird, Joe."

Stuffing his pipe, Goodluck nodded. "I might try for a mule deer in a few days," he said.

"When can we expect the first string of cows?" Duffy said to Parsons.

"Two days probably," Parsons said. "Then, like I said, expect ten a night just about every night. I know Goodluck can handle the branding, and I expect you two to handle the wrangling and provide protection."

"We'll hold up our end. Don't worry about that," Cavill said.

"I'm not worried about anything except what to do with all my money when this is over," Parsons said.

"That's a good thought to go to sleep on," Cavill said.

CHAPTER TWENTY-FIVE

"Well, gents, I'll see you when the time comes to move out the herd," Parsons said. "If all goes well, I'll send one of the boys with the word."

After Parsons was gone, Goodluck removed a rolled fishing line from his saddlebags. "I have extra line if you want to try your luck at the creek," he said.

"What the hell, we got nothing else to do today," Cavill said.

Each with rolled fishing lines and hooks, they walked to the creek, where Goodluck dug up a dozen worms.

Goodluck smoked his pipe, Cavill a cigar.

"This is a fine way to pass the time," Cavill said.

"I haven't fished in years," Duffy said.

Goodluck caught the first fish, a fine river trout.

"What did you mean yesterday when you said you defeated yourselves?" Cavill said to Goodluck.

Putting a fresh worm on his hook, Goodluck said, "I'm fifty of your years old. I was born in the state you now call Texas, just north of the Canadian River."

"I got one," Duffy said and pulled in another trout.

"Go on, Goodluck," Cavill said.

"My earliest memories are of our tribes warring with each other," Goodluck said. "Entire villages wiped out, women and babies killed and burned, men tortured every way possible. In those days, Mexico controlled Texas, and not many whites dared cross the Canadian River. I think I was maybe ten before I even saw my first white man. How could we be expected to defeat the white army when we were too busy fighting each other."

Goodluck pulled up another trout. "I think nine should do for a nice lunch," he said.

After lunch, while Cavill took a nap and Duffy cleaned his revolver and Winchester rifle, Goodluck inspected all of his branding irons.

"That's quite a collection you have," Duffy said.

"Over the years, working for the army and various ranches, I put together enough irons to make or change any brand," Goodluck said.

"Mind a question?" Duffy said.

"No."

"How did you get mixed up with Parsons?"

"In my last ten years in the army they paid fifty dollars a month," Goodluck said. "I was working for the ranchers in Arizona when Parsons appeared and told me I could make three, four, and even five thousand in a year working for him. If I make that much money, I will retire to the reservation in Oklahoma and live out my days hunting. Maybe find a young wife to take care of me in my old age."

"Sounds like a fine plan," Duffy said.

"What I said to the big man, that was something Parsons said for me to do," Goodluck said. "He said he wanted to test your courage."

"I know it. So does Jack," Duffy said.

Goodluck set the irons aside and took out his pipe and tobacco pouch. "Are you wanted by the law?" he said.

"No, neither of us," Duffy said. "Like you, we got tired of working for twenty-five dollars a month. We met this fellow, Cassidy, and sort of stumbled into this."

Goodluck lit the pipe with a wood match. "The big man,

where did he learn to use his fists like that?"

"Like you said, he's a big man," Duffy said.

Putting his revolver back together, Duffy looked over at Cavill, who was still napping. "What happens to big men is they get picked on more than regular men, so they better learn how to defend themselves. Jack learned how to do it better than most."

"As my jaw still hurts, I have to agree," Goodluck said.

Late in the afternoon, Goodluck went scouting for signs of deer.

Duffy gathered wood for a fire and made a pot of coffee.

Cavill lit a cigar, then he and Duffy sat against their saddles with cups of coffee.

"Jim, I'm thinking something a bit crazy," Cavill said.

"You'll get your chance to fight Sullivan," Duffy said.

"Not that. About Goodluck."

"I'm probably thinking the same thing," Duffy said.

"That you don't want to arrest him?" Cavill said.

"Yeah."

"Prison would kill a man like him, or worse, he could get the noose," Cavill said.

"He's here on his own accord, Jack," Duffy said.

"I know that, but look at the circumstances," Cavill said.

"In all the years we've been partners, have we ever turned an outlaw loose because of the circumstances?" Duffy said.

"Cassidy and that kid just the other day," Cavill said.

"That was different. If we hadn't, we wouldn't be here right now," Duffy said.

"I know that, Jim, but . . ."

"Jack, what are you saying? We should turn him loose?"

"That's what I'm saying," Cavill said. "And if you can't see the circumstances, then you're blind as a Mexican bat."

"I agree," Duffy said.

"Just for once in your life, put away the stupid law books and . . . What did you say?"

"I said I agree," Duffy said.

"Well damn, just say that," Cavill said.

"I did."

"So how do we handle this?"

"I don't know."

"Well, we better think of something quick," Cavill said.

Joey and some of her men took a large wagon into Helena for supplies. Joey rode her horse while her men piloted the wagon.

The men took the wagon to the hardware store while Joey stopped by the general store for supplies and then the post office for the mail.

Mixed in with the regular mail was a letter from Cavill.

She sat on the bench outside the post office and tore open the envelope.

Joey, well it's me. I'm not much for writing letters in general, but I just want to let you know that as soon as this assignment is over, I will come to see you. I don't really know what else to say except that when I come back, I hope you'll still want me. Take care, Jack

"Take care?" Joey said aloud. "You stupid oaf, you don't say 'take care' to the woman you're courting."

For a few seconds, Joey was furious. Then she smiled and started to laugh. "We'll work on your romantic presentation when you return," she said aloud.

Close to sundown, as Duffy built a fire, Goodluck returned.

"There's enough mule deer in these hills to feed an army," he said.

"The first of the cows should be here sometime tomorrow.

Why don't you get us one in the morning?" Duffy said.

"Those cows will need to be branded," Goodluck said.

"They'll come in the late afternoon I expect," Duffy said. "You can't brand at night, so we might as well eat good while we work."

"All right, I agree," Goodluck said. "We might as well eat good while we work."

"Speaking of eating, what's going in the pot tonight?" Cavill said.

After breakfast, Goodluck rode his horse into the hills to hunt for deer.

Duffy and Cavill lingered over coffee.

"The first of the stolen cattle will be here sometime today, and we don't have a plan about Goodluck," Cavill said.

"There is only one way to play this," Duffy said.

"You mean tell him the truth?" Cavill said.

"Do you see it any other way?" Duffy said.

"No."

Shortly after noon, a lone cowboy slowly came into view a hundred yards away.

"Company," Cavill said.

Duffy grabbed his Winchester, as did Cavill.

The rider stopped and shouted. "Hello to camp," he yelled. "Name is Moon. One of Parsons's men. I got the first delivery."

"Come ahead," Duffy shouted.

Moon rode in and dismounted at the campfire.

"Is that coffee fresh?" he said.

"Help yourself," Cavill said.

Moon filled a cup and took a sip. "My men are waiting on the signal," he said.

"Go ahead and give it to them," Duffy said.

Moon set the cup down and cupped his hands. "Come ahead,

boys," he shouted.

Two riders with ten cows appeared and rode toward camp.

"From here on, expect forty head a day," Moon said.

"We were about to fix lunch," Duffy said. "You boys are welcome to join us."

After lunch, Cavill inspected the ten cows.

"These girls are going to need some fattening up," Cavill said.

"That's your job," Moon said. "Our job is to steal them."

Later in the afternoon, Goodluck returned with a fully dressed deer slung over his saddle. He dismounted and looked at the ten cows.

"A bit on the thin side," Goodluck said.

"I expect the rest will be, too," Cavill said. "As they are targeting the drags."

Goodluck looped a rope around the deer's rear legs and then hung it from a tree branch to bleed out overnight.

"We can start the branding tomorrow morning," Goodluck said. He opened a saddlebag, removed a cloth sack, and set it down near Cavill. "For tomorrow morning," Goodluck said.

Cavill picked up the sack and looked inside. "Eggs," he said.

"A dozen of them," Goodluck said. "I'm partial to over easy."

Just before nightfall, the second delivery of cows arrived, led by a rider named Frog.

"Me and the boys been riding all day. Can you spare us some supper for the ride back?" Frog said.

"Break out your plates," Duffy said.

"Some of these cows weigh less than me," Cavill said as he looked over the newest additions.

"With the grass you got around here, they'll fatten up in no time," Frog said. He looked at Goodluck. "Is the Indian your brander?"

"I am the brander," Goodluck said.

"We'll be keeping you plenty busy," Frog said.

"Hand me your plates," Duffy said.

After Frog and his two men left the camp, the moon rose. Cavill, Duffy, and Goodluck inspected the twenty cows carefully.

"Ain't a one of them weighs a thousand," Cavill said.

"They will by the time they clean this valley up," Duffy said.

"I'll start my work right after breakfast," Goodluck said.

CHAPTER TWENTY-SIX

When Goodluck opened his eyes, he looked down the barrel of Duffy's Smith & Wesson .44 revolver.

"Don't move, don't twitch, don't even breathe," Duffy said. "Jack, get his guns."

Cavill scooped up Goodluck's revolver, knife, and rifle.

Duffy stepped back a few feet.

"What's the idea of this?" Goodluck said.

"Coffee's hot. Go have a cup," Duffy said.

Goodluck stood, went to the fire, and filled a cup with coffee. "Can I smoke my pipe?" he said.

"Go ahead," Duffy said.

Goodluck took out his pipe and pouch, stuffed the bowl, and lit it with a wood match.

"A good cup of coffee and a fine bowl of tobacco is not a bad way to die," Goodluck said.

"What?" Duffy said.

"That's what this is about, isn't it?" Goodluck said. "You're going to kill me and keep my share for yourselves."

"No, of course not," Duffy said.

"Then what is this about?" Goodluck said.

"Can you read English?" Cavill said.

"I was an army brander and scout. Of course, I can read English," Goodluck said. "I can also read French and Spanish. Can you?"

Duffy nodded to Cavill, and Cavill handed Goodluck his and

Ethan J. Wolfe

Duffy's identification.

"Then read this," Cavill said.

Goodluck took the papers and read them both. "Detectives with the Illinois Detective Agency? I don't understand."

"We were hired by the Montana Stock Growers Association to investigate the rash of cattle thefts," Duffy said. "We're also licensed constables with all the powers of law enforcement."

"Now I'm really confused," Goodluck said.

"We don't want to have to arrest you for cattle theft," Duffy said. "We don't know what to do with you just yet, as you haven't actually committed any crimes so far."

Goodluck took a sip of coffee, puffed on his pipe, and said, "My right boot."

"What?" Cavill said.

"Reach inside my right boot," Goodluck said.

Cavill picked up Goodluck's right boot, reached inside, and removed a folded envelope.

"Read it," Goodluck said.

Cavill removed a letter written on the official stationery of Colonel Glenwood, the commanding officer of Fort McKinney in Wyoming. It officially authorized Chief Scout Joe Goodluck to work undercover on behalf of the United States Army and United States Government as an agent to investigate the widespread cattle thefts in the western states and territories. The letter was signed by Glenwood with his official seal imposed above the signature.

"I'll be damned," Cavill said.

"What?" Duffy said.

Cavill handed Duffy the letter.

"I'll be damned," Duffy said.

"I already said that," Cavill said.

190

"So what now?" Goodluck said.

"Let's sit down, have some breakfast, and talk," Duffy said.

Eating fried eggs with bacon and bread, Goodluck said, "The army is worried that a cattle war will break out if something isn't done to catch this bunch. Glenwood estimated seven thousand head have been stolen in Montana, the Dakotas, Wyoming, New Mexico, Arizona, and Nebraska during the last eighteen months. We knew about Parsons and came up with the idea he would need a top brander and find me, but we didn't know about Cassidy and the Bighorns until I linked up with Parsons."

"Have you been there?" Duffy said.

"No, but I was hoping to go there on this trip," Goodluck said.

"Any idea who the top man is?" Cavill said.

"No. That's another thing I'm hoping to find out," Goodluck said.

"What about Mexico? What do you know?" Duffy said.

"More than half the cattle are sold in Mexico for as much as thirty dollars a head," Goodluck said. "The rest are sold at various auction houses scattered about Wyoming, New Mexico, Arizona, Nebraska, and even Texas."

"Parsons brings them to auction with the story he is representing groups of ranches too small to bring them in themselves," Duffy said. "And so far, the ploy has worked."

"Somebody is making a hell of a lot of money," Cavill said. "And seems hell bent on making a hell of a lot more."

"We need to get Parsons to lead us to the man at the top," Duffy said. "And the only way to do that is to play along and hope he either slips up or learns to trust us enough to bring us inside his circle."

"There's something else," Goodluck said. "Parsons recruited

me as a brander, because the men he was using have disappeared. I believe he killed them to keep them from talking, and I believe he will do the same to me when the job is complete. The same can be said for the men he uses as wranglers. He promises them wealth and delivers them only death."

"We figured he'd make his move after we delivered the cattle to the Bighorns," Duffy said. "For several reasons. One being he's not going to want living witnesses, and recruiting more men with the promise of riches is easy enough. Two being: to keep the secret location a secret. Three is greed."

"About what I figure," Goodluck said.

"Greed is something my people and yours seem to share," Cavill said.

"I can't argue that point," Duffy said.

"We'll need a plan," Cavill said.

"Let's start by sketching the brands we have, and then sketching the re-brand so we can identify them later," Duffy said. "I'll get my sketchbook. Jack, build up the fire for Joe's irons."

Branding full-grown cattle was no easy task. Once Goodluck, Duffy, and Cavill agreed on the right iron to change the existing brand, Goodluck had to judge the correct temperature of the iron.

If the iron was black, it was too cold; red, it was too hot. Gray was the ideal temperature to burn the hair and permanently mark the skin with the brand.

Since they lacked a cattle squeeze, Cavill had to wrestle each cow to the ground by the neck. Once the cow was down, Duffy put his body across its hind legs to keep the animal still while Goodluck applied the iron.

The procedure was slow, as after each cow was re-branded, Goodluck had to heat the iron back to the right temperature.

By noon, ten cows were re-branded, and the three men took a break to have lunch.

Moon and Frog arrived with twenty more cows and stayed long enough to share a meal.

By four in the afternoon, twenty cows were re-branded, and Duffy began making sketches of the new arrivals.

"Jack, how is your back holding up?" Cavill said.

"We got enough daylight to tackle five more," Cavill said.

"Five more, and I'll carve us some steaks out of that deer," Goodluck said.

After eating a steak that weighed two pounds, Cavill fell asleep almost immediately upon sprawling out on his bedroll.

"I've never seen a man wrestle twenty-five cows in one day," Goodluck said.

"If we get an early start tomorrow, he'll do thirty," Duffy said. "Jack doesn't like to talk about it, but he grew up on a farm in Wisconsin where he wrestled cows, and even bulls, for branding."

"And where did you grow up?" Goodluck said.

"The streets of Chicago," Duffy said. "Where the only thing I learned how to wrestle was nickels and dimes from drunks on the street."

"I'm going to clean my irons and then turn in," Goodluck said.

While Goodluck cleaned his irons, Duffy rested against his saddle and watched the stars start to come out.

"Joe, we need a plan," Duffy said.

"I agree. Do you have one?" Goodluck said.

"Not yet," Duffy said.

CHAPTER TWENTY-SEVEN

By the end of the week, two hundred cows had been re-branded. Another hundred waited, with another forty on the way by the next day.

Goodluck had gone hunting in the afternoon for chickens, and three plump hens roasted on spits.

"My back feels like I went twenty rounds with John L. Sullivan," Cavill said.

As Goodluck turned the spits, he said, "I saw him fight once about a year ago in Saint Paul."

"You saw John L.?" Cavill said.

"I forget who he was fighting, but he knocked his opponent down three times in the first thirty seconds of the first round," Goodluck said. "He never got up after the third knockdown."

"Damn," Cavill said.

"Have you seen him fight?" Goodluck said.

"In Fort Wayne, in Chicago, and in Philadelphia," Cavill said. "That's my life's goal, to fight John L."

"The way you handle yourself, I think you could give him a run for his money," Goodluck said.

"Yeah, well, at the moment I can barely lift my arms," Cavill said.

"I have liniment in my gear," Goodluck said. "Rub it on after we eat, and then sleep downwind. It's the same stuff I use on my horse."

Duffy looked at the cows peacefully eating grass a hundred

or so yards away. "At the rate they're rolling in, we'll have a thousand in two weeks," he said. "I've been thinking about a plan to deal with Parsons."

"What have you come up with?" Cavill said.

"We can't kill him, that's for sure," Duffy said. "We need him to identify the top man, and he'll surrender him to escape the noose."

"Seems to me we have to fall into whatever trap he sets for us in order to trap him," Cavill said.

As he turned the spits again, Goodluck said, "Maybe the army can help?"

"Not a bad idea," Duffy said.

"The chickens are done," Goodluck said.

By the end of the following week, four hundred cows were re-branded, with two hundred more waiting their turn.

Moon and Frog arrived in time for lunch with twenty additional cows.

"Some of the ranchers have started to notice their drags missing," Moon said.

"Parsons wants to cut it off at eight hundred," Frog said. "He wants you to drive the herd to the Bighorns as soon as possible. He said he'll stop by to let you know when."

"Where is he now?" Duffy said.

"South of here, scouting out new targets," Moon said. "He'd like you to be ready in two weeks, but he'll settle for three."

"From here to the Bighorns will take two, maybe three weeks," Duffy said. "Just the three of us driving eight hundred head?"

"Eight hundred should be nothing for three experienced cowboys," Frog said. "And by the time you get there, we'll be in business again."

"Well, that's enough sitting around. We got work to do," Cavill said.

"See you boys tomorrow," Frog said.

After Frog and Moon rode away, Goodluck built up the branding fire.

"I don't like it, Jim," Cavill said. "I think the only people getting rich are the man on top, Parsons, Frog, and Moon."

"I agree," Duffy said. "The question is, where will Parsons attempt to take us out?"

Adding wood to the fire, Goodluck said, "The white man is basically a lazy creature. Given that, I doubt Parsons is going to want to move this much bovine flesh on his own. He'll wait until we do the work before making his move."

"I can't fault that thinking, Joe," Duffy said. "What better place to kill a man and dispose of the body than a secret place in the Bighorns."

Cavill looked at Goodluck. "Bovine?" he said.

Goodluck shrugged. "It's what the army horse doctor calls them," he said.

"It doesn't matter what we call them. We need to figure out how to stay alive while we move them," Cavill said.

"We're running low on a few things," Duffy said. "It might be a good time to take a trip to Greeley, pick up some supplies, and post a letter to Goodluck's commanding officer."

Goodluck and Cavill looked at Duffy.

"It might be a good time, at that," Cavill said.

Several days later, Frog arrived midmorning with ten additional head of cattle.

He dismounted by the campfire and helped himself to a cup of coffee. "You're a man short," he said.

"Jim went into Greeley for supplies," Cavill said.

"You didn't tell me that last time I was here," Frog said.

"We're going to be out here another month. We need supplies," Cavill said.

"Next time, mention it," Frog said.

"Next time," Cavill said. "In the meantime, how about lending a hand?"

"I got to get back to pick up the next bunch," Frog said. "Moon should be in shortly. I'll be back for breakfast."

After Frog left, Cavill said, "Keep the irons hot. We can get ten more in before dark."

"That should be the last trip in," Moon said. "We have eight hundred, and Parsons wants to move the herd out before the law gets winds of it."

"I thought Parsons was going to stop by and tell us himself," Cavill said.

"He'll be along soon enough," Moon said and looked at Duffy. "How was your trip to Greeley?"

"Uneventful," Duffy said. "I picked up a hundred pounds of supplies and a newspaper. As far as I can see, we're clear of the law."

"That's good to know," Moon said. "Frog should be along sometime today and we'll stay until Parsons shows up."

"Good," Cavill said. "You can help with the work."

"Soon as I have some grub," Moon said.

"I'll get some stew going," Duffy said. "Moon, you can help Jack hold the cattle still once he's got them down."

"That ain't my skill," Moon said.

"There's nothing to it," Cavill said. "Once I got the cow on the ground, you hold her across the legs so Goodluck doesn't ruin the brand."

Moon watched as Cavill wrestled a cow to the ground, and when Moon went to spread his body across the cow's hind legs, Cavill snapped his right elbow out and clubbed Moon in the jaw, knocking him unconscious.

Goodluck quickly applied the brand, and Cavill let the cow up.

"Is he out?" Duffy said.

"He's out," Cavill said.

"Carry him over to the fire," Duffy said.

When Moon woke up, Duffy, Cavill and Goodluck were eating bowls of stew.

"Welcome back," Cavill said.

Moon groaned and sat up. "What happened?"

"Cow's rear leg snapped back and clubbed you one," Cavill said.

"Have some food. You'll feel better," Duffy said.

"Got any whiskey?" Moon said. "A shot of whiskey will do me some good."

Cavill removed an unopened bottle of rye whiskey from his gear and poured an ounce into a coffee mug.

After eating, Moon fell asleep beside the fire while Cavill, Duffy, and Goodluck returned to work.

"Hello to camp," Frog called out as he rode in with a few drags.

"Still some stew in the pot for you," Duffy said.

"What happened to Moon?" Frog said as he dismounted.

"Took a back leg to the head when he was helping with the branding," Duffy said.

Frog touched Moon's shoulder with his boot. "Moon, wake up."

Moon opened his eyes. "When did you get here?"

"A few minutes ago with the last of the drags," Frog said. He looked at Duffy. "How soon before the lot is ready to travel?"

"We have three hundred left to brand," Duffy said. "Jack?"

"A week," Cavill said. "Less, if you two care to help."

"I ain't no cow thrower," Frog said.

"Don't have to be to keep the fire hot and save Goodluck some time," Duffy said. "And the three of us can rotate holding the legs still while Goodluck applies the iron."

"Well, I guess a little work won't kill us none, but just until Parsons shows up," Frog said.

"Very pretty," Parsons said as he dismounted at the campfire. "And you fattened them up some in the process."

Duffy was stirring a large pot of beans with bacon and looked up at Parsons. "Just in time for lunch," he said.

Parsons looked at Cavill, who was wrestling a cow to the ground. "When will you boys be finished?" he said.

"Oh, four days. No more than five," Duffy said. He stood up and turned around. "Jack, lunch."

Once everyone had a plate and a hunk of cornbread, Parsons said, "Frog, Moon, we're leaving for the Bighorns right after you eat. Duffy, you, the big man, and the Indian head out as soon as the last cow is branded. We'll have camp ready for the herd, and then we'll decide on Colorado or Utah as the next target."

"It doesn't matter much to us which, just so long as we get paid when the time comes," Cavill said.

"When the time comes, you will," Parsons said. He tossed Duffy a folded map. "The route to the Bighorns is marked in red. Good grazing and water, and no people living along the routes to get nosy."

"We need supplies for the drive to the Bighorns," Duffy said. "We spent most of our money already on food. We could use a hundred to resupply for the trip."

Parsons counted out five twenty-dollar gold pieces and gave them to Duffy. "Frog, Moon, let's go," he said.

Parsons, Frog, and Moon mounted their horses.

"See you boys in the mountains," Parsons said.

CHAPTER TWENTY-EIGHT

Duffy watched the stars come out as he settled into his bedroll beside the fire.

"The question is where they will hit us," Duffy said. "On the drive or in the mountains?"

"They won't hit us in the open," Goodluck said. "Too much of a risk. Someone might see it, and we have a better chance of fighting back in the open. They'd also have to bury us, and that leaves a trail."

"I agree with Goodluck," Cavill said. "They will wait until we deliver the cattle, mostly because the white man is lazy by nature."

Duffy grinned.

Goodluck said, "At last, common ground."

"I guess we'll find out soon enough," Duffy said.

"All right cowboys, we have a herd to move," Duffy said.

With ropes looped in a circle, Duffy, Cavill, and Goodluck yelled at the cattle and moved them forward.

Duffy rode point, with Goodluck in the middle and Cavill picking up the drags.

"Twenty miles by sunset is the goal," Duffy said.

They rested the horses and cattle at noon for one hour. Lunch was jerky, canned fruit, and water.

By sundown they'd traveled twenty-five miles. While Duffy built a fire and Goodluck tended to his and Duffy's horses,

Cavill backtracked to gather up the drags.

The drive went on for a week until they reached the South Platte River.

They rested for a full twenty-four hours. Duffy and Cavill shaved, and all three men took baths in the river and washed their dirty clothes.

Goodluck hunted three prairie chickens. While they roasted on spits, Duffy checked his maps.

"Joe, tomorrow morning you ride to Fort Collins and deliver the letter I will write tonight to the commanding officer. Then request to telegraph Mr. Porter at the Illinois Detective Agency and send the message I will write," Duffy said.

Goodluck turned the spits. "Where do I meet up with you?" he said.

"Not until we reach the Bighorns," Duffy said. "Ride into Cheyenne and take the railroad as far north into Wyoming as you can go and meet up with the army. If everything goes according to plan, we'll meet just outside of Cody."

"Just the two of you to drive the herd?" Goodluck said.

"We can handle it," Duffy said. "It's more important you reach the army in Wyoming and wait for us."

Goodluck turned the chickens on the spits. "I'll do as you ask, but how will I know if something has happened to you?"

"The path we're taking puts us a day's ride west of Rawlins," Duffy said. "By the time we reach it, you should be in Buffalo. We'll need supplies by then, so I'll wire you in Buffalo."

"I still don't like it," Goodluck said. "A lot can happen between here and the Bighorns."

"Just make sure nothing happens to you," Cavill said. "Are those chickens ready?"

In the morning, Duffy packed supplies for Goodluck's thirty-mile trip to Fort Collins.

"Make sure they write my telegrams word for word," Duffy said as he handed Goodluck two folded papers.

"I will," Goodluck said. "Travel well."

"We'll do our best," Cavill said.

After Goodluck rode away, Duffy said, "Let's break camp. We got a long way to go."

Free from the constraints of driving the herd, Goodluck's powerful horse covered the thirty-mile ride in one afternoon. He arrived at Fort Collins by four o'clock.

"Chief Army Scout Joseph Goodluck from Fort McKinney to see the commanding officer," Goodluck told the sergeant at arms at the front gate of Fort Collins.

Goodluck handed the sergeant his identification.

"Wait here," the sergeant said.

Goodluck held his horse by the reins as he waited. Several minutes passed before the sergeant returned with Captain Pitt, the second-in-command.

Pitt extended his right hand to Goodluck. "Good to see you again, Joseph. What brings you to Collins?" he said.

"Pressing business, Captain," Goodluck said. "I need to see the colonel right away."

"Sergeant, have Joseph's horse taken care of," Pitt said.

"Yes, sir," the sergeant said.

Colonel Ethan Strong received Goodluck and Pitt in his office.

"Joseph, it's been a while," Strong said.

"Colonel, I have two emergency reports for you to read," Goodluck said.

"Captain Pitt, will you ask the mess to bring us a fresh pot of coffee?" Strong said.

A few minutes later, as Strong read the first of Duffy's two letters, a corporal from the mess hall brought a coffee pot with three cups to the office.

Pitt filled the cups and gave one to Goodluck and Strong.

"Captain, read this," Strong said as he turned to Duffy's second letter.

Goodluck stuffed and lit his pipe while Strong and Pitt read.

"Captain, let's take a walk over to the telegraph office," Strong said.

A sergeant manned the telegraph station inside the fort. "Sergeant, send two telegrams, word for word as they're written," Strong said. "Bring the replies to my office."

"Yes, sir," the sergeant said.

Strong arranged for Goodluck to stay in the fort's private guest quarters. He was changing into a clean shirt when a runner knocked on the door.

"Chief Scout, the colonel wants you in his office right away," the runner said.

Goodluck tucked in his shirt and rushed to Strong's office where Strong and Pitt waited.

"I have two replies," Strong said and handed them to Goodluck.

"Colonel, I'll be leaving for Buffalo on the morning train," Goodluck said.

"Drop your dirty clothes off at the laundry. We'll have them ready for you in the morning," Strong said. "Dinner is at six-thirty. You'll dine at my table."

"Yes, Colonel," Goodluck said.

"Are we in Wyoming yet?" Cavill said as he wrangled several drags into camp.

"Since that last creek we crossed," Duffy said.

"What's in the cook pot?" Cavill said.

"Stew with bacon and beans," Duffy said.

"Damn, I'm missing Goodluck's chickens already," Cavill said.

"I can build a bow and arrow for you," Duffy said.

Cavill filled a cup with coffee and sat beside Duffy. "I couldn't hit a buffalo with a bow if it was standing in front of me," he said. "Do you think they wired Porter and the army in Wyoming by now?"

"My guess is, they already got replies," Duffy said.

"That son of a bitch Goodluck is sleeping in a soft bed tonight," Cavill said.

"Don't hold it against him. We sent him," Duffy said.

"I'm not holding it against him. I wish we were with him," Cavill said.

"The man who wrote this letter, James Duffy, and his partner, John Cavill. Charles Porter sent me a telegram about them," Strong said. "He said they are two of the best detectives in the country."

They were in the mess hall at Strong's private table.

"I have to agree, Colonel," Goodluck said. "Both are highly skilled, very intelligent, and fearless. This entire operation is succeeding only because they are involved."

"And it's just the two of them driving a herd of eight hundred through Wyoming to the Bighorns?" Strong said.

"They'll make it, Colonel," Goodluck said. "I wouldn't bet against them."

"What I would like to know is who is behind this operation," Strong said.

"It isn't Parsons," Goodluck said. "He's good at following orders, but he lacks the brains to organize such a task."

"Any ideas on who is?" Strong said.

"Parsons knows," Goodluck said. "Duffy thinks Parsons will exchange the head man for a lighter sentence."

"I expect he will," Strong said. "Well, shall we get some dinner?"

After supper, Duffy and Cavill sat with their backs against their saddles and drank coffee. Cavill lit a cigar.

"How long to Rawlins?" Cavill said.

"Two, maybe three days," Duffy said.

"I'll be out of cigars by then," Cavill said. "Pick me up some when you go into town."

"What about a letter? Do you want to post one?" Duffy said.

"Hell, I don't know what to write," Cavill said.

"Just tell her you're fine and looking forward to seeing her again," Duffy said.

"Are you going to write a letter?"

"I am."

"Maybe I could copy what you write?"

"I don't think Jocy would take kindly to being called Sylvia."

"You know what I mean," Cavill said.

"You got three days to write a letter," Duffy said. "After that, we might not get another chance until we reach Cody."

"Just don't forget my cigars," Cavill said.

"Captain Pitt, wire me when you reach Buffalo," Strong said. "Chief Scout, good luck."

"Thank you, Colonel," Goodluck said.

Goodluck and Pitt mounted their horses and rode toward the railroad depot in Greeley.

CHAPTER TWENTY-NINE

Goodluck and Pitt were welcomed into Fort McKinney by the sergeant of the guard.

"Chief Scout, you've been away too long," the sergeant said.

"I need to see the general right away," Goodluck said.

Goodluck and Pitt were ushered to the office of General George Crook. Behind his desk, Crook stood and was genuinely pleased to see Goodluck.

"Chief Scout Goodluck, what have you to report?" Crook said.

"Much, General," Goodluck said. "This is Captain Pitt from Fort Collins. Colonel Strong sends his regards."

"Before you report, would you gentlemen care for a drink?" Crook said.

"We could use one, General," Goodluck said. "It was a long, dry train ride."

Crook turned to the table next to his desk and poured three drinks of whiskey from a decanter. He handed Goodluck and Pitt a glass.

"General, maybe Lieutenant Gatewood should hear this as well," Goodluck said.

Goodluck took about an hour to make his full report. Crook and Gatewood listened carefully, and Crook took notes.

"So here we are, General, waiting on Duffy and Cavill to arrive with the stolen herd," said Goodluck, ending his report.

"Chief Scout Goodluck, what do you recommend?" Crook said.

"We wait for Duffy and Cavill to arrive with the herd and do as they requested," Goodluck said.

"While the army is generally not involved in law enforcement, I tend to agree with you," Crook said. "Cattle theft cannot be tolerated under any circumstances. Lieutenant Gatewood, what do you say?"

"I agree, General," Gatewood said. "Cattle theft is a federal offense, and the army is part of the federal government."

"Chief Scout, when will they arrive?" Crook said.

"A week, but they will wire from Rawlins," Goodluck said.

"Lieutenant Gatewood, you shall be in command," Crook said. "Captain Pitt, you shall serve as first officer. Chief Scout, you will assist Gatewood."

"Yes, General," Goodluck said. "Sir, I know it's late, but is it possible for Captain Pitt and me to get something to eat?"

"Lieutenant, have the mess sergeant open the mess hall and fix them a decent meal," Crook said. "In fact, I think we should join them."

Charles Porter sipped whiskey as he sat behind his desk. There was a soft knock on the office door, and he said, "Come in, Miss Potts."

The door opened and Miss Potts entered.

"It's after midnight. Why are you still here?" Porter said.

"Because you are still here," Miss Potts said.

"I've been thinking. I lose track of time when I'm thinking," Porter said. "Go home. Tomorrow morning on your way in, stop by the train station and get me a ticket to Buffalo, Wyoming. Then send a telegram to General Crook at Fort McKinney."

Miss Potts stared at Porter. "Are you . . . ?"

"Yes, Miss Potts, I am," Porter said. "Good night."

"Good night, Mr. Porter," Miss Potts said.

After breakfast, Duffy studied his map and said, "I can make Rawlins in about two hours. I'll wire Goodluck and Mr. Porter, post our letters, and be back in time for lunch."

"Don't forget my cigars," Cavill said.

"What do we need for supplies?"

"Fresh meat, some coffee, bacon, beans, and flour," Cavill said. "Some cornbread and canned fruit."

"I'll be back for lunch," Duffy said as he mounted the saddle. "Try not to lose the herd while I'm gone."

After Duffy rode off, Cavill built up the campfire and made a fresh pot of coffee. He checked his stash in his saddlebags and found two cigars. When the coffee boiled, he filled a cup and lit a cigar.

Armed with cigar and coffee, he walked among the cattle and inspected them. They had gained a considerable amount of weight and would easily fetch twenty dollars a head at auction.

In the distance, he spotted twenty mounted riders. They were still on their horses and watching him. Cavill walked to his saddlebags, pulled out his binoculars, and zoomed in on the riders.

They were Shoshone soldiers, probably from the Wind River Reservation.

Cavill replaced the binoculars, then removed his gun belt and placed it over his saddle. He looked at the Shoshone riders and waved to them. One rider took the lead and rode toward Cavill.

The others followed.

Cavill waited beside the campfire until the twenty riders arrived. Only one rider dismounted. He was as tall and nearly as stout as Cavill. "I am Kuruk, of the Shoshone people," he said.

"The bear," Cavill said. "Well, you certainly look the part."

"You speak Shoshone?" Kuruk said.

"Some."

"How are you called?"

"Cavill. Jack Cavill."

"And Cavill means?"

Cavill grinned. "I'm English and Scots," he said. "Our names don't mean a damned thing. Have some coffee?"

"Have you sugar and milk?"

"I have. Sit. I'll fix you a cup."

Kuruk took a seat, and Cavill fixed him a cup of coffee.

"Cigar?" Cavill said.

"Yes, thank you."

Cavill gave Kuruk his last cigar and lit it with a wood match.

Looking at the six deer slung over the back of six horses belonging to Kuruk's soldiers, Cavill said, "I see you've had a successful hunt."

"It's a good time to hunt," Kuruk said. "While the herd is full before the cold arrives."

Cavill sipped coffee, as did Kuruk.

"You make good coffee, Jack Cavill," Kuruk said. "We watched your partner ride off toward Rawlins."

"We need supplies," Cavill said.

"So many cows. Where are you taking them?"

"Eventually they will wind up with the army," Cavill said. "I'll tell you what. I have a feel for some fresh deer meat. I'll trade you two cows for one deer."

Kuruk puffed on his cigar for a few seconds. "Three. Three cows," he said.

"Deal," Cavill said.

"We have a trade?" Kuruk said.

"We have a trade," Cavill said. "Pick out the three cows you want."

Kuruk and Cavill stood, and together they walked through the herd while Kuruk picked three large cows.

"Good choice," Cavill said.

"Pick your deer," Kuruk said.

Cavill chose a large buck, and the mounted soldier slid it off the saddle to him.

"Travel well," Kuruk said.

"And you," Cavill said.

Rawlins was a town of about fifteen hundred residents and named after Union General John Rawlins, who once camped in the area in 1867.

Duffy's first stop was at the general store for supplies. The store also served as the post office, and he mailed the letters to Sylvia and Joey.

Across the street from the general store was the telegraph office. He entered and paid a dollar and sixty-five cents to send telegrams to Goodluck and Porter.

About to mount up and ride out of town, Duffy remembered Cavill's cigars and he returned to the general store.

"I almost forgot cigars," Duffy told the clerk. "What have you got in the way of really good ones?"

"I just got these in the other day," the clerk said. "Came all the way from the island of Cuba down near Florida. They're expensive at a dollar apiece."

"How many in a box?" Duffy said.

"Twenty-four."

"I'll take a box," Duffy said.

At his desk, Porter loaded his old Colt revolver and gently placed it into the well-worn, brown leather holster he'd first strapped on almost three decades ago.

Miss Potts tapped on the office door, quietly opened it, and entered.

"I have your ticket, Mr. Porter," she said. "And this telegram just arrived from Mr. Duffy."

Porter took the telegram.

"They're in Rawlins," he said. "Expecting to arrive in Buffalo in about one week."

"Shall I send a reply?" Miss Potts said.

"No need," Porter said. "What time does my train leave?"

"Two o'clock."

"Ah, we have time for lunch."

"Lunch, Mr. Porter?"

"You do eat lunch, don't you?"

"Yes, of course."

"Let me get my jacket, and we'll be off," Porter said.

Goodluck was in the stables grooming his horse, when a runner entered and said, "The general wants to see you right away."

Pitt and Gatewood were in Crook's office when Goodluck arrived.

"Chief Scout, we received a telegram from Duffy and Cavill," Crook said. "They will be here in about a week."

"Sir, I'd like permission to ride out in five days and meet them on the trail," Goodluck said.

"I thought you'd say that," Crook said. "Captain Pitt and Lieutenant Gatewood will ride with you."

"Very good, General," Goodluck said.

"Take a bottle of my finest whiskey with you," Crook said. "I have a feeling those men could use a good drink."

CHAPTER THIRTY

When Duffy returned to camp, Cavill was cutting the deer carcass into steaks.

"I know you didn't go hunting, so where did the deer come from?" Duffy said as he dismounted.

"I traded for it with a Shoshone hunting party. Did you get my cigars?" Cavill said.

"What did you trade?" Duffy said. He reached into a saddlebag for the box of cigars and tossed it to Cavill. "And they came from Cuba."

Cavill inspected the box. "Cuba, huh? I traded some beef, what did you think? My dirty underwear?"

"I guess we're having venison for supper tonight," Duffy said.

Cavill removed a cigar from the box and sniffed it. "I wonder if these are any good," he said.

"Let's move the herd after lunch and put some distance between us and Rawlins," Duffy said.

After sixteen hours on a train, Porter was ready to stretch his legs. Late in the afternoon, the small town of Buffalo was crowded with pedestrians and soldiers from Fort McKinney.

Situated in Johnson County, Buffalo was cattle country. Porter walked the streets for a bit and decided to rent a buggy to ride to the fort.

The livery had several nice buggies for rent, and he got directions to the fort from the livery manager.

The ride was pleasant enough along the Powder River. He reached the gates of Fort McKinney in forty-five minutes.

"Charles Porter, owner of the Illinois Detective Agency, to see your commanding officer," Porter told the guard on duty at the gates.

"We expect them inside a week, maybe less," Crook said. "Captain Pitt and Lieutenant Gatewood and Chief Scout Goodluck will ride out in five days to escort them to the fort."

They were at Crook's table in the mess hall for the evening meal.

"Mr. Goodluck, you were with my men for several weeks, is that correct?" Porter said.

"More like a month or more," Goodluck said.

"Do we know where the stolen cattle came from?" Porter said.

"Not the individual ranches, but Mr. Duffy sketched each brand before we changed it so the cattle can be traced back to its owner," Goodluck said.

"This Parsons, he isn't the man in charge," Porter said. "The man in charge is never a man on a horse."

"We are hoping Parsons can lead us to the man in charge," Crook said.

"How many head have been stolen by now, Mr. Goodluck?" Porter said.

"Parsons said around seven thousand, half of which went to Mexico," Goodluck said.

"We're talking hundreds of thousands of dollars," Porter said. "This isn't being done out of greed for money."

"I'm not sure I follow you Mr. Porter," Crook said.

"The money is a means to an end," Porter said. "Whoever the head of this snake is, he wants the money for some higher purpose."

213

"Mr. Duffy said a very similar thing," Goodluck said.

"Mr. Duffy is a very smart man," Porter said. "Did he mention he will take the bar exam soon?"

"No, he didn't," Goodluck said. "What's a bar exam?"

"It's a very difficult test a man must take in order to become a lawyer," Porter said. "Only the smartest pass it."

"I have no doubt Mr. Duffy will," Goodluck said.

Porter looked at Crook. "General, when Chief Scout Goodluck and your officers leave the fort to escort my men in, I will ride with them."

"Mr. Porter, there is no need of that," Crook said. "My men and Chief Scout Goodluck are—"

"Duffy and Cavill are my men, General. I will ride to greet and escort them to the fort," Porter said.

"Very well, Mr. Porter," Cook said. "In the meantime, you shall be my guest here at the fort."

Porter and Goodluck sat on a bench outside Porter's guesthouse. Each had a small glass of whiskey.

Porter lit a cigar and offered one to Goodluck.

"Mr. Goodluck, what does the army pay a chief scout?" Porter said. "Fifty, seventy-five dollars a month, plus room and board?"

"About," Goodluck said.

"After this cattle business is secure, I would like you to come work for me," Porter said. "As one of my detectives. You'll earn ten times that in a month, and I'll supply you with a nice apartment near the office."

"In a city?" Goodluck said.

"Springfield isn't much of a city, but yes," Porter said. "Although I'm sure you will be out west most of the time on assignment."

"Can I think about it?" Goodluck said.

"Of course," Porter said. "It's a big step. I would expect a man to think it over carefully."

"I will," Goodluck said. "And thank you."

Porter lifted his glass. "I'll see you in the morning, Chief Scout," he said and tossed back his whiskey.

CHAPTER THIRTY-ONE

While Cavill backtracked to bring up the drags, Duffy built a campfire and put on lunch. Venison stew with beans, cornbread, and coffee.

As he stirred the stew in the pot, Duffy noticed something in the distance. He grabbed his binoculars from his saddlebags and took a look.

"Well, how about that?" he said aloud.

By the time Cavill returned with the drags, the riders in the distance were visible.

As he dismounted, Cavill said, "My eyes must be going bad, because I swear I see Charles Porter on a horse with Goodluck."

"Along with two army officers," Duffy said. "Which is why I put on a second pot of stew."

"What in the hell is Charles Porter doing out here?" Cavill said.

"Wait a few minutes and ask him," Duffy said.

Cavill filled a cup with coffee and lit a cigar. He noticed the Cuban cigars were stronger, more flavorful, than the American cigars he usually smoked.

"Mr. Duffy, Mr. Cavill, I hope you made enough for the four of us," Porter said when he and the others arrived.

"Who hunted the deer?" Goodluck said as he tasted the stew.

"A fellow by the name of Kuruk," Cavill said.

"Kuruk?" Goodluck said.

"Know him?" Cavill said.

"He's one of the great Shoshone warriors who gave the army a run for its money," Goodluck said. "What did you trade for the deer?"

"Three cows," Cavill said.

"For one deer? Shrewd trade," Goodluck said.

"He seemed a nice enough fellow," Cavill said. "And three cows will go a long way on the reservation."

"Mr. Porter, what are you doing here?" Duffy said.

"After I received your last telegram, I realized this cattle-rustling operation is much bigger than I originally envisioned," Porter said. "I thought I would come take a look for myself."

"I'm afraid I'm going to have to ask you, Captain Pitt, and Lieutenant Gatewood to ride back to the fort ahead of us," Duffy said.

"General Crook asked us to escort you to the fort," Gatewood said. "I can't defy his orders."

"By tomorrow night, we will be within range of the southern Bighorns," Duffy said. "We have no way of knowing if they will have lookouts in place, but if they do and spot army personnel, we might as well keep going all the way to Canada."

"Parsons is no dummy," Cavill said. "He'll post lookouts to let him know when we've entered the Bighorns. He's expecting to see us and Goodluck, and that's what we'll show him."

"Lieutenant Gatewood, Captain Pitt, I assume you can read a map," Duffy said.

"Of course," Gatewood said.

Duffy removed a folded map from his saddlebags and spread it out. He used his finger to trace a path.

"This is where we will enter through the secret pass in the southern Bighorns," Duffy said. "I've highlighted the secret entrance to the northern Bighorns in red. They won't expect us to enter that way because we'll lose several days' traveling time."

"We'll delay our arrival at the southern Bighorns to give the army time to enter the northern pass and take up position around the secret outlaw camp. When we arrive, you'll be able to watch us from the surrounding cliffs," Cavill said. "It's critical that Parsons doesn't discover you're there. Our lives depend upon it."

"Have some snipers at the ready," Duffy said. "You'll know when to use them."

Porter looked at the map. "I see you've given this much thought, but I would have expected no less," he said.

"We'll return to the fort right after I have another bowl of this stew," Gatewood said. "I'll square it with the general. I'm sure he'll agree with your plan."

"Mr. Porter, would you like a Cuban cigar for the ride?" Cavill said.

"Why, yes, I would," Porter said.

"Take two," Cavill said.

"I'm not entirely sure this is a good idea," Gatewood said to Porter as they rode back to the fort.

"Duffy and Cavill are two of the best men in the business," Porter said. "I trust their abilities and their judgment. Our best bet to get to the bottom of this cattle business is to allow them to do their job."

"It seems to me we're allowing them to walk directly into a trap," Pitt said.

"Captain Pitt, in case you haven't figured it out as yet, that is exactly what they are relying upon," Porter said.

"We might as well stay here and give them a good head start," Duffy said.

"How was it, sleeping in a nice, soft bed for a week," Cavill

218

said to Goodluck.

"My cot is anything but soft, but I do miss the army chow," Goodluck said. "We have several hours of daylight left. I think I'll see what I can hunt up for supper."

"I'll go with you," Cavill said.

Cavill and Goodluck walked to the surrounding hills, where Goodluck used his experience and tracking ability to locate the trail of a large hare. They followed the trail for about a quarter of a mile until Goodluck spotted a brown hare sitting in a field of wildflowers about two hundred yards away.

Slowly Goodluck aimed his bow at the hare. He held his breath before releasing the arrow, and then let it fly. The arrow struck true, and the hare fell dead.

They walked to the hare and Goodluck picked it up by the ears. "A fine, fifteen-pound snowshoe hare," he said.

"I thought snowshoe hare were white," Cavill said.

"In the winter they're white," Goodluck said. "During the summer months, they turn brown to blend in with their surroundings."

When they returned to camp, Duffy was reading one of his law books.

"Snowshoe hare stew for supper tonight," Cavill said.

"I thought snowshoe hare were white," Duffy said.

"Only in the winter, Mr. Law Books," Cavill said. "In the summer, they change color to blend in with their surroundings."

Goodluck looked at Cavill, and Cavill shrugged his shoulders.

"Jack, we need some wood," Duffy said.

"I saw a felled tree on the way back," Cavill said as he grabbed the ax from his gear. "I won't be long."

Sylvia Trent didn't sort through the mail until she and her father returned home from Miles City. She spotted the letter from

Duffy and hid it from her father. She didn't open it until she had snuck off to her room.

Duffy wrote that he hoped to conclude the job in a few weeks, and then planned to return to Miles City to ask permission of her father to officially court her.

Sylvia felt giddy and light-headed, but she knew that was the young, inexperienced girl in her, the side most people never got to see.

She wished she could write him back, but to where? She would just have to be patient and wait.

She folded the letter and tucked it away in her vanity with the first one.

"Fine hare stew," Cavill said.

"I could do with a beefsteak," Goodluck said.

"Don't let the ladies hear you say that," Cavill said. "They're still sulking because I gave three of their cousins away."

Looking at his maps, Duffy said, "We could reach the southern entrance to the Bighorns by tomorrow night. Camp out and reach the secret outlaw camp by midday."

"Is that enough time for the army to enter through the north?" Cavill said.

"They should be in place before we arrive," Duffy said.

"If they're not?" Goodluck said.

"Then I wouldn't count on celebrating your next birthday," Duffy said.

"I still could do with a nice beefsteak," Goodluck said.

Joey was surprised to find a letter from Cavill mixed in with the regular mail her men brought back with them from a trip to town for fencing supplies.

She opened the letter at the table and read it over a cup of tea.

He couldn't say much about where he was or where he was going, just that he hoped to conclude the job within a few weeks. He said he thought about her every day, maybe too much, as it was bad to get distracted when on a job. He missed her and hoped to see her soon. He ended the letter with, *Love, Jack.*

"I could use an *I* and a *you* in there, but I'll take it," she said aloud.

As they had after-supper cups of coffee, sweetened with a bit of whiskey, Duffy, Cavill, and Goodluck rested against their saddles in front of a campfire.

Cavill gave Goodluck and Duffy a Cuban cigar. They smoked quietly for a while as they enjoyed the fire and cigars.

"Mr. Porter offered me a job," Goodluck said.

"With the agency? That's a fine idea," Duffy said.

"I'm not sure I can live in a city back east," Goodluck said.

"I wouldn't call Springfield, Illinois, exactly back east," Duffy said. "And besides, you'd be on assignment in the west most of the time anyway."

"You'd make ten times the money," Cavill said.

"Of which I have little use," Goodluck said.

"But your people on the reservation do," Cavill said. "Think of the good some extra money could do."

Goodluck puffed on his cigar. "I will think about it carefully," he said. "If, after tomorrow, I am still alive."

CHAPTER THIRTY-TWO

Nestled comfortably on their stomachs, Lieutenant Gatewood and Captain Pitt used binoculars to watch the outlaw camp some four hundred yards away.

There were several cabins, a barn, a corral for horses, and a water pump.

Behind the cabins, a thousand or so cows grazed in a wide-open field of green grass.

"Six horses in the corral," Gatewood said.

"Another two on the way," Pitt said.

From the southern entrance, two riders approached, leaving a trail of dust as they raced along.

"Lookouts approaching," Gatewood said.

"Which means they are on their way in," Pitt said.

Gatewood backed away from the edge, stood, and walked a hundred feet to where General Crook, Charles Porter, and forty-two soldiers from the fort were camped.

"Two riders approaching, General," he said.

"We anticipated lookouts," Crook said. "They must be on the way in with the herd."

"I would guess, General," Gatewood said.

"When you see them, notify us immediately," Crook said.

"Yes, sir."

Gatewood returned to the cliff and took his position beside Pitt.

About thirty very slow-moving minutes passed before they

saw the first clouds of dust in the pass.

Gatewood stood and returned to Crook.

"They're approaching, General," Gatewood said.

Crook and Porter stood up from their field chairs.

"Sharpshooters, take position twelve feet apart," Crook said. "Everybody else, take your Winchesters."

Once everybody was in place, they watched as four men took a position behind some rocks at the entrance to the outlaw camp.

"They're closing the back door," Crook said.

Duffy, Cavill, and Goodluck drove the cattle into the outlaw camp to the field where a thousand other cattle were grazing.

Then they turned and rode to the cabins where Parsons, Cassidy, and two other men waited. Cassidy and two men held Winchesters.

Cavill looked at Cassidy. "I see you didn't follow our advice. Where's the kid, Parker?" he said.

"Parts unknown," Cassidy said.

"The kid's smarter than you," Cavill said.

Parsons stepped forward. "I thank you for the hard work, but I'm afraid our company must now part ways," he said.

The four men hiding behind rocks came out and walked up behind Duffy, Cavill, and Goodluck.

"Now, be good boys and step down off your horses," Parsons said.

The four men cocked their Winchesters.

Duffy turned and glanced at them.

"I have to ask again, and they'll shoot you off," Parsons said.

"If it's all the same to you, I'd rather die in the saddle," Cavill said. "What do you say, Joe?"

"No better place for a Comanche to die," Goodluck said.

Parsons sighed. "Suit yourself," he said.

"Before you kill us, I'd turn around and take a look at the hills," Duffy said.

Parsons turned just as the four sharpshooters fired. One second later, the four men behind Duffy, Cavill, and Goodluck fell dead.

Parsons looked at Duffy.

"Still want us to get off our horses?" Duffy said.

Parsons sat at the table in the main cabin. Crook and Porter sat opposite him. Duffy and Cavill, Gatewood and Pitt stood in the background.

Goodluck and Crook's soldiers guarded Parsons's men outside the cabin.

"Mr. Parsons, I will personally see to it that you swing from a rope unless you tell us who the man behind this operation is," Crook said.

"In exchange for what, twenty-five years in Yuma?" Parsons said. "I'll be an old man like you when I get out, *if* I get out. No thanks, I'll take a rope and get it over with quick."

"Have you ever seen a man hang?" Porter said. "It's a ghastly sight indeed. If you're lucky, your neck snaps and you die immediately. Most times, though, you hang there and choke to death as the rope squeezes the life out of you. I've known cases where a man took thirty minutes to die on the rope, suffocating slowly while he soiled his pants. If that's what you'd prefer, so be it. We're done here."

"Mr. Porter, we've come too far to give up on this now," Duffy said.

"What do you suggest?" Porter said.

Duffy moved closer to the table and looked at Parsons. "What will it take, Parsons, to get you to talk?"

"Immunity," Parsons said.

"Ridiculous," Crook said. "As Mr. Porter said, we're done here."

"I've killed no one, and that's the price for the head man," Parsons said.

"Three years at a minimum-security penitentiary," Duffy said.

"In Florida," Parsons said. "I hate cold weather."

Duffy looked at Porter, and Porter nodded.

"Talk, Mr. Parsons," Duffy said.

"I want it in writing first," Parsons said. "Signed by your boss and the general."

Crook turned to Gatewood. "Lieutenant, get my writing paper and a pen with ink from my gear."

A few minutes later, Crook, Porter, and Parsons sighed the document stating that, in exchange for his testimony and co-operation, Parsons would receive the reduced sentence of three years in a Florida minimum-security prison.

"All right, Mr. Parsons, let's hear it," Porter said.

"Mr. J. Paul Sims," Parsons said.

"Who?" Porter said.

"He's a Scotsman," Parsons said. "He showed up in sixty-nine with dreams of building the biggest ranch in Arizona Territory. Except Henry Hooker was there first. I went to work for Sims about eight years ago as his foreman, and I've never seen anything eat at a man the way it does Sims that Hooker, and not he, has the biggest spread."

Gatewood and Pitt set coffee cups before Crook, Porter, and Parsons.

Parsons rolled a cigarette and lit it with a wood match.

"Please continue, Mr. Parsons," Porter said.

"A couple of years ago, Sims got this idea of becoming the first governor of Wyoming when it becomes a state," Parsons said. "He said the talk was, it would happen inside of several years. I'm not sure if Sims is a genius or a madman."

"Explain that," Porter said.

"A few years ago he started buying land in Wyoming, wherever and whenever he could afford it," Parsons said. "He's got a fair spread, but he's no Henry Hooker or John Chisum, so when his money ran out, he figured he'd go get more money another way. He devised a plan where we'd steal what we need to finance his operation in Wyoming. He figures to own more land in Wyoming than anybody when it comes time to vote for statehood. He figures who better to be the first governor than the man who owns the most land in the new state."

"The man is plumb crazy," Crook said.

"That's what I thought," Parsons said. "At first. But he bought an auction house in Cheyenne, another in Dodge City, another in New Mexico, and a fourth in Old Mexico just across the border."

"You mean he sells the stolen cattle to himself and then turns around and sells them to slaughterhouses for a profit?" Porter said.

"And in the process, without the upkeep of raising the cattle, he's become a very rich man," Parsons said. "And in a few years, rich enough to buy himself an election for governor."

"Where is Sims now?" Crook said.

"At his place in Arizona," Parsons said. "He keeps a few hundred head for show."

"We should contact the US marshals immediately," Crook said. "The army can serve as a—"

Parsons started to laugh.

"I fail to see what is so humorous about this situation," Crook said.

"The auction houses are all legitimate," Parsons said. "There isn't an ounce of proof any of the cattle are stolen, except my word and your men's word. There's two thousand head outside.

If they don't reach Cheyenne inside of two weeks, Sims will wonder why. If I don't telegram him from Cheyenne that I'm delivering the money, he'll know something is wrong. He'll close up the operation, and all you'll get is me and the boys outside and nothing to tie it all to Sims. In the meantime, he'll have made hundreds of thousands of dollars right under your noses, and his auction houses will go right on making him more. By the time Wyoming is made a state, he could very well wind up as governor."

"My men will testify in court to your cattle theft," Porter said.

"Sure, but all they have is me," Parsons said.

"He's right, Mr. Porter. All we have is him," Duffy said. "We can't prove a word of this. In court, a defense attorney will say Parsons and the others lied to get a reduced sentence."

"I sense a proposal, Mr. Duffy," Porter said.

"Allow me, Jack, Goodluck, and Parsons to deliver the cattle to Wyoming so as not to alert Sims," Duffy said. "The money will go to the ranchers who lost the cattle. Parsons can get us to Sims's ranch in Arizona as part of his crew. Once we're there, we can obtain enough evidence to get an indictment."

"Now why would I do that?" Parsons said.

"I'm sure you've squirreled away quite a tidy sum from this," Duffy said. "If you get out in eighteen months and you get to keep that tidy sum, is that a good enough reason?"

"I keep my money and do just eighteen months?" Parsons said.

"That's my offer in exchange for Sims," Duffy said.

"Deal," Parsons said.

"When you deliver the money, does your crew go with you?" Duffy said.

"Most times," Parsons said. "Tucson is a good place for the boys to let off some steam after months in the saddle."

"Is that where his ranch is, Tucson?" Duffy said.

"Just south of the Gila River," Parsons said.

"Does he know your men by name?" Duffy said.

"I use a different crew each job. You know that firsthand," Parsons said.

Duffy looked at Porter. "We'll deliver the cattle to Cheyenne and then ride to Tucson to deliver the money," he said. "We know the cattle are stolen because we helped steal them. Once Sims accepts the money for stolen cattle, we'll have enough to arrest him for cattle theft, conspiracy, murder, fraud, and possibly treason."

Porter looked at Crook. "What do you say, General?"

"I don't see what you have to lose at this point," Crook said. "I'd like Lieutenant Gatewood to go along. Undercover, of course."

Duffy turned to Gatewood. "What do you say, Lieutenant, feel up to driving a herd to Cheyenne?"

"I'm afraid I have no civilian clothes with me," Gatewood said.

"You're about my size. You can wear some of mine until we reach Cheyenne," Duffy said.

"General, I'd like to go along," Gatewood said.

"It's settled then," Crook said.

Porter looked at Cavill. "Mr. Cavill, you've been strangely silent."

Cavill stepped forward and looked at Parsons. "Understand this. If you cross us or even think about it, I will bury you on the spot. I won't say by-your-leave or ask the time of day. I will simply kill you and leave your corpse for the coyotes and buzzards. Do we understand each other?"

Porter looked at Duffy. "Is he always like this in the field?"

"Mostly," Duffy said.

"Good," Porter said.

Parsons rolled a fresh cigarette. "Eighteen months in the Florida sun, and I come out with the money I went in with. I'm no fool. I'll give you no reason to kill me, no reason at all."

"Then we understand each other," Cavill said.

"Gentlemen, let's have a drink," Porter said.

Chapter Thirty-Three

Goodluck shook his head. "More cows," he said.

In the main cabin, Duffy and Cavill placed two tables together for supper. Porter, Crook, Gatewood, Pitt, Goodluck, Cavill, and Duffy sat in chairs and ate roasted chicken, compliments of Goodluck's skill with his bow.

Crook's soldiers, Parsons, and his outlaws had to settle for beans, bacon, and cornbread outside the cabin.

"Tomorrow, I shall return to McKinney with those outlaws and hold them in our brig until this matter is settled," Crook said. "Lieutenant Gatewood, although you will be traveling as a civilian, I expect you to conduct yourself as an army officer at all times."

"Yes, General," Gatewood said.

"Don't worry, General, we'll make him toe the line," Cavill said.

Duffy stood up, went to the counter beside the woodstove, and returned with a bottle of bourbon whiskey. He went around the table and added two ounces to each glass, then took his chair.

"Mr. Porter, when you get home, can you see what you can find out about this Sims?" Duffy said. "I'll wire you from Cheyenne. The information on him may prove useful."

Porter looked at Cavill. "I want this Sims character alive, Mr. Cavill. Alive and prosecuted for his crimes. Is that clear?"

"Yes, Mr. Porter," Cavill said.

"After dinner, I'd like a few more questions with Parsons," Duffy said.

By oil lantern, Duffy sat opposite Parsons at the table. Porter, Cavill, and Crook sat next to Duffy.

"Drink?" Duffy said.

Rolling a cigarette, Parsons said, "Why not?"

Duffy poured bourbon into a glass and slid it across the table to Parsons.

Parsons struck a match and lit the cigarette. "Thanks," he said.

"What does Sims look like?" Duffy said.

"He's around forty or so," Parsons said. "Like I said, he showed up in sixty-seven when he was young with the hopes of being the biggest rancher in the west."

"That doesn't tell me what he looks like," Duffy said.

"Maybe your height, slim like you, regular-looking guy," Parsons said. "It won't be necessary for me to point him out to you; you'll know him when you see him. He's top dog on his ranch."

"And he'll be there, on his ranch?" Duffy said.

"Waiting for me to arrive with the money from the last drive to Cheyenne," Parsons said.

"When he accepts the money for the stolen cows, you have him," Porter said.

"Finish your drink, Mr. Parsons," Duffy said.

Parsons tossed back his drink, stood, and walked outside.

Duffy turned to Porter. "Mr. Porter, can you meet us in Cheyenne in ten days with whatever information you can dig up on Sims?" he said. "I'd like to give you the money from the sale of the cattle, and for you to give it to the Stock Growers Association so they can return it to the ranchers the cattle was stolen from."

231

"A fine idea, James," Porter said. "Is ten days enough time?"

"We could make Cheyenne in ten days if we leave in the morning, but better make it twelve, just to be safe," Duffy said.

"I believe I'll have another drink before I turn in," Porter said. "Would you care to join me, General?"

Duffy, Goodluck, and Gatewood entered the second cabin to find Cavill at the table with Parsons's revolver and gun belt. With pliers, he was removing the lead bullet from each cartridge, dumping the gun powder, and then replacing the bullet back into the empty cartridge.

"What are you doing with Parsons's gun?" Duffy said.

"Fixing to give it back to him in the morning," Cavill said. "It might appear a bit odd, having a cowboy come off a drive going un-heeled."

"Armed but without firepower," Duffy said.

"Unless he cares to throw the bullets, that's the general idea," Cavill said.

"Sleep is the only general idea I want right now," Goodluck said.

"We got an early start in the morning, Jack, which bed do you want?" Duffy said.

"Save me the biggest," Cavill said as he pulled apart another cartridge.

After breakfast, Crook's soldiers broke camp and prepared to transport the prisoners to Fort McKinney.

"Mr. Duffy, Mr. Cavill, I shall see you in Cheyenne," Porter said. "Mr. Goodluck, you have their backs. See that nothing happens to them."

After Porter and the army left toward the north passage, Duffy, Cavill, Goodluck, Gatewood, and Parsons mounted their horses.

"All right, Mr. Parsons, let's find out what kind of cowboy you are," Duffy said.

As they rode to the field where the cattle were grazing, Cavill tossed Parsons his gun belt. "Don't get the wrong idea," Cavill said. "The cartridges are blanks. It's just for show."

"No worries, big man," Parsons said. "I can do eighteen months standing on my head, and when I get out, I'm going to take my money and start over in California."

"Glad to hear it," Duffy said. "Now let's move some cows."

As they camped along the Wind River, Cavill took a bath while Duffy guarded Parsons and Goodluck went off hunting.

The nearly two thousand head of cattle grazed in the open range near the river.

"Go ahead, Jim, grab a bath," Cavill said when he emerged from the water.

"I could use one, too," Parsons said.

"Go ahead, but watch your step," Cavill said.

While Duffy and Parsons were in the water, Goodluck returned with three large hares. He dismounted, went to the fire, and filled a cup with coffee.

"We're being dogged," Goodluck said.

From the water, Duffy said, "Who?"

"Eight men, camped about ten miles north of us," Goodluck said. "They've been on our tail for at least two days."

Duffy emerged from the water and grabbed his towel. "They're after the herd," he said.

"Well, they're not out here for the sunshine and view," Cavill said.

Grinning, Parsons emerged from the water and grabbed his towel. "You're not going to let them steal our stolen cattle, are you?" he said.

"You shut up," Cavill said.

As he dressed, Duffy said, "We can't outrun them driving a herd, and we're a hundred miles from the nearest law."

"And they know it, too," Cavill said.

"Looks like we're in for a fight," Goodluck said.

Scouting ahead, Gatewood returned and dismounted. "We have good water the next fifty miles or so," he said.

"That's not all we have," Cavill said.

"Eight men camped ten miles behind us, and it's not because they want our company," Duffy said.

"They're after the herd?" Gatewood said.

"You ladies best be careful, or you'll get the drizzles," Parsons said.

"Nobody asked you a damn thing," Cavill said.

"We'll have to make a stand if they come for the herd," Duffy said.

"They'll come, all right," Cavill said. "Forty thousand dollars of free beef for the taking; they'll come to take it."

"The question is, will they come in daylight or in the dark?" Duffy said.

"Daylight's too risky," Cavill said. "Even if they take us, some of them could get killed, and they won't vote for that. No, they'll come at night and ambush us in our sleep."

"Jack?" Duffy said.

"I know. More killing," Cavill said.

"Goodluck, do you think you could manage to get close enough to hear their conversation without getting spotted?" Duffy said.

"Of course," Goodluck said.

"All right, go," Duffy said. "And while he's gone, we best get prepared."

"And cook these fine hares," Cavill said.

The eight men never saw or heard Goodluck as he came up

behind them. He left his boots with his horse a thousand yards to their left and silently made his way behind their camp as only a Comanche could.

Goodluck listened for about thirty minutes and then backtracked to his horse, where he put his boots on and rode back to camp.

As he filled a cup with coffee, Goodluck said, "They put it to a vote. They will hit us tonight while the moon is dark."

Duffy sighed. "Well, we best get ready then," he said.

"While we're getting ready, let's eat," Cavill said as he turned the hares on the spit.

The eight outlaws waited five hundred yards away from the campfire until they were sure everybody was in their bedrolls and asleep.

Then they rode closer, dismounted, armed themselves with rifles, and walked quietly to the campfire.

In the dim light of the small campfire, five outlines in bedrolls were visible.

One of the eight outlaws held up his left hand and motioned to fire. Eight rifles shattered the silence of the night as they pumped bullets into the five bedrolls.

After the last shot fired and the echo faded, the man who gave the order to fire said, "Check them, and make sure they're all dead. If they ain't, kill them."

Three men walked forward and removed the blankets from the bedrolls.

"Why, it ain't nothing but some logs," a man said.

"It's a trap," another man said.

From behind them, Duffy said, "And you walked right into it."

"Move an inch, and you'll be full of holes," Cavill said.

"Drop the rifles and gun belts," Duffy said.

The eight men dropped their rifles.

"The gun belts," Duffy said. "Do it."

Slowly they removed their gun belts and let them fall, except one who caught his revolver before the holster hit the ground, spun, and fired a shot that went wide into the darkness.

Cavill killed the man with one well-placed shot to the chest.

The echo of the shot faded, and for several seconds the night was silent.

Then, Cavill erupted.

He tossed his rifle to Duffy and lunged forward at the man who gave the orders. "I am so sick and tired of having to kill asshole outlaws like you," Cavill shouted. He hit the man in the jaw with a powerful right hook that sent the man flying. Immediately, Cavill turned to another of the outlaws. "Are you stupid?" he shouted. "Is that it? You're stupid?"

The man backed away, and Cavill felled him with a left hook to the gut.

Immediately, Cavill turned and grabbed another of the outlaws and began pummeling him with powerful punches that sounded like thuds.

"Jack, enough," Duffy said.

Cavill continued raining punch after punch on the man, and Duffy said, "Gatewood, pull him off."

"Me?" Gatewood said.

"Jack. Enough!" Duffy shouted.

Cavill released the man, and he fell to the ground.

"What is wrong with you people?" Cavill shouted and kicked one of the men on the ground.

Duffy tossed Cavill his rifle. "Go cool off," Duffy said.

"The man sure can fight," Gatewood said.

"You don't know the half of it," Goodluck said.

"All you men sit down," Duffy said. "Gatewood, Goodluck, get your rope."

"What about Parsons?" Gatewood said.

"Get him, too," Duffy said.

As the sun rose, Duffy stirred two pans of beans and bacon. Cavill sipped coffee and smoked a cigar.

Gatewood looked at the seven prisoners bound at the wrists and ankles and looped together with rope.

"What do we do with them?" Gatewood said.

"We can't take them with us and we can't exactly let them go," Cavill said.

Filling a cup with coffee, Parsons said, "You got a future in politics, big man."

"Goodluck's returning," Gatewood said.

Walking, Goodluck held his hat in his hands. When he reached camp, he set his hat on the ground. "Seventeen chicken eggs," he said.

Duffy looked at the roped outlaws. "Enough to feed the whole bunch," he said.

"Well, gentlemen, it's eighty miles to Riverton," Duffy said. "You got food, you got water, and most important, you got your lives."

"What about our guns?" one of the seven outlaws said.

"You'll find them on the ground about ten miles south of here," Cavill said. "I'm afraid we'll have to keep your horses though."

"That ain't right, putting a man afoot," another of the outlaws said.

"Neither is shooting a man in the dark when he sleeps," Cavill said. "Be grateful you got what we gave you, bushwhacker."

"Let's go," Duffy said. "Goodluck, you take the point. We got a herd to move."

"We left you a shovel. Don't forget to bury your friend," Cavill said.

CHAPTER THIRTY-FOUR

As they rode into Cheyenne, Duffy turned to Parsons and said, "I'll give you this much, Parsons, you know how to cowboy, but you should have stuck to doing it honestly."

"Let's get these cattle penned and find Porter," Cavill said.

They drove the herd to the stockyard pens just outside of town where the auction house was located.

Duffy dismounted. "Parsons, you come with me. Jack, you too."

They entered the auction house and went to the manager's office.

"Mr. Parsons, what have you for me this trip?" the manager said.

"Eighteen hundred head, give or take, from independent ranchers in Nebraska and Colorado," Parsons said.

"I'll certify them in the morning," the manager said. "Representatives from Omaha, Saint Louis, and New York slaughterhouses will be bidding in two days."

"Sounds good," Parsons said. "I could use a few days to unwind."

"I'll see you at eight o'clock tomorrow morning," the manager said.

"I'll be here," Parsons said.

Duffy and Cavill led Parsons outside where they met Gatewood and Goodluck.

"Any sign of Mr. Porter?" Duffy said.

Ethan J. Wolfe

"No," Goodluck said. "But he's probably at a hotel."

"Let's take a look around town," Duffy suggested. "Knowing Mr. Porter, he's staying at the best hotel in town."

Porter was registered at the Hotel Cheyenne, the most expensive hotel in town. He had reserved two rooms in Duffy and Cavill's names, with one room having three beds.

"Your lucky day, Parsons," Cavill said. "A soft bed and three squares, and you don't have to pay for it."

"Do you have your own bathtubs and barber?" Duffy said.

"Yes, on the first floor in the rear," the desk clerk said.

"Get five tubs ready while we drop off our gear in our rooms," Duffy said.

"And the barber?" the clerk said.

"If he's available for five shaves," Duffy said. "We could use him."

"We could use a drink, too," Cavill said. "Can you send us a bottle?"

As they soaked in tubs of hot, scented water, Cavill lit a cigar and sipped his drink.

"Tell me something, Parsons," Duffy said. "Is that manager at the auction house in on Sims's scam?"

"No," Parsons said. "He's from back east somewhere. He doesn't know a thing about Sims. He auctions cattle and takes his cut from the sales."

The door to the tub room opened and Porter walked in.

"None the worse for wear I see," Porter said.

"It was touch and go for a while with some rustlers," Cavill said. "But we pulled through it."

"What did you do with the rustlers?" Porter said.

"We set them afoot and brought their horses to town," Cavill said.

"We figured to sell them and donate the money to charity," Duffy said.

"Whenever you're ready, I'll see you for dinner in the hotel dining room," Porter said.

As he cut into a steak, Porter said, "Mr. Parsons, are you prepared to surrender yourself once you reach the Sims ranch?"

"I'm ready to surrender right now and start my eighteen months," Parsons said.

"That will have to wait a while longer, as we need you to get to Sims," Duffy said.

"Your cooperation will be duly noted, and I will write a letter on your behalf," Porter said. "You might wind up with an early parole."

"I've no love for Sims," Parsons said. "Personally, I think he's crazy, but his greed put a fair amount of money in my pockets. I guess it's his greed that'll be his downfall."

"I think you'll find all men of greed eventually fall," Porter said. "Mr. Gatewood, Mr. Goodluck, will you escort Mr. Parsons to his room and wait with him so I may discuss business with Mr. Duffy and Mr. Cavill after supper?"

Porter, Duffy, and Cavill took drinks in the hotel lobby bar.

"Forty-one thousand acres of land in Wyoming are registered to Sims," Porter said. "His ranch in Arizona is another six thousand acres. It's been operational since sixty-nine. His average herd is about a thousand sold at auction, enough to pay his hands and keep afloat, but nothing like the illegal activity he's been involved in."

"What about the land he owns in Wyoming?" Duffy said.

"Good land for cattle, but it's not developed," Porter said. "If Parsons is correct, Sims intends to keep buying land in Wyoming until it's close to statehood and then set himself up for a run as governor."

"How much did the forty-one thousand acres cost?" Duffy said.

"Two dollars an acre," Porter said.

"So he hasn't spent nearly close to what he's made with his scheme," Duffy said.

"No, which means you have to shut him down quickly before he gets the chance to buy more land," Porter said.

"How do you want us to handle it?" Duffy said.

"Once Parsons gets you onto his ranch, arrest him and take him to the US marshal in Phoenix," Porter said. "I'll have the Stock Growers Association meet you there with a federal prosecutor. It then becomes their headache."

"Should we alert the marshal in Santa Fe beforehand?" Duffy said.

"No," Porter said. "We don't yet know how well-connected Sims is in Arizona, and without proof of the crime, they really can't act. You bring them the proof wrapped in a neat, little bow."

"And Parsons?" Duffy said.

"The Stock Growers Association and I will work out his deal with the federal prosecutor before you bring them to Santa Fe," Porter said.

"Mr. Porter, I'm just curious," Cavill said. "What kind of final bill will you submit to the Stock Growers Association for all this?"

Porter grinned. "Considerable, Mr. Cavill. Considerable."

"So we can afford another drink then?" Cavill said.

In the hotel room, Goodluck added an ounce of whiskey to three coffee cups and gave one to Gatewood and Parsons.

"To a short eighteen months," Parsons said and took a sip.

"Mind a question?" Gatewood said. "How much do you have put away from all this?"

"Fifteen thousand in a bank in Santa Fe, where it will be collecting interest until I get out," Parsons said.

"So you'll be set up pretty well when you get out," Gatewood said.

"Like I said, I have no love for Sims," Parsons said. "It was all business, and now I have to think of myself."

"Get us to Sims and then hold up your end, and you'll get a fresh start with enough money to do whatever you want," Gatewood said.

"About how I see it," Parsons said.

There was a knock on the door. It opened and Duffy and Cavill entered.

Cavill held a pair of handcuffs. "Time for bed, Parsons," he said. "We need to be at the auction house before eight."

By ten-thirty, the representatives from Omaha, Saint Louis, and New York, as well as the auction house manager, had certified the herd and approved it for bidding.

"You should fetch between eighteen and twenty-two for the herd," the manager said. "Will you be wanting it in cash as usual?"

"Yes. I have to pay the ranchers in cash," Parsons said. "But I have good people around me for protection."

The manager nodded. "The big one looks like he could wrestle a buffalo."

"I believe he already has," Parsons said.

In the hotel room, Duffy, Cavill, Parsons, and Gatewood played cards at the table. Goodluck went to the livery to have their horses shod with new shoes after the considerable wear put on the old ones.

"I could use some lunch," Parsons said.

"Not a bad idea," Cavill said.

"When Goodluck gets back," Duffy said. "So Parsons, say the herd brings twenty a head, what would your end be?"

"Sims has always been generous to me," Parsons said. "On this herd, he'd let me keep five percent. On a bigger one going to Mexico, I've kept as much as ten percent."

"So the obvious question is, why not just keep the entire haul for yourself?" Duffy said. "Take the thirty-five or forty thousand and just run."

"And spend the rest of my days looking over my shoulder for the bounty hunter Sims would hire to track me down? No thanks," Parsons said. "Besides, Sims had plans for me."

"What kind of plans?" Duffy said.

"A ranch with a hundred thousand acres needs a good fore-man," Parsons said. "We talked about it on more than one oc-casion."

"Him as governor and you running the biggest ranch in the new state," Duffy said.

"Well, that's over now, or will be when we get to Tucson," Duffy said.

"Maybe that's over, but you're not yet forty and have a decent kick in the bank to build an honest life when you get out," Duffy said. "Make the most of this second chance."

Goodluck opened the door and stepped inside.

"Mr. Porter wants to know if we'll join him for lunch," he said.

After lunch, Duffy mailed his letter to Sylvia and Cavill's letter to Joey, and then he met Cavill and Parsons on the front porch of the hotel.

"Mr. Porter went to the telegraph office," Cavill said.

"Gatewood and Goodluck are at the livery checking on the horses."

"I stopped by the railroad station on the way back and checked schedules," Duffy said. "Tomorrow, after the auction, we can get a three o'clock train to Tucson that gets us there in twenty-four hours."

"From Tucson to the Sims ranch is how long?" Cavill said.

"About four hours," Parsons said.

"What do you say, Jack? Feel like a stretch of the legs?" Duffy said.

"I was thinking that very thing," Cavill said.

They walked to the livery, met Gatewood and Goodluck, and saddled the horses.

"Where are we going?" Goodluck said.

"A ride in the country," Duffy said.

Ten miles outside of town, Duffy picked a shady spot along the banks of the Crow Creek and dismounted.

"This looks like a good spot," Duffy said.

"For what?" Goodluck said.

"I'm wondering that myself," Parsons said.

"A private conversation," Duffy said.

Once everyone had dismounted, Duffy said, "We know you can cowboy. We've seen you. And we know you're smart. Can you shoot?"

"At what and with what?" Parsons said. "My gun has blanks, remember?"

Duffy drew his Smith & Wesson revolver, cocked it, and fired at a birch tree twenty-five feet away. "Mine doesn't," he said and tossed the revolver to Parsons.

"Put a group around my shot," Duffy said.

"Aim anywhere else, and you'll wish you hadn't," Cavill said from behind Parsons.

Parsons rapid-fired five bullets at the tree, putting a tight group around the bullet Duffy fired, then he tossed the empty revolver back to Duffy.

"Nicely done," Duffy said as he emptied the spent rounds. "How are you with your mitts?"

Parsons glanced at Cavill, who was removing his gun belt.

"With him?" Parsons said.

"Can you last one minute?" Duffy said. "With him?"

Cavill tossed his gun belt to Goodluck and rolled up his sleeves.

"Is there a reason I should find out?" Parsons said.

"If I was you, I'd defend myself for the next sixty seconds," Duffy said.

Parsons spun around and punched Cavill in the jaw while Cavill was still rolling up his left sleeve.

Cavill's head snapped back, but then he looked at Parsons and smiled.

"Well, shit," Parsons said.

"Fifty seconds to go," Duffy said as he looked at his watch.

Outsized and outclassed in skill, Parsons did his best to ward Cavill off, but in the next fifty seconds, Cavill knocked Parsons down three times.

Each time, bloodier than the last, Parsons got up.

"Time," Duffy said.

"Thank God," Parsons said.

Duffy tossed Parsons a canteen. Parsons rinsed his mouth with water and spat blood. "Mind telling what this was all about," he said.

"Jack?" Duffy said.

"He's no coward, and he can take a punch," Cavill said. "Can he stay honest?"

"What's this about?" Parsons said.

"Consider it your audition," Duffy said.

Wiping blood from his mouth and nose with a neckerchief, Parsons said, "Audition for what?"

"A job with the Illinois Detective Agency when you get out," Duffy said.

"What?" Parsons said.

"Why not put your talents to good use for once?" Cavill said. "Porter can always use a good man like you, if you stay honest."

Parsons rubbed his jaw. "How much can a man make working for Porter?"

"We'll make about fifteen thousand this year," Duffy said. "It depends on how much you care to work."

"It's something to think about during the next eighteen months besides Florida mosquitoes," Cavill said.

"I'll be damned," Parsons said.

"Maybe so, but remember that second chance I spoke of," Duffy said.

"You mean you?" Parsons said.

"And Jack," Duffy said. "Except for Mr. Porter, we might be in the next cell over to yours. Think on it."

CHAPTER THIRTY-FIVE

The auction started promptly at eight and was over by ten-thirty. The entire herd was purchased by the Omaha, Saint Louis, and New York slaughterhouses for thirty-six thousand dollars.

Porter, Duffy, and Cavill walked the money to the Bank of Cheyenne, where Porter deposited it.

Duffy and Cavill returned to the hotel where Parsons, Gatewood, and Goodluck were on the porch.

"Where is Mr. Porter?" Goodluck said.

"Telegraph office, sending a telegram to the Montana Stock Growers Association to send a representative to his office in Springfield," Duffy said.

"Let's get packed and wait for Mr. Porter and then have lunch before we leave," Duffy said.

"Send me a telegram from Tucson," Porter said. "I'll have a federal prosecutor and the Stock Growers Association standing by for when you bring Sims to the US marshal in Tucson."

"Will do," Duffy said.

Porter looked at Parsons's face. "Judging from those bruises and fat lip, I'd say you passed your audition," he said. "And that was my idea, by the way. Write me from prison if you're interested in a job when you get out."

"I will," Parsons said. "And thank you for your trust."

"Let's get going. We got a long train ride ahead of us," Duffy said.

Gatewood and Goodluck shared a sleeping cabin, while Duffy, Cavill, and Parsons occupied a suite for the twenty-four-hour ride to Tucson.

In their cabin, Goodluck and Gatewood relaxed on their beds. Each had a cup of coffee. Goodluck smoked his pipe.

"You didn't have to come this far with us," Goodluck said.

"I follow the general's orders," Gatewood said.

"When you return to the fort, I expect you'll pursue Geronimo and his people," Goodluck said.

"Like I said, I follow the general's orders," Gatewood said.

"You know him, don't you?" Goodluck said.

"Yes, I know him," Gatewood said. "The general and I visited him on the reservation not long ago. We spoke of many things. The purpose of the visit was for the general to learn what Geronimo's people needed. They needed seed to farm and rifles to hunt. Geronimo said to me that he is a great hunter, but that he is a poor farmer."

"That's his way of telling you blood will be spilled," Goodluck said.

"I know," Gatewood said.

"He will lose," Goodluck said.

Gatewood looked at Goodluck. "I know."

There was a knock on the door and Cavill said, "We reserved a table in the dining car for supper. Seven o'clock."

After dinner, as they lingered at the table, Duffy took his notebook out of his jacket pocket and set it on the table. He handed Parsons a pencil.

"Draw the Sims ranch layout," Duffy said.

Parsons opened the notebook to a blank page. He made an

X. "That's Tucson," he said. He drew a straight line across the page. "This is the southeast road out of town. It forks about here, after about ten miles." He drew a line directly south at the fork. "Another ten miles or so takes you to Sims's ranch. There's an archway on the road. Once you cross under it, you're on his land."

"What's the layout at the house?" Duffy said.

"The house, barn, corral, bunkhouse for the hands," Parsons said. "Nothing fancy, but suited to the purpose."

"How many hands?" Duffy said.

"This time of year, probably four," Parsons said. "No gun hands, just twenty-five-dollar-a-month cowboys. You won't have any trouble out of them."

"They're just going to sit on their hands while we arrest Sims?" Cavill said.

"Would you risk a bullet or prison for twenty-five a month?" Parsons said. "I expect they'll just ride on to the next ranch and the next job."

"Something I'm curious about," Duffy said. "That day in Colorado when you left with Frog and Moon, you said you'd meet us in the Bighorns, but Frog and Moon weren't there."

"I sent them ahead to the next location," Parsons said. "By now they know I'm not coming."

"Ahead to where?" Duffy said.

"Utah, near Vernal," Parsons said. "I expect they'll head back to the Bighorns when I don't show."

Duffy looked at Gatewood.

"I'll wire the general when we reach Tucson," Gatewood said. "He'll send a patrol to pick them up."

Duffy nodded and put a finger on the notebook. "From the archway to the house is how far?"

"I never timed it, but I'd guess about two miles or so," Parsons said. "No more than that."

"What are you thinking?" Cavill said to Duffy.

"The best way to handle Sims without shooting," Duffy said. "We want to arrest and prosecute him, but we can't do that if he's dead."

"His hands won't fight, like I said, but Sims will," Parsons said. "If he has a reason to."

"Let me ask you, when you deliver the money after an auction, do you always ride in with some of your men?" Duffy said.

"Most times," Parsons said. "Sometimes they'll relax in Tucson until I get back."

"So he doesn't know all your men?" Duffy said.

"Not all, no," Parsons said. "Except for Frog and Moon, I rotate the men."

"So he won't be suspicious if he sees us riding with you?" Duffy said.

"No, he won't," Parsons said. "He knows I recruited an Indian as a brander, so he won't think anything of it when he sees Goodluck."

"I want to trust you," Duffy said. "So I want you to think about that short prison sentence and what's waiting for you when you get out. I also want you to think about the alternative."

"He means a rope," Cavill said.

"You said it yourself, I'm not a stupid man," Parsons said.

"Let's go to the gentlemen's car, have a drink, and play a few hands of cards," Duffy said.

CHAPTER THIRTY-SIX

Tucson was a sprawling town of about seven thousand residents. The dry heat was a slap in the face as they stepped off the train. Residents were on the streets, but nobody seemed to be moving too quickly.

"Let's get the horses and find a hotel for the night," Duffy said. "We'll leave for Sims's ranch first thing in the morning."

"If you see anybody you know in town, best sing out right away," Cavill said to Parsons. "I'm in no mood to be shot in the back."

They retrieved the horses from the boxcar and walked them to a large livery stable near the railroad depot.

"Give them plenty of food and water and groom them," Duffy said to the livery manager. "We'll need them fresh in the morning."

As they walked down Main Street, Duffy said, "What's a good hotel?"

"I never stayed in Tucson," Parsons said. "I always just rode out to Sims, but some of the boys liked the Presidio."

The Presidio stood four stories tall with balconies on every room on the third and fourth floor.

They took two rooms on the fourth floor, where the balcony faced Main Street.

"I'm going to send a telegram to Mr. Porter," Duffy said. "I think it's a good idea we take supper in our rooms tonight, on the odd chance there is someone in town who might recognize Parsons."

Duffy left the hotel and walked several blocks to the telegraph office. Across the street was the town sheriff's office. On the same block as the telegraph office was the US marshal's office.

Duffy sent a telegram to Porter to let him know they'd arrived in Tucson.

When he returned to the room, Cavill, Parsons, Goodluck, and Gatewood were playing cards at the table.

"Pull up a chair," Cavill said. "We need something to do to kill time."

"I got something to do," Duffy said. "It involves a bar of soap and a tub of hot water."

"Not a bad idea," Cavill said. "Gatewood, Goodluck, keep the game going. We'll be back directly."

Cavill smoked a cigar as he soaked in a tub of hot water. He looked at Duffy in the next tub.

"Let's have it," Cavill said.

"Do you trust him?" Duffy said.

"Parsons? No, but we don't have a choice if we want evidence on Sims."

"So far he hasn't done anything to make us believe he can't be trusted," Duffy said. "And that's exactly why I don't trust him."

"We come this far to end this thing. I don't see we have a choice but to keep going," Cavill said.

"At the first sign of trouble, be ready to shoot," Duffy said.

"Sims?" Cavill said.

"Everybody but him," Duffy said.

"I don't profess to be a lawyer, that's your department, but without Parsons to testify against Sims, it seems to me we don't have much of a case against Sims," Cavill said.

"All right, don't shoot either of them," Duffy said. "Anybody else is up for grabs."

Cavill blew a smoke ring to the ceiling. "We best convey that to Goodluck and Gatewood," he said.

"Right," Duffy said.

Duffy and Cavill watched Parsons take a bath and then returned to the room so Goodluck and Gatewood could take their turn.

They ordered steaks for supper and ate in their rooms.

Afterward they played cards and then turned in by ten o'clock.

Duffy handcuffed Parsons to the brass headboard.

"Sorry to keep doing this to you, but it won't be for much longer," Duffy said.

"The situation I am in is of my own doing," Parsons said. "So, no hard feelings."

"I appreciate that," Duffy said,

They had breakfast in the hotel dining room when it opened at five-thirty in the morning and were riding out of town before sunrise.

They took the southeast road as instructed by Parsons.

The morning temperature was a comfortable sixty-five degrees, but as soon as the sun rose, it started to heat up. By the time they reached the fork in the road, the temperature was close to ninety.

As they turned onto the fork, Goodluck slowed his horse to a stop and dismounted.

"What is it?" Duffy said.

Goodluck lifted the right leg of his horse. "He's favoring his leg a bit," he said. "I think he's all right."

Goodluck mounted the saddle, and they proceeded along the road.

The scenery was bleak and harsh.

"How do you raise cattle in this country?" Duffy said.

"A tributary of the Santa Cruz River runs right through his property," Parsons said. "Keeps the land green and he has year-round water for the cattle."

"A Garden of Eden in a wasteland," Cavill said.

"You'll see," Parsons said.

Several miles down the road, the harsh terrain slowly turned to green grass and richer soil.

"How far to this archway?" Duffy said.

"From here, less than a mile," Parsons said.

"Hold up," Goodluck said and dismounted.

Goodluck checked the horse's right front leg again. "He'll go lame if I don't change this shoe," he said. "That blacksmith in Cheyenne put on a bad shoe."

"We have extras," Duffy said.

"I have some," Goodluck said. "Go on ahead. I'll catch up."

"All right, but don't be too long," Duffy said.

Duffy, Cavill, Gatewood, and Parsons continued riding and reached the archway. A simple sign hung from the top that read *Sims Ranch.*

"All right, Parsons, take us to the house," Duffy said.

The next two miles took them past several green fields where hundreds of cattle grazed peacefully.

"No hands about," Duffy said.

"It doesn't take much to see to these cattle," Parsons said. "What hands there are most likely are at the bunkhouse, or putting up fences."

"We'll see," Duffy said.

They continued riding and reached the house, bunkhouse, and corral.

"Five horses in the corral," Duffy said. "Call them out from the bunkhouse. Sims, too."

Parsons dismounted.

"Jack, Gatewood, get ready," Duffy said as he pulled his Winchester. "And Parsons, keep in mind if anything goes wrong, you die first."

"Hey, boys, it's Bill," Parsons shouted. "Come on out, boys."

"And Sims," Duffy said.

"Mr. Sims, it's Bill Parsons. Come on out, Mr. Sims," Parsons shouted.

After thirty seconds of silence, Cavill said, "Looks like nobody is home."

"Gatewood, keep your rifle on Parsons," Duffy said as he replaced his Winchester.

Duffy and Cavill dismounted and drew their sidearms. They walked to the bunkhouse and stepped onto the porch.

Cavill stood at the door, nodded to Duffy, and then kicked the door inward. He stepped inside, Colt cocked and ready, looked around, and stepped back outside to the porch.

"Nobody," Cavill said.

"Let's try the house," Duffy said.

They walked to the house; Cavill tried the door and found it unlocked. Cautiously, they entered. The house was small. They checked the bedrooms, kitchen, and living room.

They holstered their sidearms and returned to the porch.

"Empty," Cavill said. "Parsons, you have some explaining to—"

A shot fired. A red hole appeared in Cavill's chest on the left side. A smaller man would have been blown off his feet, but Cavill absorbed the blow and stayed upright.

"Now drop your guns," Parsons said.

Duffy looked at Gatewood. Frog was behind him with a rifle in his hands. Standing beside Parsons, Moon grinned. Two men armed with rifles emerged from the barn and walked to Parsons.

Duffy and Cavill removed the guns from the holsters and

dropped them to the porch floor.

"Come to me," Parsons said to Duffy and Cavill.

Duffy and Cavill stepped down off the porch and walked to Parsons.

"Now I owe you," Parsons said. "Thanks to you, me and the boys are unemployed. Of course, a quarter million goes a long way toward easing our pain."

"There is no Sims, is there?" Duffy said.

Parsons motioned to one of the two men from the barn. "Tony, your Colt," he said.

The man identified as Tony flipped his Colt revolver to Parsons. "Now, to answer your question, Mr. Duffy, there is no Parsons," Parsons said and shot Tony and then the other man standing next to Tony.

Moon cracked up laughing and started to cackle.

"Now, you two get on your knees," Parsons said.

"Screw you," Cavill said.

"One bullet isn't enough, huh," Parsons said. "Moon."

Moon drew his revolver, cocked it, and placed it against Duffy's skull.

"On your knees," Parsons said. "You, too, big man."

"Like Jack said, screw you," Duffy said.

"Ah, pride," Parsons said. "Foolish pride. It must really hurt to be outsmarted by a man like me, but to tell you the truth, I wouldn't have gotten on my knees either."

"Want me to shoot them now?" Moon said.

"Let's get it over with and get out of here," Frog said.

"Go ahead and kill us, but you'll be hunted forever by the law and by the army," Duffy said.

"I don't think so," Parsons said. "You see, who will they hunt? Bill Parsons or Sims? By the time they figure it all out, me and the boys will be in California, living high off a quarter million. It's a shame I won't get to be governor, though, but you never know."

"Enough talking, Bill," Frog said. "Let's kill them and get going already."

"Moon, allow me," Parsons said.

Moon lowered his revolver as Parsons cocked his and took aim at Duffy. "Well, boys, *adios*," Parsons said. "It was fun riding with you, but like the poet said, all good things must come to an end."

An arrow struck Parsons square in the back. A second later, another arrow hit Frog in the neck.

Gatewood grabbed his fallen rifle, cocked the lever, and shot Moon dead.

Parsons slumped to his knees and looked up at Duffy and Cavill as another arrow struck him in the back.

"Forgot about him, didn't you?" Cavill said.

Gasping in pain, Parsons turned and looked at Goodluck, who now stood beside Gatewood.

"Your horse," Parsons said. "There was nothing wrong with him, was there?"

"No," Goodluck said.

"It must really hurt to be outsmarted by men like us," Duffy said.

Parsons gasped one final time and then fell to the ground, took one last look at Duffy and Cavill, and died with his eyes open.

Duffy looked at Cavill. "How's that wound?"

"It's a through and through," Cavill said. "You can sew it up like all the others."

Goodluck and Gatewood walked to Duffy and Cavill.

"Joseph Goodluck, welcome to the agency," Duffy said.

ABOUT THE AUTHOR

Ethan J. Wolfe is an award-winning author and the author of a dozen historical western novels, including the popular *The Regulator* series.

The employees of Five Star Publishing hope you have enjoyed this book.

Our Five Star novels explore little-known chapters from America's history, stories told from unique perspectives that will entertain a broad range of readers.

Other Five Star books are available at your local library, bookstore, all major book distributors, and directly from Five Star/Gale.

Connect with Five Star Publishing

Visit us on Facebook:
  https://www.facebook.com/FiveStarCengage

Email:
  FiveStar@cengage.com

For information about titles and placing orders:
  (800) 223-1244
  gale.orders@cengage.com

To share your comments, write to us:
  Five Star Publishing
  Attn: Publisher
  10 Water St., Suite 310
  Waterville, ME 04901